THE CANADIAN CHILDREN'S TREASURY

THE
CANADIAN
CHILDREN'S
TREASURY

KEY PORTER BOOKS

CANADIAN CATALOGUING IN PUBLICATION DATA

Main entry under title:

The Canadian Children's treasury

ISBN 1-55013-066-8

1. Children's literature, Canadian (English). *

PS8233.C36 1988   jC810 ' .8 ' 09282
C87-095176-9   PR9194.4.C36 1988

Key Porter Books Limited
70 The Esplanade
Toronto, Ontario
Canada M5E 1R2

Contributing editors: Frances Hanna,
    Sandra Martin
Design: Marie Bartholomew
Typesetting: Vellum Print & Graphic Services Inc.
Printed and bound in Italy

Arti Grafiche VINCENZO BONA S.p.A. - Torino

88 89 90 91 6 5 4 3 2 1

Contents

Foreword

A real treasury of Canadian writing for children needs in it everything from that old-time children's favourite, "The Song My Paddle Sings," to the science fiction of Suzanne Martel and Monica Hughes. Here is that treasury: a collection of stories, poems and excerpts from novels that moves through time into the many worlds of the Canadian imagination.

How different these worlds are from one another, and how different the styles and sensibilities of the writers who describe them! In his west-coast Tse-shaht fable, "How the Human People Got the First Fire," George Clutesi dances the reader straight into the tent of the fierce wolf people with the brave Ah-tush-mit who has come to steal their fire. "Hop, hop, hop, stiff-legged," he enters the tent. "Kiyaaa, tlin, tlin, tlin, tlin," he chants. In this immediate, vivid language, Clutesi tells a story of his own people.

In contrast to Clutesi's style, Eva Martin's retelling of "Goldenhair" is measured and spare. "Goldenhair" is a fairytale that came to Canada with the French, and Martin is as faithful to its heritage as Clutesi is to Ah-tush-mit's. The contrast is exciting, as contrast is with flowers of different colours and scents, which are never as rich as when they are gathered in the same bouquet.

There are other contrasts as interesting: the nonsense verse of Dennis Lee and sean o huigin and the dark social commentary of Margaret Atwood; the gentle, rain-soft writing of Joy Kogawa and the cheerful, ironic prose of Leacock. But, in that same bouquet — keeping, for a moment, the metaphor of flowers — there are hybrids, particularly in the stories from Quebec. These are stories that began in France centuries ago, but have been so long and so firmly rooted in their new ground that they are now almost as indigenous as Roch Carrier's or Gabrielle Roy's. Cyrus Macmillan's story, "The Baker's Magic Wand," is one of these, a genuine Quebec folk tale, though its European origin is readily traceable.

While the backgrounds of the stories in this anthology are varied, and the natures of their creators are highly individual, they are all strong and compelling. They reflect, together, a many-faceted whole that is very Canadian.

There is, for instance, that pawky sense of humour so pronounced

among the Scots, Irish, Welsh and Breton French that is the hallmark of
W.O. Mitchell's, Farley Mowat's and Roch Carrier's writing. Mitchell's
"Auction Fever" tells of a series of dealings at an auction from which both
Jake and the kid come off better than either dreamed they might. Farley
Mowat brings forth a more ridiculous, more obvious kind of nonsense in
"Mutt Makes His Mark," while Carrier's "What Language Do Bears
Speak?" is almost a shaggy dog story. "Long Skinny Minny," Gabrielle
Roy's reminiscence of a most determined cat, touches the same funny bone
that Roch Carrier touches, only more delicately.

The other side of this kind of humour, the black side that sometimes
shows through the hilarity, is dominant in much of Morley Callaghan's
writing. In "The Shining Red Apple," a hungry boy is watched closely by a
jaded fruit seller, in a cat-and-mouse story that is bleak and heartbreaking.
Duncan Campbell Scott's "The Pedler" is horrifying, while Ernest Thompson Seton's "The Springfield Fox," with some of the same ingredients —
kindness and unkindness — is neither as sharp nor as bleak as these other
two. What Seton does say is that foxes have finer natures than humans.

The other aspect of the Canadian character that shows up here, as
clear and bright as the morning sun, is a down-to-earth common sense. It
informs fantasies like Suzanne Martel's "Luke in the Forest," and Monica
Hughes's "Chris and Sandy," and humorous pieces like Stephen Leacock's
"The Conjurer's Revenge," as definitely as it does the realistic adventures
of Anne Shirley in "Matthew Cuthbert is Surprised," and *North Lay Freedom*, an excerpt from Barbara Smucker's fictional account of two black
children escaping slavery before the American Civil War.

The anthology is more like an old-fashioned peep-show than a
chronological collection. There are five sections, beginning with *The First
People*, ending with *Here, Now*. This may sound chronological, but *The
First People* has in it Pauline Johnson's poem "The Song My Paddle Sings,"
so familiar to everyone who was a child thirty or forty years ago, George
Clutesi's indigenous fable, native tales retold by Christie Harris, William
Toye and Elizabeth Clark, and James Houston's contemporary Inuit adven-
ture, "Akla gives Chase." The other four sections have in them a similarly
piquant assortment of stories and poems, and the whole is ended with Jean
Little's short, happy poem, "My Own Day," as a sort of grace note.

It is good to see stories like the excerpt from *Anne of Green Gables* comfortably ensconced in the same treasury with the animal stories of Charles G.D. Roberts, R.D. Lawrence, Ernest Thompson Seton and Sheila Burnford, traditional legends, fairy tales and a healthy number of contemporary stories. And it is fun to find the poems sprinkled through the whole like surprises in a birthday cake.

This is a rich treasury, its editors reflecting in their choices those same facets of the Canadian imagination that the writers reflect in their stories and poems. Surely Canadian readers, consciously or unconsciously, of whatever ages, will recognize themselves, and be pleased.

JANET LUNN

THE FIRST PEOPLE

The Origin of Stories

ELIZABETH CLARK

In a Seneca village long ago there was a little boy whose mother and father had died when he was only a few months old. This little boy was cared for by a woman who had known his parents. She gave him the name Poyeshao, which means "Orphan Boy."

When the boy was old enough, his foster mother gave him a bow and some arrows and said, "It is time for you to learn to hunt. Tomorrow, go to the woods and kill all the birds you can find."

She took ears of dry corn, shelled off the kernels, and parched them in hot ashes from the fire. Next morning she gave the boy some of the corn for his breakfast and rolled some of it in a piece of buckskin.

"Take this with you," she said. "You'll be gone all day and you'll get hungry."

Orphan Boy started off and soon found plenty of game. At noon he sat down to rest and eat some of his corn. Then he continued hunting. When he began to head for home, he had a good string of birds.

The next morning Orphan Boy's mother said to him, "Always do your best hunting. If you become a good hunter, you'll always be well off."

Orphan Boy thought about what his mother had told him. "I'll do as she says and someday I'll be able to hunt big game." That night when he returned home, he had more birds than before. His mother smiled and thanked him, saying, "Now you've begun to help me get food."

Each day Orphan Boy started off with his bow and arrows and his little bundle of corn. Each day he went farther into the woods and brought home more birds than the day before. On the ninth day he killed so many that he had to carry them home on his back. His mother tied the birds in little bundles of three and four and shared them with her neighbours.

On the tenth day the boy started off as usual and went even deeper into the woods. About noon the sinew that held the feathers to his arrow came loose. When Orphan Boy looked for a place where he could sit down and fix the arrow, he found a small clearing. Near the centre was a high, smooth, round stone with a flat top. Orphan Boy jumped up on the rock and sat down. He unwound the sinew and put it in his mouth to soften it. Then he arranged the feathers on his arrow. Just as he was about to tie them on, a voice near him asked, "Shall I tell you stories?"

Orphan Boy looked up, expecting to see someone. No one was there. He looked behind the stone and around it. Then he began to tie the feathers to his arrow.

"Shall I tell you stories?" asked a voice right there beside him. The boy looked in every direction but saw no one. When the voice asked again, "Shall I tell you stories?" the boy found that it came from the stone.

"What is that?" he asked. "What does it mean to tell stories?"

"It is telling what happened a long time ago. If you will give me your birds, I'll tell you stories."

"You may have the birds," Orphan Boy said.

Right away the stone began telling what happened long ago. When it finished one story, it began another. The boy sat with his head down and listened. Toward night the stone said, "We will rest now. Come again tomorrow. If anyone asks about your birds, say you've killed so many that you have to go a long way to find one."

On the way home the boy killed five or six birds. When his mother asked Orphan Boy why he had so few, he said that they were getting hard to find.

The next morning Orphan Boy started off but he forgot to hunt for birds. He was thinking of the stories the stone had told him. If a bird landed near him he shot it, but really he was heading straight to the stone.

When he got there, he put his birds on the stone and called out, "I've come back! Here are the birds. Now tell me stories."

The stone told story after story. Toward night it said, "Now we must rest until tomorrow."

On the way home the boy looked for birds, but it was late and he found only a few.

That night his mother told the neighbours, "Orphan Boy used to bring home a lot of birds, but now he brings home only four or five even after being in the woods from morning till night. Maybe he throws the birds away or gives them to some animal. Or maybe he just fools around and doesn't hunt at all."

Orphan Boy's mother hired an older boy to find out what her foster son was doing. The next morning this boy followed Orphan Boy, keeping out of sight. Orphan Boy killed many birds, then he suddenly took off toward the east, running as fast as he could. The older boy followed him to the clearing in the woods. He saw Orphan Boy climb up a large round stone and heard him talking to someone. He couldn't see whom Orphan Boy was talking to; so he went up and asked, "What are you doing here?"

"Hearing stories," replied Orphan Boy.

"What are stories?"

"Stories tell about things that happened long ago," said Orphan Boy. "Put your birds on this stone and say, 'I've come to hear stories.'" The other boy did, and right away the stone began. The boys listened until sundown. Then the stone said, "We'll rest now. Come again tomorrow."

That night the boys returned home with only a few birds. When Orphan Boy's mother asked the reason, the older boy said only, "I followed him for a while. Then we hunted together but we couldn't find any birds."

The next morning the older boy went hunting with Orphan Boy again. By noon they each had many birds. They gave the birds to the stone and listened to more stories. That night they tried to find birds on the way home, but it was late and they didn't find any.

Now, this went on for several days. Finally the mother hired two men to follow the two boys. The men watched the boys hunting and they followed the boys to the clearing, hiding behind trees so that they couldn't be seen. They saw the boys put their birds on the stone, then climb up and sit there with their heads down listening to a voice. Every now and then the boys said, *"Mmm Hmm!"* One man said to the other, "Let's go and find out who's talking to those boys."

They walked up quickly to the stone. "What are you boys doing?" they asked.

The boys were surprised, but Orphan Boy said, "You must promise not to tell anyone." When the two men had promised, Orphan Boy said, "Jump up and sit on the stone." So the men did.

Then Orphan Boy said to the stone, "Go on with the story. We are listening."

All day the four sat listening to the stone tell story after story. When it was almost night, the stone said, "Tomorrow all the people in your village must come and listen to my stories. Have each person bring something to eat. Then clear away the brush so that they can all sit on the ground near me."

That night Orphan Boy told the chief about the storytelling stone. The chief sent a runner to give the message to each family in the village.

Early next morning everyone in the village followed Orphan Boy, walking in single file through the woods. When they came to the clearing, each person put meat or bread on the stone. Then they cleared away the brush and sat down.

When all was quiet, the stone said, "Now I will tell you stories of what happened long ago. There was a world before this one. The things I am going to tell about happened in that world. Some of you will remember every word that I say, others will remember some of the words, and the rest will forget them all. From now on you must tell these stories to one another. Now listen."

The people bent their heads and listened to every word the stone said. Once in a while the boys said, *"Mmm Hmm!"* When the sun was almost down, the stone said, "We'll rest now. Come tomorrow and bring meat and bread."

The next day when the people returned, they found that the food they had brought the day before was gone. They put fresh food on the stone and sat down in a circle to listen.

When all was quiet, the stone began to tell stories. Late that afternoon it said, "I have finished! You must keep these stories as long as the world lasts. Tell them to your children and your grandchildren and your great-grandchildren. Some people will remember them better than others. When you go to a man or a woman to ask for one of these stories, take something to pay for it — bread or meat or whatever you have. I know all that happened in the world before this. I've told it to you. When you visit one another you must tell these things. You must remember them always. I have finished."

So it has been ever since that time. From this stone came all the knowledge that the Senecas have of the world before this one.

The Loon's Necklace

WILLIAM TOYE

An old man who had recently gone blind lived with his wife and young son near a salmon stream. It was winter and they were starving because he could no longer hunt. One morning his wife went looking for berries, leaving the boy to care for his father. The unhappy old man sat in the sun, thinking of his days as a great hunter.

Suddenly the boy spotted a bear on the other side of the stream. If only he could find a way to kill it!

He had an idea.

He guided his father to the water's edge and put a bow and arrow in his hands. "I am going to help you kill a bear," he said.

"But how can I aim?" his father asked.

"I will be your eyes."

The boy stood on a rock and pointed the arrow at the bear's heart. "Shoot!" he cried.

The old man pulled hard and the arrow flew through the air. It hit its mark and the bear fell dead.

Before the boy could tell his father that he had killed the bear, an old hag appeared. She lived by herself near their clearing and was feared for her magical powers. Upon seeing the dead bear across the stream, she thought of the meals it would give her — enough to last all winter long.

"Good for you, old man!" she sneered. "You hit a log." Then she called to the boy, "Come with me!", and stepped into his canoe.

Afraid to refuse, he got in and they crossed the stream together. "If you tell your father that he killed a bear," said the hag, "I'll give you a beating. I might even do something worse!"

She and the boy skinned the bear. Then they made a fire and cooked some meat. "Why should that old man have food?" she muttered, gorging herself. "He is blind and useless." She did not notice the boy hide some meat in his robe.

When he got back to the clearing and the hag had disappeared with a joint of meat, the boy told his father that he had killed the bear. "The old woman said she would beat me if I told you, but I saved this piece of meat."

His father did not touch it. "Keep it for your mother," he said. "I want to go to the lake." He reached for the boy's arm and stood up. "I will visit Loon there. He is a wise and magical bird who might help me."

When they reached the lake, the old man sat down close to the shore. "Now leave me," he said.

"Let me stay with you, Father."

"No, you must go back. Your mother will return soon."

Left alone, the old man began to sing about his misery and helplessness. "*Ha-no ha-no hi-hi-ye-ee!*" he chanted over and over again. "*My heart is breaking with grief!*"

After many hours had passed, another song reached his ears. Heard from afar, it was sad and lonely. But the old man smiled because he knew it as the song of Loon.

He heard it a second time, louder and closer, and a third time closer still.

In a little while the bird perched at the water's edge. "You sing of troubles," Loon said. "How can I help you?"

"O Loon, I am old and blind. My family are starving and I can't feed them. I do not ask to be young, but I would not be so helpless if I could see. I would give my most precious possession to see again."

Loon said: "First you must enter the water with me. Hang onto my wings as I dive and bury your eyes in my feathers."

The old man did as he was told. He grasped Loon's wings and together they dove — down, down, down.

Then they floated up, up, up.

They reached the air just as the old man thought his lungs would burst.

"Can you see?" Loon asked.

"A little," he replied. "I can see the shape of some trees."

"Dive with me again!"

Down, down, down they went. And up, up, up — just like the first time.

"I can see!" cried the old man.

He yanked a shell necklace from his chest and tossed it to the bird. It fell on Loon's neck, while a sprinkling of loose shells covered his back. Where the shells touched his black feathers, beautiful white markings appeared. Loon preened himself and swam away.

When the old man returned to the clearing it began to rain. Hurrying inside the house, he found his wife consoling their son, who was weeping.

"Why are you crying?" he asked.

"The old woman beat me. She found the meat I brought you."

"Forget about your beating. I can see again, my son. Now we will never want for meat and you needn't fear the old woman any more."

The air filled with thunder and lightning, and rain came down in torrents. The old man and his wife blocked the entrance to their house to keep dry.

Soon they heard the hag's voice outside. "Let me in! The rain has destroyed my hut!"

The old man had had enough of her cruel ways. He was silent.

"Take pity on me, I beg you!" There was still no answer.

The next day the clearing by the stream was deserted — except for a sleeping owl never seen there before. It was the hag, who had turned herself into an owl to annoy the old man and his family by screeching at them all night long.

They stood this for one night, then another, then another. Finally they decided to leave the clearing forever.

Spring arrived.

Now that the old man could see again, his family never went without food.

When Loon called to them from far away, his cry was no longer always sad and lonely. Often it was a long, joyful trill.

"Loon is laughing!" the old man would say. "How proud he is of my necklace."

The Song My Paddle Sings

E. PAULINE JOHNSON

West wind, blow from your prairie nest
Blow from the mountains, blow from the west.
The sail is idle, the sailor too;
O! wind of the west, we wait for you.
Blow, blow!
I have wooed you so,
But never a favour you bestow.
You rock your cradle the hills between,
But scorn to notice my white lateen.

I stow the sail, unship the mast:
I wooed you long but my wooing's past;
My paddle will lull you into rest.
O! drowsy wind of the drowsy west,
Sleep, sleep,
By your mountain steep,
Or down where the prairie grasses sweep!
Now fold in slumber your laggard wings,
For soft is the song my paddle sings.

August is laughing across the sky,
Laughing while paddle, canoe and I,
Drift, drift,
Where the hills uplift
On either side of the current swift.

The river rolls in its rocky bed;
My paddle is plying its way ahead:
Dip, dip,
While the waters flip
In foam as over their breast we slip.

And oh, the river runs swifter now;
The eddies circle about my bow.
Swirl, swirl!
How the ripples curl
In many a dangerous pool awhirl!

And forward far the rapids roar,
Fretting their margin for evermore.
Dash, dash,
With a mighty crash,
They seethe, and boil, and bound, and splash.

Be strong, O paddle! be brave, canoe!
The reckless waves you must plunge into.
Reel, reel,
On your trembling keel,
But never a fear my craft will feel.

We've raced the rapid, we're far ahead!
The river slips through its silent bed.
Sway, sway,
As the bubbles spray
And fall in tinkling tunes away.

And up on the hills against the sky,
A fir tree rocking its lullaby,
Swings, swings,
Its emerald wings,
Swelling the song that my paddle sings.

How the Human People Got the First Fire

GEORGE CLUTESI

Long, long time ago the human people had no fire.
There was no fire to cook the food,
The people ate their food cold.
There was no fire to dry their clothes,
No fire to warm them at winter time.
There was no fire to give them light when the moon would not.

It has been said there was no fire at all amongst the human people. No one had fire, except the Wolf people.

The Wolf people were the most dreaded people in all the land.

"No other people shall ever have our fire," they would say, and they guarded it with care, for they alone owned the precious fire.

"No one shall have it," they declared.

The human people wanted and needed the fire very much. Great chiefs and their wise councillors would sit and make plans and more plans to find a way in which to capture the wondrous fire.

"Let us call all the strong and brave men," the wise men would say.

So the great chiefs from all the land would command that all men come forward and try to capture the fire. The strongest would boast that he would go forth to the land of the Wolf people and force his way into their village and bring the fire back. He was strong. The brave knew no fear. He would go forth and capture the fire.

The wise one would say, "I will find a way to win the fire. I am wise."

The fastest would boast, "I will run off with the fire and bring it here to you all. I am fast."

One by one they would go out to capture the fire, and one by one they would come back with the same story. It cannot be done!

The strongest would say, "I could not even get near the village of the dreadful Wolves. They have guards all over the place of the fire. No one can ever enter their village. We can never have the fire. The Wolves are too smart for us."

The fastest would say, "I got so close to their village that I could smell the food roasting in their great fires, but I could not enter their great house."

The wise old one would say, "I'll think of a way."

The great chief was very sad. His best men had failed him and all the people of the land.

"What shall we do? What can we do? We shall be cold again this winter. We shall again eat cold, raw food. We shall be blind by night when the moon will not give us light, and there is no fire to light the way. We must have the fire! We must!" cried the great chief in despair.

No one spoke. No one moved. All eyes were cast down. All had tried and all had failed. All the people were very sad indeed.

But there was really no great need for sadness, for all the while the great council had met — the many trials to capture the fire — young Ah-tush-mit, Son of Deer, had the real secret of how to procure the fire from the Wolf people.

All throughout the great struggle for the possession of the fire Ah-tush-mit had been gambolling about the beach, racing, leaping and hopping about on his long spindly legs. He had seemingly paid no heed to all the great fuss about the fire.

He was racing past the people, as he had done so many times before, when suddenly he stopped directly in front of the chief and announced very simply in a small, small voice, "I'll get you the fire."

"You will what? What did that little boy say?" There was anger in the loud queries from the great braves and the strong men.

Then from the foolhardy ones a loud hee-haw went up — "Ho-ho-ho-ho-ho-ho."

"I'll get you the fire," the small boy repeated quite unabashed and not a bit frightened of the braves and the strong men, for he knew they had all tried and had failed to capture the fire.

Looking the great chief full in the face, Ah-tush-mit repeated again, "I'll get you the fire."

The little boy stood there, so small, so tiny and foolish looking among the great strong men. The wise chief was solemn while the others chuckled and laughed.

Ah-tush-mit, the Son of Deer, began twitching his long, long ears and rolling his big eyes as he looked this way and that way — but still he held his ground.

"I'll get you the fire," he persisted.

At last the great chief looked up and said, "Choo — all right — Ah-tush-mit, my strongest, bravest, fastest and wisest have all failed. Do the best you can."

Ah-tush-mit called the womenfolk together.

"Make me the most colourful costume you can," he commanded. "I am going to dance for the great Wolf chief."

"Dance? Who wants to dance at a time like this?" all the women wanted to know. "The boy is really foolish. He is wasting our time," they all declared.

"Obey and do everything Ah-tush-mit says," the wise old chief commanded his people. "Let the boy try. Give him a chance as I did to all of you," he continued.

Thus the womenfolk made him a head-band, a sash for his belt, bands for his knees and elbows, and for his ankles too. All these were made from the inner bark of the cedar tree, and dyed the colour of the young cohoe salmon — as red as red can be.

Ah-tush-mit fitted and worked with his regalia until it was just right. He paid especial attention to the bands for his knees. He kept remarking these knee-bands had to fit exactly right — not too tight, not too loose — just right so that he could dance well for the great Wolves.

While he was paying special attention to the knee-bands no one noticed that he tucked something into them between the bark and his skin. He worked with the knee-bands and finally they were smooth and exactly to his liking.

"Now I want the best drummers and singers," he announced. "Come with me to the outskirts of the Wolf village. Do not enter with me. When I give the signal you must all run back home as fast as you can."

"We shall go before dark so that you can reach your homes before the night blinds you," he assured the brave men and women drummers and singers who were to risk their very lives to accompany him to the outskirts of the Wolf village.

At last everything was in readiness. Evening came. Ah-tush-mit sallied forth to capture the fire for the human people from the most dreaded people in the land, the Wolf people.

"Show yourselves. Do not hide or sneak in any manner," he warned. "The Wolf people are wise and cunning. They would be sure to see us anyway, even if we were to try and sneak in by the dark of the night."

So the odd little company sang and beat their drums with all their might and main. The Wolf people heard them from a long distance off, they sang so lustily. One strange thing took place. Ah-tush-mit did not take the lead as everyone had expected. Instead he hid himself behind the company of drummers.

"Ah, the foolish boy is now too frightened to show himself?" the women asked one another.

Finally the group of singers and drummers reached the outskirts of the great village of the dreaded Wolves. The huge doors of the house opened slowly, and the biggest, fiercest-looking Wolves bounded out to see what all the noise and din was about.

The humans could see the large fire burning and blazing inside the great house of the Wolves. They could almost feel the heat and the smoke smelled so sweet as they inhaled with all their might, for they had never before seen or smelled the fire.

What a wondrous beautiful sight! Great sparks burst and escaped through the smoke hole on the top of the great roof. What a wonderful thing! So bright and beautiful in the gathering gloom of the dark night. These were the thoughts that ran through the minds of the awe-stricken humans.

Suddenly, Ah-tush-mit sprang forward from his place of conceal-ment. He was on all fours as he began his dance. He sidled towards the door of the great Wolf house. It was fast getting dark. The flickering light from the fire reached out to him and cast pleasing shadows all around as he danced and sprang about on his four spindly legs. Suddenly, he made the signal and the singers and drummers stopped their din abruptly and fled for home as they had been instructed.

Little Ah-tush-mit was left all alone with the fire and the fierce Wolves. There were no more drums nor singers to give him courage, and he was very frightened. He was very, very frightened indeed.

He could hear the Wolf chief asking, "What is all the noise about?"

A Wolf guard answered, "It is only young Ah-tush-mit dancing."

"Send him away," the chief growled.

"Ah, what a jolly little boy! Bring him in. Do let him in," the Wolf chief's wife called out.

"Let us see him dance for awhile, then send him home," the chief agreed.

Ah-tush-mit increased the pace of his dance. Towards the great doors he pranced, hopping straight up and down, with no bend to his knees. Hop, hop, hop, hop, he went, sidling ever closer to the opening of the doorway, and as he circled around he sang a rollicking ditty:

Kiyaaa tlin, tlin, tlin, tlin,
Kiyaaa tlin, tlin, tlin, tlin,
Ooo nootl sahshh keeyah-qwa-yup
    qwatlin,
Hee yah ahh haaa ya-yaulk
    tah khaus ti-nah-is,
Kiyaaa tlin, tlin, tlin, tlin,
Kiyaaa tlin, tlin, tlin, tlin.

Break, crack, crack, crack, crack,
Break, crack, crack, crack, crack,
Do I break yon stakes with
    these I wear?
My flints, my sandstone hooves,
Break, crack, crack, crack, crack,
Break, crack, crack, crack, crack.

Ah-tush-mit's voice was small, but he sang with all his heart. He sang with all his might. He was singing to capture a spark. Ah-tush-mit was singing for his life!

Hop, hop, hop, hop, stiff-legged, he entered the doors. Once inside he could see the fire burning brightly and all about it was a bed of stakes made of broken bones implanted into the earth, as sharp as mussel shells they were. This was what his little song was all about. Up to this very minute no human who had ever tried to get past that awful bed of bone stakes had lived to tell the tale.

Ah-tush-mit danced with all his heart. He danced as he had never danced before. He danced so he might capture a tiny spark. Ah-tush-mit danced for his life.

"Kiyaaa tlin, tlin, tlin, tlin," he sang as he sidled ever closer towards the awful trap made with broken bones. Skirting its edges in a half circle, he danced towards a far corner, closer to the fire, but where the bones were neither so large nor too plentiful in the ground.

Suddenly, he had arrived at his chosen spot and with a mighty leap he was among the broken bones, hopping higher and ever higher as he picked his way among the sharp spear-like bones. His sharp little feet seemed to fit around and pass between the dangerous bones harmlessly. His long shanks and slim legs kept his plump little body safely away from the sharp, sharp points and thus he was saved from being torn to shreds.

"Do I break yon stakes of bones with these I wear? My flints, my sandstone hooves," he sang.

The Wolf people were completely fascinated. Their big and awful jaws hung open in wonderment. Ah-tush-mit had won the cheers and applause of the Wolf people.

The little fellow's bright costume glowed in the firelight.

"Break, crack, crack, crack, crack," his little song floated over the great fire. "With these I wear my flints, my sandstone hooves," he carolled as he suddenly sprang right beside the great fire.

Ah-tush-mit sang louder and louder; he leaped higher and ever higher; he was dancing to capture a spark; he was dancing for his very life.

"Ah, what a jolly little boy! He is a dancer, a good dancer," the mamma Wolf beamed.

Then it happened — as quick as a flash — before your eyes could blink. Ah-tush-mit had turned towards the roaring fire and with a mighty leap he sailed into the air — right over the roaring fire sailed he.

"Ho-ho-ho-ho-ho," roared the Wolves. "Ah-tush-mit is on fire. Ho-ho-ho-ho-ho."

Ah-tush-mit had indeed caught on fire. His little legs smouldered between the knees. He stopped his dancing and bounded through the great doors with a mighty leap. Once clear of the great Wolf house he raced for his life towards home as fast as he could run.

All around the leaping, roaring fire the Wolves sat bemused. The whole action of little Ah-tush-mit had happened so quickly and seemingly without intent that they were taken completely by surprise. Before they realized what had occurred Ah-tush-mit was well away from the Wolf village. Ah-tush-mit, the Son of Deer, the fleetest of them all, had completely outsmarted the Wolves, the most dreaded people of the land.

With a spark smouldering between his knees he had captured the fire! With his sharp pointed feet, his flints and sandstone hooves he had successfully run the sharp broken stakes of bones.

Yes indeed, with his colourful costume, his captivating dance, he had outwitted the most cunning people of the land. Ah-tush-mit, Son of Deer, the small one, had captured the fire for the human people.

The secret something Ah-tush-mit had tucked between his knees had been a small bundle of very dry sticks he had gathered from the undermost branches of the spruce tree. It was this that had caught fire since it was dry as dry can be, and even some of the spruce gum still stuck to the twigs. When the sticks caught fire the cedar bark bands had smouldered until he reached home with the tiny sparks of fire. This was where the tinder had come from and where the human people first came to know about fire.

But Ah-tush-mit had burned himself. The inside of his knees were badly scorched. Thus it is to this day that the inside of all deers' knees are singed black. That is how the human people got their first fire.

In the growing season, when all living things burst out in bloom
Sit in the glade of the wood at even-tide.
If your own heart be open to love be there for Ah-tush-mit
you will hear the thump and the beat of his little song:
Thump, thump, thump, thump.

Akla Gives Chase

JAMES HOUSTON

Upik and Pitohok are two Inuit children whose father has died. Now they must fetch food for the rest of the family, or starve. The previous autumn, their grandfather shot a caribou which he was unable to carry home, but left hidden. It is a long journey to the hiding place, but the children are the only hope of their mother, their two baby sisters, and their grandfather. They find the caribou, but on the long journey home they are pursued by Long Claws, or akla — a grizzly bear that is hungry, too.

The evening sun turned red as it slid down and touched the long, flat white horizon. Pitohok looked back then and groaned beneath the heavy weight of caribou. "Long Claws is still coming after us. Give him a fish. Hurry and fling it back toward him."

Upik did as she was told. Pitohok looked again, then slowed his pace. "He's lying down," Pitohok gasped. "He's eaten the trout. He looks now as if he's going to sleep." It was growing dark and Pitohok was staggering with weariness. "Hold onto me," he groaned. "Help me. I've got to make my feet carry me over that next snow ridge so the akla won't see us stop to build our igloo."

When they were beyond the huge bear's sight, Pitohok collapsed, letting the caribou fall to the snow. Upik helped him up, but Pitohok was so exhausted that he could scarcely rise. With the snow knife Upik cut a shallow gravelike hole and they slid the caribou in and carefully covered it with snow. They built their igloo on top of it.

Once inside, Pitohok wedged a snow block firmly into place, trying to jam the entrance. "Let us share our one last fish," he said. "I have never been so hungry or so tired in all my life."

Even while they were eating, they listened carefully. But they did not hear the akla. Upik could not finish her share of the fish, so exhausted was she from their terrible journey. They rolled themselves into the caribou robe and slept, not knowing if the akla would let them live to see the next day dawn.

When Pitohok awoke, he said, "The weather's changed. Can you not smell and feel spring's dampness in the air?"

Cautiously he cut away the entrance block and crawled outside. Upik followed him. The land was blanketed in lead-gray fog that hung heavily above the snow, hiding everything from view. The huge akla might have been very close to them or very far away.

Pitohok dug up the caribou and, cutting a larger entrance in their igloo, shoved the frozen animal outside.

"There is Long Claws. He is waiting for us," Upik whispered with terror in her voice.

Pitohok looked up and saw the dark outline of the akla standing watching them. It was less than a stone's throw away, its wide back glistening with silver hoarfrost, which made the coarse hair on its massive shoulders bristle like countless needles.

"Shall I try to shoot him now?" Pitohok whispered to his sister.

"No," she said. "No! I'm afraid that last bullet will break and the noise will only anger him."

"Then hurry," he cried. "Help me get this caribou up onto my back. I don't know how far I can carry it today. My legs feel weak as water. But we've got to get it home."

Swaying its huge head back and forth, the grizzly let a low growl rumble in its throat. It was so close now that for the first time Upik could see the akla's long, sharp claws. They cut deep furrows in the snow when it came shambling toward them. Its beady black eyes watched every move they made.

"Leave our caribou sleeping skin in front of the igloo. That may fool him," Pitohok whispered. "If he goes inside, he will surely smell the place where the caribou lay last night. He may stay there digging long enough for us to lose him."

Together they hurried away, trying to hide themselves from Long Claws in the heavy ice fog. They walked and walked until they came to a riverbed that seemed familiar to them. Violent winds had blown one bank free of snow, but in the swirling fog they could not tell where it would lead them. Pitohok struggled up onto the stones that formed the bank of the frozen river. His sister had to help him by pushing at his back.

"Be careful not to leave a single track up here," Pitohok gasped. "Step from rock to rock," he warned her. "The wind is at our back. If the akla cannot see us or smell our footprints, we may lose him."

Together they traveled on the stony river bank until about midday, following a twisted course, leaving no path behind them.

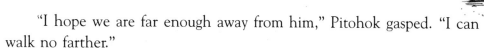

"I hope we are far enough away from him," Pitohok gasped. "I can walk no farther."

He sank to his knees and let the heavy weight of the caribou sag down until it rested on the wind-cleared stones. He lay against it, his chest heaving as he tried to catch his breath. Although the air was stinging cold, Upik had to kneel and wipe the frost-white sweat from her brother's face.

"He's gone." Upik sighed, glad to rest the heavy rifle in the snow. She looked around in the still-thick fog. "Which way do we go now?"

Pitohok peered over his shoulder and felt cold sweat trickling down his spine. He could see no sign of the sun. Everything was hidden by a wall of fog.

"I . . . I don't know," he admitted. "I was trying so hard to get away from the akla that now . . . we're lost!"

Pitohok struggled painfully onto his knees and looked in all directions. He saw nothing but gray ice fog that drifted in phantom swirls along the frozen river.

"Oh, I wish someone would help us," Upik whispered aloud, and as if in answer to her words, the snowy owl came toward her, winging low out of the fog. Upik saw the owl turn its head as though it had seen the bear, then stare at her with its huge golden-yellow eyes. Suddenly the owl changed its wingbeat, hovering as if by magic at the very edge of the smokelike mists. It seemed to signal Upik. Then, turning sharply to the right, it flew off, cutting a dark trail through the ice-cold wall of fog.

Upik stood up, and, using all her strength, helped her brother heave the caribou onto his back. She struggled to ease the heavy burden as she stood upright.

"We should follow her," said Upik. "I think she knows the way."

Her brother's answer was a moan when the full weight of the frozen caribou settled on his tired, cramped shoulders. "Yes, follow the owl," he whispered.

Upik tried to steady Pitohok while they walked. She looked back only once at the zigzag trail they left in the snow as her brother's strength grew less and less. Both of them had lost all sense of distance and of time. Upik followed the owl's course through the dense fog, wondering if they would ever reach their home.

They had not gone far before Upik heard the sound of heavy breathing. She turned, then screamed in terror. The huge grizzly, its heavy head rolling, its tongue lolling out of its mouth, came padding after them. It was only a pace behind Pitohok. Upik saw Long Claws raise its head and sniff at the rich burden of caribou, which had softened a little because of the heat of Pitohok's body. The grizzly stretched out its neck and licked the frosted nostrils of the caribou.

"What's the matter?" Pitohok asked her. Then turning, he, too, saw the bear. His voice caught in his throat. "You've got to . . . to try and shoot him," Pitohok gasped. "I can't do it. My arms are too tired. My whole body is trembling from carrying this weight. Let him get close to you," he said, "then shoot him . . . in the head."

Upik stopped, raised the heavy rifle and tried to sight along its wavering barrel. "I can't," she said. "I am afraid . . . afraid this last stone bullet will break." She was weeping. "Drop the caribou," Upik begged her brother. "Let Long Claws take it. We can walk away alive. It will stop and eat. Please drop the caribou. I am afraid that the akla is going to kill you for that meat."

Pitohok hunched his shoulders and struggled forward, as if he had not heard her plea. But now Upik could see that he held his short knife in his hand and that he would not give up their prize of meat without a fight.

Once more she heard an angry rumble in the grizzly's throat and saw it reach out with one terrible paw and rake the caribou along the whole length of its back. As its claws hooked against the caribou's antlers, Pitohok was thrown off balance and stumbled sideways, falling onto his knees. The big bear moved closer. Driven by fear and desperation, Pitohok rose and continued walking, his eyes narrowed, his mouth drawn down with strain.

The huge akla, with lips drawn back to show its enormous teeth, came after him again. Upik once more raised her grandfather's rifle and looked along its sights. The bear must have heard the safety catch click off, for it stopped, turned its head and stared straight up the gun barrel at

her. At that moment, looking into its eyes, Upik realized that the bear was neither good nor evil. It was a hunter like themselves, desperate to feed itself and remain alive in the lonely, snow-filled wilderness. She lowered the rifle. She could not bring herself to try to kill the bear.

At that moment, Pitohok whispered hoarsely, "I see the owl again! She's sitting on our family's empty food cache. Can it be?" he sobbed. "Are we . . . almost home?"

The bear moved in again behind him and, rising up on its hind feet, struck out angrily at the caribou's plump haunches. Pitohok reeled from the heavy blow and staggered to his knees. He tried to rise, then sank back onto the snow.

"I can't go on," he said. "I'm finished." He had lost his knife. There were tears in his eyes, but his teeth were clenched in anger. He tightened his grip upon the caribou.

"Let go," Upik begged her brother. "Let him have the meat."

"No," Pitohok said. "If I lose this caribou to that bear and return home with nothing, none of us will live, and I, myself, would die of shame."

He turned away from the hot breath of the snarling grizzly whose great swaying head was not more than an arm's length from his face.

"Run!" Pitohok whispered to his sister. "Run for the igloo and save yourself."

Upik bent and grabbed her brother underneath the arms, trying to help him up, but he was too weak. Then she turned around so that she stood directly between him and the akla's gaping jaws.

"No — don't do that," Pitohok gasped. He was hunched over like an old man. "Put the rifle under the caribou to help me support this weight," he moaned, "or I . . . shall never rise. You run!" he begged his sister. Pitohok wept aloud as he whispered, "I can't do any more. All my strength has gone. It's going black . . . I'm going to . . ."

"You are coming with me, now!" cried Upik. "I can see our igloo. It's not far from us. Can you not see it through the fog?"

The big grizzly raked its claws through the snow. Upik put her left shoulder underneath the caribou and her arm around her brother's waist and strained with all her might. Together they rose from the snow and staggered off toward their family's house. Pitohok stumbled once again and fell onto one knee. He hung there gasping for breath.

The akla snarled and opened its mouth wide to take the caribou's leg and Pitohok's mitted hand between its crushing jaws.

"*Unalook! Kukikotak!*" Upik screamed at the bear. "We shared our fish with you. Don't you dare to harm my brother. He must take this food home to our family. They are starving . . . don't you understand?"

The huge bear let go of Pitohok's hand and the caribou's leg and stood there glaring back at her.

"Quick! Get back on your feet," Upik whispered. "We have only a little way to go."

The grizzly must have seen the snowhouse, too, for suddenly it shambled around in front of them, blocking Pitohok's way.

"I warned you not to hurt my brother," Upik screamed again.

As if ruled by magic, the huge bear stepped back and let them pass.

"Mother! Mother! Come and help us!" Upik wailed.

Long Claws turned its head and stared at her when Upik's mother burst out of their igloo entrance. She saw the great humped shoulders of the akla and, like her daughter, screamed at it, then turned and rushed inside again.

Upik tried to take half of the caribou's weight on her own shoulders while pulling Pitohok to his feet. Slowly he rose, but his knees would scarcely support him.

"Don't drop it now," Upik said in a stern voice. "We're almost there."

Together they staggered painfully toward the igloo.

"Everything is whirling around," cried Pitohok. "It's going black again . . . I'm falling. . . ."

Because she no longer had the strength to hold him, Upik and her brother collapsed together on the snow. She shook him, but Pitohok seemed to have lost the power to hear or move or speak. Upik tried to drag him toward the igloo, but his arms remained locked tight around their precious burden of meat.

Long Claws turned once more and shambled after them, snarling like a huge and angry dog. It grasped the caribou's neck in its powerful jaws and started backing away, dragging the carcass and Pitohok, pulling both of them into the swirling fog.

The snow knife, the rifle and Pitohok's short knife were gone. Upik had no weapons but her hands and teeth. She turned and saw her grandfather crawling out of the igloo on his hands and knees. In his left mitt he held his huge curved bow and in his mouth a pair of arrows. Right behind him came their mother, her parka hood puffed out with icy wind, screaming aloud, raging to protect her children, ready to do battle with the enormous bear. Her hands outstretched like claws, their mother raced forward to attack.

Upik heard her grandfather call out, "Stop, woman. Hold! If you help me, we can pierce him right from here."

The grandfather knelt unsteadily and notched an arrow to the braided string. His hands shook with strain when he tried to draw the powerful bow. But he could not. In desperation Upik's mother knelt and helped to draw the heavy weapon almost to full curve. The point of the arrow wavered wildly when the grandfather tried to aim.

"Don't!" Upik cried, spreading her arms and running between her grandfather's unsteady arrow and the bear. "You might hit Pitohok."

Looking back, she saw her brother still being dragged across the snow behind the bear. In sudden anger she whirled around and ran straight between her brother and the akla, screaming, *You let go of him! Let go!*

Surprised, the huge grizzly released the caribou for a moment and raised its head.

"Here, this is for you," she yelled and reaching into her parka hood, she snatched out the last piece of frozen trout that she had saved and flung it beyond the bear.

The akla looked at her, grunted, then turned and moved away from Pitohok, who still clasped the caribou as fiercely as an Arctic crab. The grizzly snatched up the piece of fish. Then, with its hips and frosted shoulders rolling, it disappeared into the silver wall of icy fog.

Pitohok's mother and his grandfather knelt beside him, trying to unlock his arms from the caribou.

Pitohok opened his eyes and stared at them. "I thought that akla would surely snatch the caribou away from me," he whispered.

"I, too, believed that he would take it from you," his grandfather agreed. "But no human knows exactly what the animals will do."

"Upik was afraid of the akla. We were both afraid of him, and yet she ran and put her body between me and the grizzly's snarling jaws. Grandfather, did you believe my sister would do that?"

"No. I did not know what she would do. Nobody knows the strength or courage that humans possess until real danger comes to test them."

The Princess and the Geese

CHRISTIE HARRIS

Once it was a supernatural princess who vanished. But she had not been tricked into trouble. She had vanished because she was unhappy about living with humans.

This is the way it happened.

It was in the time of very long ago, when things were different in the vast green wildernesses of the Northwest. It was at a time when Mouse Woman was living on the Haida islands.

It was early in the spring. Geese were filling the northern flyway with their wild calls as they moved toward their summer feeding grounds in great flying wedges.

A chief's son was out alone, watching the mighty travellers of the air with longing eyes. For not even the biggest and finest of the Haida canoes could venture as far as the great birds. He was looking up at the birds with shining eyes when he heard a chattering of geese at a nearby lake.

Eager to observe the mighty visitors at close range, he glided warily toward the sound. But there were no geese. There were only two maidens swimming near the shore. They were swimming and laughing and chattering merrily.

The young man caught his breath. For there was something geeselike about the chattering. And, shining silver in the sun, two large gooseskins lay at the edge of the lake.

"Goose maidens!" He scarcely breathed it. For these were supernatural maidens. Narnauks. And they were as beautiful as a summer sky.

He longed to speak to them. But he knew that they would take flight at the first sign of a human being. Unless — His eyes widened with a thought. The goose maidens could not take flight without their flying blankets. He crept warily toward the gooseskins.

A startled cry told him he was discovered.

Wild to speak to the two beautiful maidens, he threw himself down on the gooseskins so that they could not take them.

The elder maiden came at him, hissing like an outraged gander. But the younger maiden only looked shyly at him.

Caught in the spell of her eyes, the youth rose to his feet, picking up the gooseskins.

The elder maiden almost snatched hers from his hand. But the younger one stood looking at him with great wondering eyes. And a wild thought leaped up in the young man. Perhaps she would marry him.

With the courage born of his yearning, he held her gooseskin out toward her. "If you will marry me, Princess, I will give you your flying blanket."

The elder maiden hissed in outrage at such presumption. "Marry you? YOU! A mere human!" But the younger one still looked at him.

"I will marry you," she whispered.

The elder maiden hissed at both of them. Angrily she put on her gooseskin. And then she was a goose, flapping furiously out into the lake. With a great thunder of wings and a fury of wild calls, she rose. She flew up, up, up, up until she was lost in the vast blueness of the sky.

"She has gone home to Skyland," the younger maiden whispered. And her shining eyes were shadowed with concern.

"I will take you home to my village," he assured her. "You will be warmly welcomed by my family." But now a shadow darkened *his* eyes. For the beautiful princess was a narnauk. His family would look askance at her. Unless they did not know she was a narnauk.

Putting her flying blanket on the ground, the youth took off his top martenskin robe and laid it gently on her shoulders. Then he folded up her gooseskin and hid it under his second robe. "May we keep this as our secret, Princess?" he begged.

The goosemaiden nodded, though her eyes were still anxious.

They started toward the village. And when they were nearing it, the youth hid the supernatural gooseskin in the heart of an old cedar tree.

"Keep it safe!" the maiden murmured to the tree.

The youth looked at her with a moment's sadness. "You will be so happy with my family that you will not want it again, Princess."

For a time she was happy with his human family.

Her husband could see the questions in his parents' eyes. But they were a proud and proper people. They did not pry into their daughter-in-law's concerns. They recognized the nobility in her bearing and in her manners. They noted the richness of her broad black neck ring. Obviously she was a princess who had been spirited away from her own people and was now keeping herself secret from some dreaded enemy. But she did walk a little oddly, they confessed to one another.

"Since my wife came in springtime, with the geese," her husband suggested, "let us call her Goose Princess." He caught her grateful and loving glance.

Food was her first problem; for she did not like their food, until a woman chanced to steam the roots of plants she had gathered near the mouth of the creek. Goose Princess ate those with relish. "Though I do wish they weren't cooked," she confided to her husband.

For some time, she seemed happy enough in her new home.

Then her husband began to notice something. Often at night she glided silently out of the house. And when she returned she was cold. Cold as the night air. Cold as the seawater.

One night he stealthily followed her. He saw her take her supernatural flying blanket from the heart of the cedar tree. He watched her fly off to graze on sea grasses. And as he went back to the house so that she would not know he had watched her, his heart was heavy. Goose Princess was not satisfied to be a human.

Summer passed. And winter came. A desperately cold winter. Fierce gales uprooted trees and set the sea smoking with blown spray. Canoes could not go out on the sea for food. Snow and ice locked in the land. And people in the great cedar houses grew hungry. For, in the Haida islands, no one was prepared for such a winter.

One day when they were outdoors, Goose Princess said, "Sh!" to her husband. And she seemed to listen to the sky; though he could hear nothing but the wind. "My father is sending food to us," she told him.

To the amazement of the whole village, a great flying wedge of geese came out of the south. And when they had gone, there was a mound of roots and grasses behind the house where Goose Princess lived.

"Strange food for *people*!" envious neighbors muttered. There was fear and scorn — as well as envy — in their voices. For people do not like unaccountable happenings.

Again and again during the bitter winter, flying wedges of geese came out of the south, bringing more roots and grasses for the princess's family.

"That family will be turning into gaggling geese," a man muttered. And his friends laughed. For there was now much gossip in the village. There were sly little goose walks and goose hisses. And there were many sidelong glances at the mysterious princess who had come from no-one-knew-where. She did walk very oddly, people whispered to one another.

Goose Princess heard the whispers. She caught the sidelong glances and the sly little goose walks and goose hisses. "They are mocking me," she told her husband. And for the very first time, she hissed at him. "They are mocking me; for humans are always suspicious of people who are different." Then her eyes blazed with anger. "And they are mocking the geese, who are greater than they are." She raced out of the house. But, after a while, she came back.

Then the worst of the storms was over. It was early in the spring. Geese filled the northern flyway with their wild calls as they moved toward their summer feeding grounds in great flying wedges. And as she watched their high passing, Goose Princess was sad and quiet. Her eyes were full of yearning.

One night, she slipped out of the house.

Alarmed by what might happen, her husband followed her. But she seemed to fly on the wings of her longing for her own kind. And as he fell farther behind, she reached the cedar tree. With a quick, grateful word to the tree, she snatched up her supernatural gooseskin and put it on. Then, with a great thunder of wings and a trumpeting of wild calls, she rose. She flew up, up, up, up until she was lost in the vast darkness of the sky.

Her husband sank to the ground in despair. He knew he had lost his beautiful goose princess.

At long last, he went sadly back to the village.

Next day, the rumors flashed from house to house. Goose Princess had vanished as mysteriously as she had come.

"She was not a proper woman," people whispered to one another. And now there was fear in their voices. For they had offended a narnauk. And who knew what would happen to them? They began to turn angry glances on the young man who had brought the narnauk to their village. It was his fault that they were now in danger.

The young man neither heard the whispers nor saw the glances. For he was lost in grief.

When he finally stirred himself, he made his way to the remote house

43

of a shaman, a witch doctor who had almost left the ways of man to have closer contact with the spirit world.

"My wife has vanished," the young man told the shaman. "So I wish to find the Trail to her father's village."

The old man's glittering eyes seemed to pierce into the young man's innermost being. "Your wife's father is a Great One almost beyond the thinking of a human being," he said in his strange, old, cracked voice.

The young man nodded. He knew that his father-in-law was a Supernatural Being. "Where is the Trail to his village?" he insisted.

The old medicine man pierced him again with his glittering wild eyes before he said, "You are a worthy man. The Trail runs behind my house."

Pausing only long enough to present the old shaman with a small, but beautifully carved box, the young man raced out to seek the Trail, the Spirit Trail that would lead him to Skyland.

Growth was so dense on the Haida islands that men seldom ventured into the depth of the forest; they clung to the seacoast. But now a Trail seemed to open before him as he moved. And it closed behind him.

His heart was pounding. For who knew what would happen along such a Trail? He pushed from his mind the old stories of fearsome Beings who lived there.

As he moved along the Trail, he seemed to have left even time behind him. For his world was a world of summer.

He had gone a long, long way when he came upon the mouse. A white mouse! It had cranberries in its mouth. And it was vainly trying to get over a huge tree that had fallen across its pathway.

With instant compassion for the small creature, he picked it up and lifted it over the fallen tree. He watched it scurry off into a stand of large ferns.

Then he heard a voice, a squeaky little voice. "Come in and speak to the Chief-woman!" it commanded.

Startled by the words, the young man lifted a leaning fern. And there, to his amazement, was a house. A huge, underground house.

"Come in!" It was a sharp command in the same squeaky voice.

He went in. And there was the tiniest of old women cooking cranberries in a hot-stone box. She was watching him with big, busy, mouse eyes.

"You are a worthy man," she said to him in the same sharp voice. "And since you have helped me, I will help you. Though it is not a proper marriage," she added tartly.

"It is a marriage, Grandmother," he protested.

"It is a marriage," she conceded. "And I owe you assistance." For of course, this was Mouse Woman. And of course Mouse Woman knew the obligation of a gift. If help had been given, the helper must be compensated.

She marched off to a corner of her house and began to open a nest of five carved chests. From the innermost chest, she took out a tiny mouseskin.

"I wore this for hunting when I was young," she told him, with just a little sigh for her long gone days of hunting. She held it out to him.

"Wear it!" she commanded.

"Wear . . . that?" The young man looked at the tiny mouseskin. He looked at his own big body.

"Wear it!" she repeated.

To humor her, he took the mouseskin. And to his utter amazement, he could enter it the way the reflection of a giant tree can enter a tiny puddle. He could move around in it, as if he were a mouse.

"Practice wearing it!" she commanded. And she pointed toward the outdoors.

The young man, now seeming to be a mouse, scampered around logs and mosses for a brief time. Then he went back into the house.

"Now," the tiny old woman said, "as soon as you have eaten, be on your way! Though it is not a proper marriage."

"It is a marriage, Grandmother," he answered.

Removing the supernatural garment, the young man ate and went on his way.

This time he met only one creature — a strange little man with one leg, one arm, and half a head.

"Master Hopper!" he gasped, watching the halfman hop boisterously around the base of a red pole that seemed to reach up and up forever, beyond the highest treetops. He had heard about Master Hopper, but he had not believed in him.

Then his gaze fastened on the pole. He had heard stories about that, too, and had scarcely believed them. *This* was the red pole that reached up to Skyland. Where Goose Princess was.

Without a moment's hesitation, he entered his magical mouseskin and scampered up the red pole. He climbed up and up and up beyond the treetops, up and up and up beyond the eagles, up and up and up beyond the clouds, up and up and up until he reached the door into Skyland.

It was an alarming door. It opened, and shut again, as fast as the blink of an eye. He watched it for a long time. And only when he had caught the rhythm of its opening, did he ready himself to leap through.

As a mouse, he leaped through.

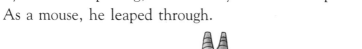

Then, as a man, he looked about him.

Skyland was dazzling. Houses as blue as the sky and as white as the clouds were decorated with tiny stars.

Before the biggest house, he saw the Goose pole.

Then he saw Goose Princess running toward him. Goose Princess was embracing him. She was taking him into the house of her father who was Town Chief.

"You will be happy here," she told him.

And for some time, he was happy.

Then he began to long for the great sea where he had gone sea-hunting. He began to long for the smell of the cedars, the scream of the seagulls, the sound of the rain on the roof. He began to long for his family.

"My son-in-law is not happy here," the Town Chief told his daughter.

She nodded in sad agreement. "He is not happy here." As she had not been happy living among humans.

"I will send him back to his own kind," the Town Chief told her. And again she nodded in sad agreement. She understood his yearning for his own kind.

The Town Chief summoned Eagle and Raven and Heron and Seagull to consult about the manner of the young man's return to earth. And it was agreed that they could carry him back while he was sleeping.

So it was that the young man woke up next morning in his own house in his own village.

"Did I dream it all?" he asked himself, glancing about at the familiar walls and smokehole.

Then he saw the mouseskin. And he reached out a hand for it.

But as he reached, the mouseskin vanished.

He blinked his eyes to clear them.

But the mouseskin had truly vanished. And he thought he heard a small, sharp-voiced mutter, "It was not a proper marriage."

Indeed, it was not a proper marriage. But, as long as he lived, the Goose Princess's husband watched the high passing of the geese with a great yearning. He went often to lonely waters. But he never again found a goose maiden swimming.

The Boy of the
Red Twilight Sky

JULIET HESLEWOOD

On the shores of the Great Water, far out in the west, there is little to view but endless sea and the high, arching sky. There was a time when all seemed flat and colourless and the ceaseless moaning of the waves only added to the world's great gloom. The sky held no rose, no blue; it reflected the sad greyness of the sea and shore. To live there could be very lonely. One young wife, left to herself all day while her husband fished in the ocean, found her isolation almost unbearable.

"If only I had children I should not feel so bad," she said. "I could talk and I could busy myself with all sorts of occupations that caring for a child would bring me."

One evening, she saw a lively kingfisher swoop and dive for minnows not far from where she sat on the shore.

"O sea-bird with your bright blue wings and white collar; how I wish we had children like you."

The kingfisher heard her plaintive call and replied, "Go and look you in the sea-shells; look you in the sea-shells."

The next night, as she stared at the dull, low clouds, she saw a white sea-gull circle in the air. She followed its course as it bobbed and nosed the waves with smaller birds, just like itself.

"O sea-gull; how I wish we had the company of children such as yours," she said sadly. The gull, hearing her mournful appeal replied:

"Go and look you in the sea-shells; look you in the sea-shells."

She couldn't help but wonder what this twice-told advice might lead to and as she rose to make her search, she heard a strange cry from the sand-dunes behind her. Weaving her way through the spiky grasses and treading the cool, soft sand that streamed between her toes, she soon came across a large, pink shell. To her amazement and deep concern she found inside it a tiny boy. He was crying inconsolably. Without thinking how he came to be there, she lifted him in her arms and cradled him until his murmurings ceased. She then hurried home with him, anxious to await her husband and show him what she'd found. Since they both wanted children so much, they agreed that this boy should stay and live with them as their son.

They were all three very happy. His mother chatted and laughed and played with the boy. He accompanied his father on fishing trips. He helped them both in their small home, sharing with them all their household duties. He was practical and often made good use of household objects, transforming them to serve other needs. Armed with a new bow, he was able to go out hunting alone and their admiration grew when he returned from his chase with food such as they had never known before.

As he grew older he naturally changed in appearance. But instead of taking on a freckled or ruddy look as you would expect from such a hard, outdoor life, his face became refined and soft. In time it was quite golden. The warmth of his skin shone outwards so that it seemed he was surrounded by a deep, rich glow. Wherever he went he left a brilliant haze as one might trail a shadow on all sides.

"Why do you shine so brightly?" asked his mother.

"I cannot tell you yet."

One day, a loud storm raged over the Great Water. To try to fish was impossible in such weather and the family feared they would go hungry. The torrents of wind and rain hemmed them to their house.

"Don't be afraid," said the boy, "for I can calm the Storm Spirit. Come with me and I will show you."

His unwilling father unbolted the door and stood tremulous, unsure if this was wise. But the boy took his hand and led him to their boat that was moored by the dunes on the shore. They put out to sea in the howling gale and the boy looked up at the sky.

"See! See! The mad Storm Spirit is keen to overthrow us!"

The Spirit heaved and blew and tried to upset their boat, but the boy stood firm and soon the sea around them dropped and remained still.

Angered by his defeat, the Storm Spirit called to the south west.

"O nephew Black Cloud — come and do your darkest work!"

Almost immediately they saw a deep shade hurtling across the sky towards them. The boy's father cried aloud in fear.

"Don't be afraid; watch," said the boy.

As soon as he had reached the boat, Black Cloud saw the gleaming boy and felt his rays pierce through him utterly. He hurried away with speed.

At this the Storm Spirit rolled in the air with fury. Then he roared to the corners of the earth:

"O Mist of the Sea, come spread yourself and shield their view of the land."

The boy's father crouched in the boat and moaned:

"This is the worst of all. This is the greatest enemy of fishermen. He obscures our sight and leads us to confusion."

"Don't be afraid; watch," said the boy.

As a pale light streamed around them, the boy sat down and smiled. Beams of gold spread out from his face and pushed the Mist of the Sea back to where it had come from. And with that, the Storm Spirit also left, screaming with rage into the distant sky.

"How have you done this?" asked the boy's father.

"When I am with you, they cannot harm you. Soon I shall tell you why."

Remembering their present needs, they set out for the nearest fishing grounds. There the boy taught his father a magic song and as he sang it he was astonished to see, below in the water, large shoals of fish gliding into his net.

"What is the secret of your power, my son? You can lure the fish and banish the darkest weather threats."

"Tomorrow I will tell you."

Standing on the shore with his mother and father beside him, the following morning the boy tried his skill at shooting birds. One by one his targets fell to the earth. He tenderly skinned each bird and dried their skins with the utmost care. Across the bare sands lay all colours of feathers.

The boy, discarding his normal clothing, then dressed himself as a plover. And soon, as he waved his arms and looked across the water, he

flew up into the sky. He reeled and swooped and the sea below him turned grey-white like the colour of his wings.

He descended to the shore and this time covered his body with the bright feathers of the blue jay. Up into the sky he went and the sea turned as blue as his plumage.

A third time he changed; the bright tones of the robin now covered him from head to toe and when he circled the air, the sky and the sea gleamed deepest red.

He returned to the shore once more and addressed his parents.

"My powers were tried yesterday; today they have been proved. It is time for me to leave you and return to my true home; for I am the sun's offspring. But don't think that you will not see me again. When you stand on the shore, find something white; an offering that I may see from my home in the west. For I shall be waiting and looking out for you. And you need not feel lonely. Whenever you have need of me I shall appear in the twilight sky and the sea shall reflect my glory."

As a parting gift, the boy gave his mother a wonderful robe that contained part of his power. Wearing it loosely, she could summon the Storm Spirit, Black Cloud or the Mist of the Sea. But when she sat on the sea-shore, she preferred to wrap it close about her as she watched, as she waited.

Sometimes, in the late autumn, when the evenings were chill and a greyness spread from the sky, the father and mother of the boy stood together by the sea. They threw into the air tiny white feathers and shells. They called towards the sky:

"It is dreary and dull on the shore tonight and the earth yearns for a sight of your face!"

As they watched, they saw the clouds part. The chill sea breezes touched their cheeks. Then a rose-tinged light fell from where the sky was now clear, the clouds having dispersed. It shone into their eyes and they blinked. They then looked out upon the Great Water and saw it streaked with colour; the golden glow they remembered in their son and the crimson-dappled waves of evening.

OTHER WORLDS

Goldenhair

EVA MARTIN

In a land far away, a homeless young man, Jean-Pierre by name, travelled on his white horse through the land. One day he came to a castle that had been built in an ancient forest. "It is the castle of a king," the white horse told Jean-Pierre.

"Do you think he would hire me?" said Jean-Pierre, a homely lad who wore a grey sheepskin wig on his head.

"You can only go and ask him."

Jean-Pierre went up and knocked on the castle door. The king himself answered the door, and when Jean-Pierre offered his services as a gardener, the king hired him, for a king can never have too many servants. Jean-Pierre was given a little hut at the edge of the garden to live in. It was near the stable so he could look after the white horse. Every day he fed the white horse hay and oats and brushed him from head to foot.

Now, the king had two daughters, of whom the youngest was the most beautiful. The window of her bedroom looked out onto the garden. Every day she carried meals to the new gardener. One fine morning she saw Jean-Pierre washing his face and his hair. She saw that under the sheepskin wig he had the most beautiful hair in the world, fine golden hair that shone in the light.

When she took him his dinner that day, she asked him, "Why do you wear that funny cap?"

"Beautiful princess, I am bald. People called me 'Little Baldy,' and that made me very angry."

"You are no more bald than I am," was all the princess said but she kept the little gardener's secret.

War broke out on all fronts. The neighbouring king began to invade the kingdom. The call went out and everyone with strong feet and good eyes enlisted in the army. The white horse said to Jean-Pierre, "The king has gone to war, but he doesn't have enough soldiers, and he will lose. Do you feel like helping him?" Jean-Pierre was as brave as he was small, and he agreed. He took off his sheepskin wig and let his golden hair fall down to his shoulders. He put on a suit of white armour that he found in his horse's stall. And his enchanted horse became whiter than snow.

Jean-Pierre set off for the war at full speed. Like an arrow, he shot before his king's army. He passed close to the king and bowed deeply. Then he went on alone on the white horse to attack the army of the enemy king. Jean-Pierre and the white horse leaped one hundred feet in the air, sending off flashes of fire as they landed in front of the enemy king. Terrified by this splendid knight in white armour who attacked an entire army by himself, the enemy took flight.

Jean-Pierre returned to his king's battlefield where he again bowed deeply and then galloped off toward the castle and disappeared. The king returned to his castle, thinking, "I wonder who that golden-haired prince is. He is so strong and courageous that I won the battle, and not one of my soldiers was killed." When the youngest princess passed by he asked her, "Did you see a golden-haired prince dressed all in white pass by?"

"No, I saw no one more beautiful than the little gardener," she replied.

"The gardener! Don't talk about him in the same breath!"

The next day, the princess took Jean-Pierre his dinner. She arrived before he had finished dressing, and again saw his beautiful golden hair which shone like the rays of the rising sun. But she did not let him know that she had noticed it.

As Jean-Pierre was brushing the white horse, he heard that a second battle was about to begin. And the white horse declared, "We must help the king. Today we will wear red from head to toe."

At the appointed hour, there they were, completely attired in red. The horse's coat appeared a fiery red and the little gardener had taken off his wig. At full gallop Jean-Pierre crossed in front of his king's army, stopped briefly before the king and bowed deeply. Before the king had time to say a word, the red knight and horse had slipped away. The horse leaped two hundred feet in the air and came down in front of the enemy king, who was so astounded that he ordered his soldiers to retreat. The enchanted horse took Jean-Pierre back before his king and bowed deeply. But before the king could grab him he had disappeared in the direction of the castle.

Upon returning to his court, the king said to his youngest daughter, "I don't understand it. Once again a mysterious knight with long golden hair won the battle for me. But I do not know who he is. I tried to catch him when he returned, but he slipped away. He was even more beautiful than the white knight."

"Not more beautiful than my little gardener."

"Hold your tongue. It is not appropriate to speak of the red knight in the same breath as your 'little gardener.'"

The next morning, for a third time, the white horse asked Jean-Pierre to help the king. "Once again there is to be a great battle. Today we will attire ourselves completely in black to mark the death of our enemy king and the end of the war."

Both the horse and Jean-Pierre appeared in velvety black. Only Jean-Pierre's hair remained the richest, finest gold. Again the horse stopped in front of the king. Jean-Pierre bowed deeply, and then with his black sword clutched in his hand, he galloped ahead. Horse and rider leaped one thousand feet into the air, and landing in front of the enemy king, Jean-Pierre struck him down with the blade of his sword and routed his army so quickly that the sun was eclipsed by the dust it created.

The king was determined not to let this faithful knight slip away. "Cut him off," he cried. "We must catch him. I wish to know who he is."

This time the black knight did not take time to bow before his king, but as the horse leaped away the king hurled his lance and the point lodged in Jean-Pierre's thigh. Then the wounded man disappeared before anyone could discover who he was.

After he returned to his castle, the king plotted how he could discover who these three knights were. He decided to organize a tournament and invite all the knights for miles around to attend. Whoever brought him the point of his broken lance would have in marriage the princess of his choice from his two beautiful daughters.

Young men came from all corners of the kingdom bringing with them the ends of forks, pieces of axe, or points of a sickle, but none of these fitted the king's broken lance. The king dismissed them all. The only one who did not appear was the golden-haired knight.

One day, the white horse said to Jean-Pierre, "My old friend, the king is having a tournament today. Let us go to it dressed all in black."

They arrived just before the tournament started. They were all in black except for Jean-Pierre's golden hair which blew in the wind. The horse leaped into the air and came down in the middle of the tournament field. The king and his courtiers tried to grab him as he flew by, but he was as quick as lightning and disappeared like an arrow, leaving behind a trail of gold.

The king was very disappointed and said, "Tomorrow, there will be another tournament to which this knight is bound to come. He will not succeed again in passing under our noses like that."

Returning to the castle, Jean-Pierre led his horse to the stable, went back to the little hut and put on his sheepskin wig again. The beautiful princess saw him pass by and noticed that he limped, but she did not say a word.

The next morning the white horse said to Jean-Pierre, "Today there is to be another tournament. Let us dress in red." Together they set out, and the horse made a great leap which landed them in the middle of the tournament field. Everyone had eyes only for the red knight with the golden hair flowing down to his shoulders. The king raised his arms and cried out joyously, "There he is. He won our second battle. Don't let him get away." The handsome knight in red paraded back and forth in front of the king, but just as he was about to be surrounded on all sides, the red horse leaped up and flew away through the air like a flaming arrow.

The king was very upset. "He is swifter than a fish in the sea. But tomorrow he will not make fun of us again like that."

Jean-Pierre tended the horse and changed back into his old clothes. He put on the sheepskin wig. The young princess who had eyes only for him noticed again that he limped, but she just smiled in a knowing way.

The next morning Jean-Pierre said to his horse, "Don't you think we have been playing tricks on the king for long enough?"

"There is only one tournament left. This last time we shall dress all in white for it is our best colour."

Jean-Pierre sat on the horse radiating with light. His golden hair shone like the rays of the rising sun. Seeing them reappear on the tournament field, the king shouted, "There is the knight who won our first battle. Without him we would never have won the war. We must catch him this time."

However, the young knight was far too nimble to fall into any trap the king might set, and he escaped back to his garden. The king was very disheartened, and when he saw his two daughters he said, "My children, you have been very badly treated. Not one of those handsome knights came forward to ask for a princess's hand in marriage. You are destined to become old maids."

The king wandered dejectedly about his garden. The little gardener waited at the door of his hut for him to pass by.

"Look, Your Majesty," he said, "won't this iron piece fit exactly on the break in your lance?" The king turned around, astounded. How could a simple gardener have such pretensions? He said nothing but placed the iron piece against the break in his lance. He could not believe his eyes. He yelled at the top of his voice, "Come and see. The little gardener has found the iron piece that fits my lance."

"I found it while I was gardening."

"Never mind. I have given my word. Whoever found the broken end of my lance could choose a wife from between my two daughters. Now my little gardener, which one do you choose?"

Jean-Pierre took off his sheepskin wig and tossed it up to the castle ceiling. His golden hair fell in waves down to his shoulders. Everyone recognized in him the knight who had won the war. Without hesitation Jean-Pierre chose the younger, beautiful daughter to be his bride. People came from miles around to the wedding.

In the middle of the wedding feast, Jean-Pierre remembered his friend the white horse and went out to the stable to look after him. The white horse said, "Before we are separated forever, will you do me a favour?"

"Certainly, my white horse, for I owe you everything."

"Take that axe from that dark corner over there, and cut me in two. You will not regret it."

Although he was horrified, he could not possibly refuse. Jean-Pierre took the axe, closed his eyes, and brought it down on the white horse's head, cutting him into two pieces. A handsome prince emerged. The king was very pleased, for it meant that his older daughter would also be married. And the celebrations continued for many more days.

Bye Bye

SEAN O HUIGIN

there's a creaking
in the darkness
a groaning in
the night
there are mutters
in the next
room
oh please
turn on the
light
there are footsteps
in the hallway
there's a
croaking over
there
AAAAAAAAAARRRRGGHHHHHH
an horrid
monster
has got me
by the hair
oh please don't
eat my fingers
oh please
don't bite my
nose
oh please
somebody
save me

GLUMP

The Talking Cat

NATALIE SAVAGE CARLSON

Once in another time, my friends, a great change came into Tante Odette's life although she was already an old woman who thought she had finished with such nonsense as changing one's habits.

It all happened because of a great change that came over Chouchou. The gray cat was a good companion because he seemed quite content to live on bread crusts and cabbage soup. Tante Odette kept a pot of soup boiling on the back of the stove. She added a little more water and a few more cabbage leaves to it each day. In this way, she always had soup on hand and she never had to throw any of it away.

She baked her own bread in her outdoor oven once a week, on Tuesday. If the bread grew stale by Saturday or Sunday, she softened it in the cabbage soup. So nothing was wasted.

As Tante Odette worked at her loom every evening, Chouchou would lie on the little rug by the stove and steadily stare at her with his big green eyes.

"If only you could talk," Tante Odette would say, "what company you would be for me."

One fall evening, Tante Odette was busy at her loom. Her stubby fingers flew among the threads like pigeons. Thump, thump went the loom.

Suddenly there was a thump, thump that didn't come from the loom. It came from the door.

The old woman took the lamp from the low table and went to the door. She opened it slowly. The light from the lamp shone on a queer old man who had the unmistakable look of the woods. He wore a bright red sash around his waist and a black crow's feather in his woolen cap. He had a bushy moustache like a homemade broom and a brown crinkled face.

"Pierre Leblanc at your service," said the old man, making a deep bow.

"What do you want?" asked Tante Odette sharply. "I can't stand here all night with the door open. It wastes heat and firewood."

"I seek shelter and work," answered Pierre Leblanc. "I am getting too old to trap for furs or work in the lumber camps. I would like a job in just such a cozy little place as this."

"I don't need any help," snapped Tante Odette. "I am quite able to do everything by myself. And I have my cat."

She was beginning to close the door, but the man put his gnarled hand against it. He was staring at Chouchou.

"A very smart cat he looks to be," he said. "Why don't you ask him if you should take me in? After all, you need pay me nothing but a roof over my head and a little food."

Tante Odette's eyes grew bigger.

"How ridiculous!" she said. "A cat can't talk. I only wish — "

To her great surprise, Chouchou started to talk.

"Oh, indeed I can," he told her, "if the matter is important enough. This Pierre Leblanc looks to me like a very fine man and a good worker. You should take him in."

Tante Odette stood with her mouth open for two minutes before she could make any sound come out of it. At last she said, "Then come in. It is so rare for a cat to be able to talk that I'm sure one should listen to him when he does."

The old man walked close to the stove and stretched his fingers toward it. He looked at the pot of soup bubbling on the back.

Chouchou spoke again.

"Pierre looks hungry," he said. "Offer him some soup — a big, deep bowl of it."

"Oh, dear," sighed Tante Odette, "at this rate, our soup won't last out the week. But if you say so, Chouchou."

Pierre sat at the wooden table and gulped down the soup like a starved wolf. When he had finished, Tante Odette pointed to the loft where he would sleep. Then she took the big gray cat on her lap.

"This is a most amazing thing that you should begin talking after all these years. Whatever came over you?"

But Chouchou had nothing more to say. He covered his nose with the tip of his tail, and there was not another word out of him all night.

Tante Odette decided that the cat's advice had been good. No longer did she have to go to the barn and feed the beasts. And no more skunks crawled into her oven because Pierre saw to it that the door was kept closed. He was indeed a good worker. He seemed quite satisfied with his bed in the loft and his bowls of cabbage soup and chunks of bread.

Only Chouchou seemed to have grown dissatisfied since his arrival.

"Why do you feed Pierre nothing but cabbage soup and bread?" he asked one day. "A workingman needs more food than that. How about some headcheese and pork pie?"

Tante Odette was startled, but Pierre went on drinking his soup.

"But meat is scarce and costs money," she told the cat.

"Pouf!" said the cat. "It is well worth it. Even I am getting a little tired of cabbage soup. A nice pork pie for dinner tomorrow would fill all the empty cracks inside me."

So when Pierre went out to the barn to water the beasts, Tante Odette stealthily lifted the lid of the chest, fished out a torn woolen sock and pulled a few coins out of it. She jumped in surprise when she raised her head and saw Pierre standing in the open doorway watching her.

"I forgot the pail," said Pierre. "I will draw some water from the well while I am about it."

The old woman hastily dropped the lid of the chest and got the pail from behind the stove.

"After Pierre has done his chores," said Chouchou, "he will be glad to go to the store and buy the meat for you."

Tante Odette frowned at the cat.

"But I am the thriftiest shopper in the parish," she said. "I can bring old Henri Dupuis down a few pennies on everything I buy."

"Pierre is a good shopper, too," said Chouchou. "In all Canada, there is not a better judge of meat. Perhaps he will even see something that you would not have thought to buy. Send him to the store."

It turned out that the old man was just as good a shopper as Chouchou had said. He returned from the village with a pinkish piece of pork, a freshly dressed pig's head, a bag of candy, and some tobacco for himself.

"But my money," said Tante Odette. "Did you spend all of it?"

"What is money for but to spend?" asked Chouchou from his rug by the stove. "Can you eat money or smoke it in a pipe?"

"No," said Tante Odette.

"Can you put it over your shoulders to keep you warm?"

"No."

"Would it burn in the stove to cook your food?"

"Oh, no, indeed!"

Chouchou closed his eyes.

"Then what good is money?" he asked. "The sooner one gets rid of it, the better."

Tante Odette's troubled face smoothed.

"I never saw it that way before," she agreed. "Of course, you are right, Chouchou. And you are right, too, Pierre, for choosing such fine food."

But when Pierre went out to get a cabbage from the shed, Tante Odette walked to the chest again and counted her coins.

"I have a small fortune, Chouchou," she said. "Now explain to me again why these coins are no good."

But Chouchou had nothing more to say about the matter.

One Tuesday when Pierre Leblanc was cutting trees in the woods and Tante Odette was baking her loaves of bread in the outdoor oven, a stranger came galloping down the road on a one-eyed horse. He stopped in front of the white fence. He politely dismounted and went over to Tante Odette.

The old woman saw at a glance that he was a man of the woods. His blouse was checked and his cap red. Matching it was the red sash tied around his waist. He looked very much like Pierre Leblanc.

"Can you tell me, madame," he asked, "if a man named Pierre Leblanc works here?"

"Yes, he does," answered Tante Odette, "and a very good worker he is."

The stranger did not look satisfied.

"Of course, Canada is full of Pierre Leblancs," he said. "It is a very common name. Does this Pierre Leblanc wear a red sash like mine?"

"So he does," said Tante Odette.

"On the other hand," said the man, "many Pierre Leblancs wear red sashes. Does he have a moustache like a homemade broom?"

"Yes, indeed," said the woman.

"But there must be many Pierre Leblancs with red sashes and moustaches like brooms," continued the stranger. "This Pierre Leblanc who now works for you, can he throw his voice?"

"Throw his voice!" cried Tante Odette. "What witchcraft is that?"

"Haven't you heard of such a gift?" asked the man. "But of course only a few have it — probably only one Pierre Leblanc in a thousand. This Pierre with you, can he throw his voice behind trees and in boxes and up on the roof so it sounds as if someone else is talking?"

"My faith, no!" cried the woman in horror. "I wouldn't have such a one in my house. He would be better company for the *loup-garou*, that evil one who can change into many shapes."

The man laughed heartily.

"My Pierre Leblanc could catch the *loup-garou* in a wolf trap and lead him around by the chain. He is that clever. That is why I am trying to find him. I want him to go trapping with me in the woods this winter. One says that never have there been so many foxes. I need Pierre, for he is smarter than any fox."

The creak of wheels caused them both to turn around. Pierre Leblanc was driving the ox team in from the woods. He stared at the man standing beside Tante Odette. The man stared back at Pierre. Then both men began bouncing on their feet and whooping in their throats. They hugged each other. They kissed each other on the cheek.

"Good old Pierre!"

"Georges, my friend, where have you kept yourself all summer? How did you find me?"

Tante Odette left them whooping and hugging. She walked into the house with a worried look on her face. She sat down at her loom. Finally she stopped weaving and turned to Chouchou.

"I am a little dizzy, Chouchou," she said. "This *loup-garou* voice has upset me. What do you make of it all?"

Chouchou said nothing.

"Please tell me what to do," pleaded Tante Odette. "Shall we let him stay here? It would be very uncomfortable to have voices coming from the roof and the trees."

Chouchou said nothing. Tante Odette angrily threw the shuttle at him.

"Where is your tongue?" she demanded. "Have you no words for me when I need them most?"

But if a cat will not speak, who has got his tongue?

Pierre Leblanc came walking in.

"Such a man!" he roared gleefully. "Only the woods are big enough for him."

"Are you going away with him?" asked the woman, not knowing whether she wanted him to say yes or no. If only Chouchou hadn't been so stubborn.

"That makes a problem," said Pierre. "If I go into the woods this winter, it will be cold and I will work like an ox. But there will be much money in my pocket after the furs are sold. If I stay here, I will be warm and comfortable but — "

He pulled his pockets inside out. Nothing fell from them.

"What is this business about your being able to throw your voice to other places?" asked Tante Odette.

"Did Georges say I could do that?"

Tante Odette nodded.

"Ha! Ha!" laughed Pierre. "What a joker Georges is!"

"But perhaps it is true," insisted the woman.

"If you really want to know," said Pierre, "ask Chouchou. He would not lie. Can I throw my voice, Chouchou?"

Chouchou sank down on his haunches and purred.

"Of course not!" he answered. "Whoever heard of such nonsense?"

Tante Odette sighed in relief. Then she remembered that this did not fix everything.

"Will you go with him?" she asked Pierre. "I have made it very comfortable for you here. And now it is only for supper that we have cabbage soup."

Chouchou spoke up.

"Tante Odette, how can you expect such a good man as Pierre Leblanc to work for only food and shelter? If you would pay him a coin from time to time, he would be quite satisfied to stay."

"But I can't afford that," said the woman.

"Of course you can," insisted Chouchou. "You have a small fortune in the old sock in your chest. Remember what I told you about money?"

"Tell me again," said Tante Odette. "It is hard to hold on to such a thought for long."

"Money is to spend," repeated the cat. "Can it carry hay and water to the beasts? Can it cut down trees for firewood? Can it dig paths through the snow when winter comes?"

"I have caught it again," said Tante Odette. "If you will stay with me, Pierre, I will pay you a coin from time to time."

Pierre smiled and bowed.

"Then I shall be very happy to stay here with you and your wise cat," he decided. "Now I will unload my wood and pile it into a neat stack by the door."

He briskly stamped out. Tante Odette sat down at her loom again.

"We have made a good bargain, haven't we, Chouchou?" She smiled contentedly.

But Chouchou tickled his nose with his tail and said nothing.

That is the way it was, my friends. It would have been a different story if Pierre had not been such a good worker. So remember this: if you must follow the advice of a talking cat, be sure you know who is doing the talking for him.

The Cremation of Sam McGee

ROBERT SERVICE

There are strange things done in the midnight sun
By the men who moil for gold;
The Arctic trails have their secret tales
That would make your blood run cold;
The Northern Lights have seen queer sights,
But the queerest they ever did see
Was that night on the marge of Lake Lebarge
I cremated Sam McGee.

Now Sam McGee was from Tennessee,
 where the cotton blooms and blows.
Why he left his home in the South to roam
 'round the Pole, God only knows.
He was always cold, but the land of gold
 seemed to hold him like a spell;
Though he'd often say in his homely way
 that "he'd sooner live in hell."

On a Christmas Day we were mushing our way
 over the Dawson trail.
Talk of your cold! through the parka's fold
 it stabbed like a driven nail.
If our eyes we'd close, then the lashes froze
 till sometimes we couldn't see;
It wasn't much fun, but the only one
 to whimper was Sam McGee.

And that very night, as we lay packed tight
     in our robes beneath the snow,
And the dogs were fed, and the stars o'erhead
     were dancing heel and toe,
He turned to me, and "Cap," says he,
     "I'll cash in this trip, I guess;
And if I do, I'm asking that you
     won't refuse my last request."

Well, he seemed so low that I couldn't say no;
     then he says with a sort of moan:
"It's the cursèd cold, and it's got right hold
     till I'm chilled clean through to the bone.
Yet 'tain't being dead — it's my awful dread
     of the icy grave that pains;
So I want you to swear that, foul or fair,
     you'll cremate my last remains."

A pal's last need is a thing to heed,
     so I swore I would not fail;
And we started on at the streak of dawn;
     but God! he looked ghastly pale.
He crouched on the sleigh, and he raved all day
     of his home in Tennessee;
And before nightfall a corpse was all
     that was left of Sam McGee.

There wasn't a breath in that land of death,
     and I hurried, horror-driven,
With a corpse half hid that I couldn't get rid,
     because of a promise given;
It was lashed to the sleigh, and it seemed to say:
     "You may tax your brawn and brains,
But you promised true, and it's up to you
     to cremate those last remains."

Now a promise made is a debt unpaid,
    and the trail has its own stern code.
In the days to come, though my lips were dumb,
    in my heart how I cursed that load.
In the long, long night, by the lone firelight,
    while the huskies, round in a ring,
Howled out their woes to the homeless snows —
    O God! how I loathed the thing.

And every day that quiet clay
    seemed to heavy and heavier grow;
And on I went, though the dogs were spent
    and the grub was getting low;
The trail was bad, and I felt half mad,
    but I swore I would not give in;
And I'd often sing to the hateful thing,
    and it hearkened with a grin.

Till I came to the marge of Lake Lebarge,
    and a derelict there lay;
It was jammed in the ice, but I saw in a trice
    it was called the "Alice May."
And I looked at it, and I thought a bit,
    and I looked at my frozen chum;
Then "Here," said I, with a sudden cry,
    "is my cre-ma-tor-eum."

Some planks I tore from the cabin floor,
    and I lit the boiler fire;
Some coal I found that was lying around,
    and I heaped the fuel higher;
The flames just soared, and the furnace roared —
    such a blaze you seldom see;
And I burrowed a hole in the glowing coal,
    and I stuffed in Sam McGee.

Then I made a hike, for I didn't like
    to hear him sizzle so;
And the heavens scowled, and the huskies howled,
    and the wind began to blow.
It was icy cold, but the hot sweat rolled
    down my cheeks, and I don't know why;
And the greasy smoke in an inky cloak
    went streaking down the sky.

I do not know how long in the snow
    I wrestled with grisly fear;
But the stars came out and they danced about
    ere again I ventured near;
I was sick with dread, but I bravely said:
    "I'll just take a peep inside.
I guess he's cooked, and it's time I looked";
    . . . then the door I opened wide.

And there sat Sam, looking cool and calm,
　　in the heart of the furnace roar;
And he wore a smile you could see a mile,
　　and he said: "Please close that door.
It's fine in here, but I greatly fear
　　you'll let in the cold and storm —
Since I left Plumtree, down in Tennessee,
　　it's the first time I've been warm."

There are strange things done in the midnight sun
　　By the men who moil for gold;
The Arctic trails have their secret tales
　　That would make your blood run cold;
The Northern Lights have seen queer sights,
　　But the queerest they ever did see
Was that night on the marge of Lake Lebarge
　　I cremated Sam McGee.

The Pedler

DUNCAN CAMPBELL SCOTT

He used to come in the early spring-time, when, in sunny hollows, banks of coarse snow lie thawing, shrinking with almost inaudible tinklings, when the upper grassbanks are covered thickly with the film left by the melted snow, when the old leaves about the grey trees are wet and sodden, when the pools lie bare and clear, without grasses, very limpid with snow-water, when the swollen streams rush insolently by, when the grosbeaks try the cedar buds shyly, and a colony of little birds take a sunny tree slope, and sing songs there.

He used to come with the awakening of life in the woods, with the strange cohosh, and the dog-tooth violet, piercing the damp leaf which it would wear as a ruff about its neck in blossom time. He used to come up the road from St. Valérie, trudging heavily, bearing his packs. To most of the Viger people he seemed to appear suddenly in the midst of the street, clothed with power, and surrounded by an attentive crowd of boys, and a whirling fringe of dogs, barking and throwing up dust.

I speak of what has become tradition, for the pedler walks no more up the St. Valérie road, bearing those magical baskets of his.

There was something powerful, compelling, about him; his short, heavy figure, his hair-covered, expressionless face, the quick hands in which he seemed to weigh everything that he touched, his voluminous, indescribable clothes, the great umbrella he carried strapped to his back, the green spectacles that hid his eyes, all these commanded attention. But his powers seemed to lie in those inscrutable guards to his eyes. They were such goggles as are commonly used by threshers, and were bound firmly about his face by a leather lace; with their setting of iron they completely covered his eye-sockets, not permitting a glimpse of those eyes that seemed to glare out of their depths. They seemed never to have been removed, but to have grown there, rooted by time in his cheek-bones.

He carried a large wicker-basket covered with oiled cloth, slung to his shoulder by a strap; in one hand he carried a light stick, in the other a large oval bandbox of black shiny cloth. From the initials "J. F.," which appeared in faded white letters on the bandbox, the village people had christened him Jean-François.

Coming into the village, he stopped in the middle of the road, set his bandbox between his feet, and took the oiled cloth from the basket. He never went from house to house, his customers came to him. He stood there and sold, almost without a word, as calm as a sphinx, and as power-ful. There was something compelling about him; the people bought things they did not want, but they had to buy. The goods lay before them, the

handkerchiefs, the laces, the jewelry, the little sacred pictures, matches in coloured boxes, little cased looking-glasses, combs, mouth-organs, pins, and hairpins; and over all, this figure with the inscrutable eyes. As he took in the money and made change, he uttered the word, "good," continually, "good, good." There was something exciting in the way he pronounced that word, something that goaded the hearers into extravagance.

It happened one day in April, when the weather was doubtful and moody, and storms flew low, scattering cold rain, and after that day Jean-François, the pedler, was a shape in memory, a fact no longer. He was blown into the village unwetted by a shower that left the streets untouched, and that went through the northern fields sharply, and lost itself in the far woods. He stopped in front of the post office. The Widow Laroque slammed her door and went upstairs to peep through the curtain; "these pedlers spoiled trade," she said, and hated them in consequence. Soon a crowd collected, and great talk arose, with laughter and some jostling. Everyone tried to see into the basket, those behind stood on tiptoe and asked questions, those in front held the crowd back and tried to look at the goods. The air was full of the staccato of surprise and admiration. The late comers on the edge of the crowd commenced to jostle, and somebody tossed a handful of dust into the air over the group. "What a wretched wind," cried someone, "it blows all ways."

The dust seemed to irritate the pedler, besides, no one had bought anything. He called out sharply, "Buy — buy." He sold two papers of hairpins, a little brass shrine of La Bonne St. Anne, a coloured handkerchief, a horn comb, and a mouth-organ. While these purchases were going on, Henri Lamoureux was eyeing the little red purses, and fingering a coin in his pocket. The coin was a doubtful one, and he was weighing carefully the chances of passing it. At last he said, carelessly, "How much?" touching the purses. The pedler's answer called out the coin from his pocket; it lay in the man's hand. Henri took the purse and moved hurriedly back. At once the pedler grasped after him, reaching as well as his basket would allow; he caught him by the coat; but Henri's dog darted in, nipped the pedler's leg, and got away, showing his teeth. Lamoureux struggled, the pedler swore; in a moment everyone was jostling to get out of the way, wondering what was the matter. As Henri swung his arm around he swept his hand across the pedler's eyes; the shoe-string gave way, and the green goggles fell into the basket. Then a curious change came over the man. He let his enemy go, and stood dazed for a moment; he passed his hand across his eyes, and in that interval of quiet the people saw, where they expected to see flash the two rapacious eyes of their imaginings, only the seared, fleshy seams where those eyes should have been.

That was the vision of a moment, for the pedler, like a fiend in fury, threw up his long arms and cursed in a voice so powerful and sudden that the dismayed crowd shrunk away, clinging to one another and looking

over their shoulders at the violent figure. "God have mercy! — Holy St. Anne protect us! — He curses his Baptism!" screamed the women. In a second he was alone; the dog that had assailed him was snarling from under the sidewalk, and the women were in the nearest houses. Henri Lamoureux, in the nearest lane, stood pale, with a stone in his hand. It was only for one moment; in the second, the pedler had gathered his things, blind as he was, had turned his back, and was striding up the street; in the third, one of the sudden storms had gathered the dust at the end of the village and came down with it, driving everyone indoors. It shrouded the retreating figure, and a crack of unexpected thunder came like a pistol shot, and then the pelting rain.

Some venturesome souls who looked out when the storm was nearly over, declared they saw, large on the hills, the figure of the pedler, walking enraged in the fringes of the storm. One of these was Henri Lamoureux, who, to this day, has never found the little red purse.

"I would have sworn I had it in this hand when he caught me; but I felt it fly away like a bird."

"But what made the man curse everyone so when you just bought that little purse — say that?"

"Well, I know not, do you? Anyway he has my quarter, and he was blind — blind as a stone fence."

"Blind! Not he!" cried the Widow Laroque. "He was the Old Boy himself, I told you — it is always as I say, you see now — it was the old Devil himself."

However that might be, there are yet people in Viger who, when the dust blows, and a sharp storm comes up from the south-east, see the figure of the enraged pedler, large upon the hills, striding violently along the fringes of the storm.

The Ships of Yule

BLISS CARMAN

When I was just a little boy,
Before I went to school,
I had a fleet of forty sail
I called the Ships of Yule;

Of every rig, from rakish brig
And gallant barkentine,
To little Fundy fishing boats
With gunwales painted green.

They used to go on trading trips
Around the world for me,
For though I had to stay on shore
My heart was on the sea.

They stopped at every port to call
From Babylon to Rome,
To load with all the lovely things
We never had at home;

With elephants and ivory
Bought from the King of Tyre,
And shells and silks and sandal-wood
That sailor men admire;

With figs and dates from Samarcand,
And squatty ginger-jars,
And scented silver amulets
From Indian bazaars;

With sugar-cane from Port of Spain,
And monkeys from Ceylon,
And paper lanterns from Pekin
With painted dragons on;

With cocoanuts from Zanzibar,
And pines from Singapore;
And when they had unloaded these
They could go back for more.

And even after I was big
And had to go to school,
My mind was often far away
Aboard the Ships of Yule.

OTHER TIMES

The Baker's Magic Wand

CYRUS MACMILLAN

Once very long ago in the days when Canada was owned by the French there lived on the banks of a great river a wicked lawyer who was in love with a baker's wife. He tried in various ways to get rid of the baker, but without success. They lived not far from the Seigneur who owned all the land around and was very powerful. Now, in front of the Seigneur's palace there was a great lake of more than twelve thousand acres. One morning the lawyer went to the palace and knocked at the door. When the Seigneur came out, he said to him, "Sire, there is a man not far from here who boasts that in less than twice twenty-four hours he can change this lake into a beautiful meadow covered with grass that would give hay enough for all your horses and would be to the great advantage of the colony." Then the Seigneur said, "Who is this man?" The lawyer answered, "He is no less than the baker who furnishes your household with bread." So the Seigneur said, "I will send for him."

The lawyer went away, and the Seigneur sent a letter to the baker saying that he wanted to see him. The poor baker thought he was to get his pay for the bread he had provided for the Seigneur and all his servants and soldiers. So he was very glad, and went quickly to the palace and knocked at the door. When the Seigneur came out, he asked what was wanted of him. The Seigneur answered that he had heard of his boast that in less than twice twenty-four hours he could change all the lake into a beautiful meadow covered with grass and clover that would feed all the Seigneur's horses and would be a great advantage to the colony. Now, unless within twice twenty-four hours the lake was changed into a meadow, the baker should be hanged before the door of the palace.

Then the Seigneur turned away and the baker went out discouraged, for he did not know what to do. He walked off into the woods and sat down on a log to weep. After a long time an old woman came along and asked what was the matter. He said he was very miserable; he was going to be hanged in twice twenty-four hours; for the Seigneur had commanded him to change all the lake into a meadow, covered with grass and clover, and he was not able to do it. Now, this old woman was a good fairy in disguise and when the baker had done speaking she told him not to be troubled but to go to sleep. She gave him a wand just like a broken stick, which she told him to wave before he slept; it had great power, she said, and while he slept it would bring to pass whatever he desired. So he waved the wand and went to sleep. When he had slept an hour, he was awakened

by the smell of hay, and when he looked about him, he saw that the lake was all gone and that there was only a small river that ran through the middle of a beautiful meadow down to the great river not far away. The good fairy was still by his side. She told him to go to the Seigneur and show him what he had done. He went to the palace, and when he came near, he saw the Seigneur looking out of the window at the meadow, and all the men and horses at work making hay. He knocked at the door, and when the Seigneur came downstairs, he asked him if he was satisfied. The Seigneur said he was not satisfied, because the river had been left running through the middle of the meadow. The baker told the Seigneur that the river had been left to provide water for the animals and to help in making hay, because there was so much hay that all the horses in the land could not draw it and it would have to be brought in boats. Then the Seigneur was satisfied and sent the baker away.

Soon the wicked lawyer came again, and the Seigneur showed him the meadow and the men and women and horses making hay. The lawyer was much surprised to see all this, but he did not say so. Instead, he told the Seigneur that he had no doubt the baker could do a great deal more than that; the baker, he said, had boasted that he could make a *tiens-bon-la* for the Seigneur that would be worth a great deal more than the meadow and would be a great advantage to the colony. "What is a *tiens-bon-la?*" asked the Seigneur. "I do not know," answered the lawyer; "but the baker said he could make one." "I will send for him," said the Seigneur. So he sent for the baker, who was just making his bread. When he had put the bread into the oven, he went to the palace and knocked again, and the Seigneur came to the door. The Seigneur said: "I have heard that you boasted that you can make a *tiens-bon-la* that would be worth more than the meadow and a great advantage to the colony. Now you shall go home and make it, and unless you bring it to me in twice twenty-four hours, you shall be hanged before the palace gate." The baker asked, "What is a *tiens-bon-la?*" The Seigneur said, "I do not know, but I must have one within twice twenty-four hours." Then he went into his palace again.

The poor baker went away more sorrowful than before. He had no idea of what a *tiens-bon-la* was; but yet he knew he should be hanged unless he made one within twice twenty-four hours. He went out into the forest again and sat down on the same log as he had sat on before, and wept as hard as he could. When he had cried himself to sleep, the good old fairy came again and waked him up and asked him what was the matter. He told her that he should certainly be hanged this time, for he had been ordered to make a *tiens-bon-la* for the Seigneur, and he did not know what it was. Then the fairy said, "It is only that wicked lawyer who is in love with your wife and wants to get rid of you. You must do what I tell you and the lawyer will be punished, for we shall make a *tiens-bon-la* that will satisfy the Seigneur. Go to your home and tell your wife that you are commanded to make a *tiens-bon-la* for the Seigneur and that you have nothing to make it of. Tell her to put two days' provisions in a bag for you, and when she has them all ready, go to your room and take the latch off the window. Then say good-bye to your wife, and walk about the country until it is dark. As soon as you are gone your wife will send for the lawyer and invite him to supper. Before he comes, and after it is dark, you must come back to your house and get in at the window and hide yourself under the bed. Now, the lawyer will not eat without first washing his hands. When he comes, your wife will send him into the room where you are hiding to wash, and when he takes hold of the wash-basin you must cry out 'tiens-bon-la.' Take this wand that I will give you and anything you wave it at when you cry 'tiens-bon-la' will hold fast to whatever it is touching." Then she gave him another wand and went her way.

The baker did as the fairy had told him, and his wife was very glad to learn that he was going away; and she packed up a large bag of provisions and sent him off. As soon as he was out of the house she sent a note to the lawyer telling him that her husband was gone away for two days and that she would like to have him come to supper. The baker walked around the country until it was dark, and then came back and hid himself under the bed. His wife told the servant to set the table and prepare a nice supper, and then she went to get ready to receive the lawyer. Soon the lawyer arrived. The servant showed him into a room where he might wash his hands after his day's work before he sat down to his meal. The baker was under the bed in the room. There was some water that was not very clean in the wash-basin, and when the lawyer took hold of the basin to throw the water out, the baker, who was under the bed, waved his wand and cried out "*tiens-bon-la*," and the lawyer's hands stuck to the basin so that he could not let go and the basin stuck to the wash-stand. He called out to the servant to come and help him, but she was busy about the supper and did not hear him. So then he cried out as loud as he could, "Madame, Madame." When the baker's wife heard him, she was dreadfully frightened

and ran in to see what was the matter. When she found the lawyer stuck to
the wash-stand, which was very large and heavy, she took hold of him
with both hands to pull him away. Then her husband cried out from under
the bed "*tiens-bon-la*," and the wife could not let go the lawyer. Then the
baker went out and called in some of his friends, and they ate the supper
and drank the wine that had been prepared for the lawyer who was stuck to
the wash-stand, and the wife, who could not let go the lawyer.

When morning came, the baker took the wand that the fairy had
given him and told his wife and the lawyer that if they wanted to get loose
they must do as he told them. With his wand he loosened the basin from
the wash-stand. Then he made them go out into the street, and he started
them towards the Seigneur's palace.

As soon as they all came out into the light, the baker saw that there
was a hole in his wife's dress, so he pulled some grass and twisted it into a

wisp and filled up the hole. Presently they came to a cow that was feeding by the side of the road. There was not much grass there and the cow was hungry, so when she saw the wisp of grass sticking from the woman's dress she began to eat it; but the baker waved his wand and cried "*tiens-bon-la*" and the cow's teeth stuck in the grass and the grass stuck to the dress. They all went along until they came to a house where there was a large dog on the doorstep. When the dog saw the people, he jumped over the fence to see where they were going. The cow gave him a switch with her tail across the nose, the baker cried "*tiens-bon-la*," and the dog stuck to the cow's tail and went along with the rest. When the old woman who owned the dog saw him going off in this manner, she was very angry; she called him but he would not come; then she ran out with the broom that she was using to sweep the floor, and began to beat the dog to drive him home. But the baker cried out "*tiens-bon-la*" again and so the broom stuck to the dog and the old woman could not let go the broom. The old woman's husband was quite lame; he ran after his wife, limping along with a stick. He could not go very fast, but he went as well as he could to see what his old woman was beating the dog for. When he came up, he took hold of the woman's dress to pull her away, but the baker cried out "*tiens-bon-la*" again and the lame farmer had to go limping along with the others.

So they all went to the Seigneur's palace — the lawyer with the heavy wash-basin, the woman holding on to the lawyer, the cow trying to eat the wisp of hay, the dog barking at the cow and sticking to her tail, the old woman with her broom, and the lame farmer limping along with his stick. The baker knocked at the door and when the Seigneur opened it he said: "Oh, my Seigneur, you ordered a *tiens-bon-la* and I have brought you one, the best that was ever made. If you will be pleased to try it, I hope you will be content." The Seigneur took hold of the basin to take it away from the lawyer, the baker cried "*tiens-bon-la*" again, and the Seigneur was held to the basin as fast as the others. He tried hard to get away but the *tiens-bon-la* was good and would not let go.

Then the Seigneur asked the baker what he would take to let him off.

After a long time the baker said he would let him go if the Seigneur would give a great sum of money every year to himself and to each of his fifteen children. The Seigneur consented, but the baker said he must have a deed made by a notary. So they sent for the notary and the deed was made, and the Seigneur signed it on the wash-basin. The baker waved his wand backwards, the *tiens-bon-la* was broken, and they all went away happy again, and the baker's wife never again deceived her husband.

The House at Hawthorn Bay

JANET LUNN

Rose Larkin, an orphan, is sent from New York City to eastern Ontario to live with an aunt and uncle and four cousins she has never met. It is soon obvious that this new family is going to take some getting used to, but this is only the first of Rose's worries. She comes across an old lady who introduces herself as Mrs. Morrissay and who seems to belong to another time . . . .

In The Root Cellar, *from which this excerpt is taken, Rose is swept back to the time of the American Civil War.*

They tumbled out of the station wagon and across the yard, four boys and a round untidy-looking woman carrying two large shopping bags, a potted geranium and, under one arm, a load of books.

Halfway across the yard Aunt Nan saw Rose. She stopped. The books slipped from under her arm. "Oh dear, never mind, are you looking for someone? Are — oh my Lord, you must be Rose!" she cried. "Oh, good heavens, it's today! Isn't it tomorrow? Oh, dear!"

"Mother! I told you the letter said Monday." A tall, thin, long-legged boy was half bouncing, half dancing on first one foot then the other in front of his mother. "I told you. Now, if you'd listen to what I —"

"Shut up, George. Mother, you're losing the groceries." The second boy, not quite as tall and not nearly as wild looking, grabbed the bags of groceries and the geranium before they could follow the books to the ground. He turned to stare at Rose. Two small boys grabbed him by his arms and whispered loudly and urgently, "Is it Rose, Sam? Is it?"

"I don't know. Are you Rose?"

"Yes, I'm Rose," said Rose stiffly, feeling all their eyes on her, conscious of how ridiculous she must look in her city boots and pants and fur jacket, standing by the old pump, desperate for a place to hide. Wildly she thought of running, but her feet would not budge. "Aunt Stella couldn't stay," she blurted out.

"Oh, Rose!" Aunt Nan had got over her surprise. She rushed over and threw her arms around Rose and gave her a warm kiss.

Rose flinched as though she had been struck. No one, in her memory, had ever showed her more affection than Grandmother's occasional pats on the head and Aunt Millicent's showy little kisses in the air. Aunt Nan did not seem to notice. She went on talking. She was astounding, the way she looked and the way she talked. She was short, and as plump as an overstuffed cushion. She had a full mouth, warm brown eyes and a lot of soft brown hair coming undone from a knot at the back of her head. She had on a loose plaid dress with a big, bright green sweater over it, no stockings, and on her feet a pair of running shoes with holes in them. And she never stopped talking.

"How tiny you are," she crowed. "My goodness, I can hardly see you inside that coat. I write stories for girls. It's to get away from boys your uncle Bob says, so you can imagine how nice it's going to be to have you here. Of course the new one might be a girl." Aunt Nan patted her stomach and Rose realized that some of the plumpness was because Aunt Nan was expecting a baby.

"Not that I don't like boys." Aunt Nan's voice sounded like a xylophone going up and down the scales. "I like my boys very much. Come and meet them. Imagine being this old and never knowing each other! Boys! Boys! Come and meet your cousin. Sam! George! Twins!"

The twins, dressed in identical jeans and dark blue sweaters, looked exactly like their mother with the same round faces, the same brown hair and round eyes. They inspected Rose solemnly from the protection of their mother's skirt.

"Jimmy and Brian are the babies. They're six. That's Sam, he's fourteen." Sam was crossing the yard with the fifth load of groceries. "Hello," he said, nodded curtly towards Rose and continued on his way. The only impression Rose had of him was that he was a big, stocky boy with bushy red hair.

"And that's George." Aunt Nan laughed. "George is fifteen. He talks a lot and thinks he knows everything."

George slammed the back of the station wagon shut with his foot and came loping towards them. He had light curly brown hair, blue eyes, a wide full mouth in a small round face. In his jeans and worn brown sweater, too short at the waist and wrists, he looked like a scarecrow.

"Hi," he said in a loud, croaking voice. "Hi. I knew you were coming today. You see I read the letter and —"

"And that's all of us except Uncle Bob who had to go to a meeting this afternoon in Soames. He'll be back soon."

"How do you do?" said Rose.

"Mother!" George was exasperated. "Mother, you forgot to introduce Grim. You see, Rose, we have a cat called Grim for Grimalkin, which means grey cat —"

"Come on," said Aunt Nan. "It's starting to rain again, and the wind's coming up. We'd better get your things inside, Rose, dear. Is that all you have, just that one little suitcase?"

"There are at least four thousand more in the kitchen," said George.

"Oh, good! Rose, where's Stella? How long have you been waiting for us out here in this wet yard?"

Rose explained that Aunt Stella had been in a hurry. She was going to mention meeting Mrs. Morrissay but Aunt Nan interrupted. "Same old Stella. No time for anything. I swear someday she's going to drop dead in the middle of a TV show and when they go to pick up the body they'll find it's nothing but dust because she's forgotten to eat for three months." With one hand firmly on Rose's arm, Aunt Nan steered her through the kitchen door, talking all the while. "Look at all those boxes! Oh, my goodness, child, I expect you left New York very early. You must be exhausted. Why don't I take you right up to your room? We only found out last week, of course, that you were coming, so we haven't had a chance to do much with it. Here, give me your suitcase. The boys can carry up the big ones."

"No, thank you. I'll carry it." Rose held tightly to her overnight bag and followed Aunt Nan from the dark kitchen through another gloomy room and up a flight of steep stairs to a little room at the back of the house. Like the outside of the house, and the glimpse she had had of downstairs, the room was dismal. Its flowered wallpaper, dried and yellowed with age, was in shreds. The plaster had come away from half of one wall, and where the roof had leaked there was a large brown stain on the ceiling and running down the wall by the bed. She could see that the wide boards of the floor had once been painted dark red but the paint was almost gone and some of the boards had come loose. A brass bed stood against one wall. There was a small white dresser beside it. Opposite, next to the window, was a low desk also painted white. The room smelled musty and a little sour — Sam told Rose later he thought it was because of all the dead rats and mice in the walls.

"The dresser and the desk were mine when I was little," said Aunt Nan, "and the bed was here in the house when we came. Isn't it nice?"

Rose did not answer. She had never been anywhere, dreamed of any place uglier or more depressing than this one. As though in answer to her

bitter thoughts, Aunt Nan sighed. "You probably think we're all crazy. People do, I guess. We're a bit disorganized but we've only been here a month. Your Uncle Bob was in the forces, and he's just retired. That's why we came down here. He's the game warden for the island, and this is all so much better for him we should have done it years ago. You know the house is one hundred and sixty years old — it's going to be beautiful when we get it fixed up and — oh Lord, Bob will be home any minute. I'd better get supper started. I'll leave you to settle yourself before supper. O.K.?" Without waiting for an answer she was off down the stairs, her burbling words punctuated by the excited whispers of the twins.

Then came Sam and George struggling with two heavy suitcases each, the twins right behind them.

"What's in these things? The Statue of Liberty? Haw! Haw!" George dropped the bags with a thump, tripped over Sam and went down for more. Sam put his down, said nothing, and turned to follow George. The twins scooted after. Up they came again until all the suitcases and boxes were piled around Rose who stood in the middle of the floor in an agony of shyness, willing them to be finished.

"Well," said George, "I guess that's done." Rose mumbled "thank you" but when she said nothing more, he cleared his throat, looked around, stared at her and said, "Well, see you later," and they were gone.

Rose closed the door after them as tightly as it would close. Still in her coat and boots, she sat on the edge of the bed. For a moment the chaos of the last weeks threatened to overwhelm her. One week she had been with her grandmother on her way to Paris, steeling herself to face boarding school, three days later she had been flying home with her grandmother lying dead in the baggage compartment. Three weeks more and she was in a run-down farmhouse in Canada surrounded by a family noisier, more rambunctious than any in her worst imaginings. She clamped her lips tightly shut and reached down and unzipped her overnight bag. It had in it her nightclothes in case she and Aunt Stella had had to stop at a motel, and her treasures: her music box and her mother's old copy of *The Secret Garden*. They had been hers since her parents died, and Rose had always carried them with her, feeling that without them, and the silver rose she wore on a chain around her neck, she wouldn't be any kind of person at all.

She became aware of a noise at her door. She looked up and saw the latch moving. She turned around quickly. "Who's there?"

The door was edged open and two pairs of brown eyes peered through the opening at her. "It's us," whispered the twins.

"Yes?"

"Mother says it's supper time." They stood looking at her for a moment, let out a long sigh in unison and retreated from the door. Rose could hear them thumping rapidly down the stairs.

She took off her boots, rummaged through her suitcases, found her loafers and the plaid skirt she was used to wearing, and put them on. "I don't suppose I need to wash for dinner," she muttered, but all the same she found her hairbrush and swiftly brushed through her short curls.

On her way downstairs she passed the open doorway of the next room. She caught a glimpse of firelight and stopped to peek inside. To her astonishment a girl was busily pulling up the covers on a big, handsome four-poster bed. There was a small black stove with a bright fire between the windows, a round rag rug on the floor and a cheerful tidiness that wasn't anywhere else in the house. Hastily she backed out, puzzled, and went downstairs.

Downstairs was like turning on a radio and getting all the stations at once. The television was going in the living room. George was perched on one arm of the sofa making running comments as he watched. Aunt Nan was beating something with an electric beater in the kitchen and talking in a loud voice to someone who made an occasional rumbling response. In sing-song voices the twins were anxiously telling their mother, "We don't want any peas, we don't want any peas."

Rose stood at the foot of the stairs trying to take it all in. The living room was in worse condition than her bedroom. It was a large room full of doors and windows, cluttered with furniture that appeared to have been left wherever the moving men had deposited it a month earlier. The bare lath was exposed through large holes in the walls. She couldn't understand why the front room upstairs had been made so charming while the living room was in such a state.

She went through into the kitchen which was much more cheerful. It had been scrubbed and repaired. Along one wall there was a big old fire-place with a bake oven beside it. The other walls and the low ceiling were a honey-coloured wood that reflected softly the light from the fire burning in the fireplace and from the lamps on the mantel and the small table under the front window. Against the back wall was a big brown electric range, counters (obviously new) and a sink with small square windows over it. There were shelves for dishes over the windows — but most of the dishes were on the big table in the middle of the room or piled up dirty in the sink. An old wooden rocking-chair stood by the front window, covered — as was every other possible space — with books, magazines, rubber boots and sweaters.

Something was burning. Aunt Nan pulled a smoking pot off the stove while she talked to a man with bushy black hair and a big black moustache, who sat on a high stool just out of her way. The twins were poking their fingers into various bowls and dishes until one of them happened to turn and see Rose standing in the doorway. "Here she is," he whispered and tugged at his father's hand. His twin echoed, "Here she is, she's here!"

Rose drew back a step. Her uncle Bob looked up. He got up and walked over to her. "How do you do, Rose?" He smiled and shook hands. "I'm glad you've come to stay with us."

Uncle Bob was tall and thin like George, with those same bright blue eyes, but Uncle Bob's had wrinkles at the corners and a quiet dreaminess about them. His nose was thin and long. He asked about her trip from New York and said he was sorry about her grandmother having died.

Before she had to say anything, Nan called out that supper was ready and they sat down to eat burned spaghetti, peas and chopped cabbage salad. There was orange pudding for dessert.

Sam and George sat opposite Rose. "Do you always talk with that accent — awrange pudding?" George brayed.

Rose flushed with embarrassment. "I've never thought about it before," she said.

"Did your grandmother really die in Paris?"

"Yes."

"What did you do?"

"I'm used to Paris and they know me in that hotel. I managed," said Rose coldly. She did not want to talk to George. She did not want to talk about her grandmother dying in Paris to anyone.

"Do you — " George began.

"George!" Uncle Bob said sharply, "This is not a court martial!" He turned apologetically to Rose. "I imagine you'll find mealtime here a bit different from what you're used to."

"Grandmother and I generally ate in restaurants," replied Rose. She caught Sam looking at her, and in the quick way he turned she had the feeling he was angry. Aunt Nan kept up a steady flow of talk. The twins sat on either side of Rose and did not take their eyes from her face throughout the meal. Nobody mentioned the girl upstairs making the bed and nobody mentioned Mrs. Morrissay. Finally, when dinner was nearly over, Rose got up her courage and asked about the girl. For an answer she got six blank stares and dead silence.

"I expect she's the maid," said Rose.

"The maid?" Aunt Nan put down her fork.

George let out a yell of laughter. "The maid! That's a good one!"

"Well, as she didn't come to dinner I thought . . . ."

"What are you talking about, dear? There's nobody upstairs. Are you playing a joke?" Aunt Nan smiled indulgently at Rose.

Rose did not answer. Everyone else was laughing. She flushed with embarrassment and anger. Why were they saying there was nobody upstairs? She had seen the girl. But she wasn't going to risk another bout of George's laughter or Sam's glowering so she said no more about it, and did not ask about Mrs. Morrissay either. Instead, she asked to be excused. In her primmest voice, she said, "I've had a rather busy day. I'd like to go to bed."

Uncle Bob said approvingly, "Good soldiers need their sleep," and George called after her, "Tell the maid we need her in the kitchen if you see her. Haw! Haw!"

Rose went swiftly but sedately upstairs and straight to the front room. There was no one there. There was no four-poster bed, no stove with a fire in it, no round rag rug. The room was cold and dark and as ramshackle as the rest of the house.

She was scared. She went to her own room, closed the door and sat down on her bed with her coat over her. She wanted to be ready to run in case something horrible should happen.

"This place is very odd," she whispered into the dark night. "It's like that story about the girl who had the plague in a hotel and they took her away and nobody would say she'd ever been there. I saw a girl making that bed. I know I did. What happened to her? Why don't they want me to know about her? And I saw that old lady — nobody's said anything about her, and —" She suddenly remembered the strange vision of the house. "I saw flowers. Delphiniums. I saw them."

She sat in the dark, silently huddled under her coat, listening to the wind rattle the loose window frame and whistle through the cracks. A tree scratched on the window. The room was cold and musty. Usually, talking to herself was a kind of comfort. It was almost like having a companion, but on this night there was no comfort. She had a sudden sharp pang of loneliness for her grandmother. She did not deeply grieve for her — her grandmother had not let her come close enough for that — but she missed the comfort of their familiar relationship and the life they had known together. She ached to leave the frightening strangeness of people who were so noisy and unpredictable and whose house held in it people they pretended were not there. She choked back the tears that threatened, as she always had choked back tears, until her throat was sore, and she sat with her arms tight around her knees until she fell over fast asleep.

She was awakened hours later by a thought. "How did that old lady know my name? She talked to me as if she knew me."

Wide awake by now she sat up and listened to the quiet. It had stopped raining and the wind had died. She got up and went to the window. The clouds had gone from the sky. The moon was full. The night had washed away all colour and, outside, the world was a black and white and silver landscape.

The tall grass beyond the bushes was as soft and pale as doves' feathers. Here and there apple and thorn trees dotted the slope, their trunks and limbs twisted and black, a few late apples hanging on the boughs like tiny iridescent globes. A creek followed a meandering path to the bay, gleaming under the moon.

Down past the creek was a small wood and through it the bay was just visible, shining whitely through the trees. Up close to the house the bushes made a dark smudge. In their midst was a little glade, not much bigger in diameter than the height of a large apple tree, a circle of bright light in the dark.

Rose stared down at the glade as though hypnotized. Then she left the window, slid her feet into her shoes, opened her door and crept down the stairs, through the silent house and out into the night.

Outside she pushed her way through the dense tangle of the bushes. She emerged into the glade, scratched and out of breath. There was the creek, and beside it was a small hawthorn tree. Its bark was silvery, its delicate branches stretched out gracefully around it like a hundred arms, its twigs and branchlets forming an intricate tracery to which tiny pointed leaves and a few dark berries still clung.

The ground was covered with leaves from the hawthorn and from the lilac and chokecherry that surrounded the clearing. The creek bubbled swiftly over the stones and bits of old branches that lay clearly visible in its bed. It smelled of wet leaves and moss.

Rose had never seen any place so beautiful. She turned around slowly, absorbing it all. The glade was quite bare except for the creek and the little hawthorn tree, and an old cedar fence post close by, leaning over and half buried in dead leaves.

On an impulse she gathered a few small hawthorn branches from the ground, ones that still had leaves and a few clusters of berries, and put them into the hollow of the fence post.

"There," she whispered, "now I have a secret garden." Quietly she went back into the house and upstairs. This time she took off her clothes and got into bed — and slept soundly until morning.

Le Hibou Blanc

HAZEL BOSWELL

It was a still day late in September. The maples were glowing scarlet and gold; the ploughing had been done, and the fields lay bare and brown under the silver grey sky. Madame Blais sat on an upturned box on the narrow gallery that ran the length of the summer kitchen. She was plaiting long strings of red onions to hang in the attic for the winter. The little gallery was heaped with vegetables: great golden yellow squashes, green pumpkins, creamy brown turnips, and great piles of green cabbages and glossy red carrots.

It was a good day for work. Her husband, and Joseph her eldest boy, together with their neighbour, Exdras Boulay, had gone off to repair the old sugar *cabane*. Her sister's fiancé, Felix Leroy, who had come up from the States for a holiday, had gone with them. Not to work. He despised that sort of work, for he was a factory hand in the United States and, as he said, "made more money in a week than he would make in a month working on the land." The older children were off at school; the little ones, Gaetané, Jean-Paul, and Marie-Ange, were playing happily with old "Puppay." Me'Mère was spinning in the kitchen keeping an eye on p'tit Charles who was sleeping peacefully in his cradle. Madame worked happily. She didn't often get such a good day for work. Her mind was turning in a placid, peaceful circle, "*Que tous s'adone bien aujourd-hui.*"

Suddenly the peace was broken. Puppay had begun to bark furiously; then the barking changed to joyful yapping. The children were shouting too. Madame turned on her box and looked out to where they had been playing, but they had left their game and were racing off across the field. As her eye followed them on the far side of the field she saw her husband, Joseph, and Exdras Boulay coming out of the wood by the road to the old sugar *cabane*.

Me'Mère had heard the noise too and had come to the door. "What is it?" she asked, "*Un Jerusalem?*" "No," answered Madame, "it's the men coming home, and it's not yet four. Something must have happened."

She watched the men anxiously as they crossed the field. She noticed that Felix wasn't with them. As they came up to the house she called out, "What has happened?"

No one answered her; the men tramped on in silence. When they got to the house, her husband sat down on the step of the gallery and began taking off his *bottes-sauvages*. The other two and the children stood watching him.

"Where is Felix?" asked Madame.

"He wouldn't come with us."

"Why did you leave so early?"

Again there was silence; then her husband said, "We saw the Hibou Blanc."

"You saw him?"

"Yes," answered her husband, "that's why we came home."

"Why didn't Felix come with you?"

"He said it was all nonsense. Old men's stories."

"You should have made him come with you," said Me'Mère. "You can't remember the last time the Hibou Blanc came. But I can. It was just two years after I was married. Bonté Lemay was like Felix, he didn't believe. He stayed on ploughing when the others left. The horse got scared and ran away. Bonté's arm was caught in the reins and he was dragged after the plough. His head struck a stone and he was dead when they found him. His poor mother. How she cried. One doesn't make fun of the Hibou Blanc."

The noise had wakened p'tit Charles and he began to cry. Madame went in to the kitchen and picked him up. She felt to see if he was wet; and then sat down by the stove, opened her dress, and began to feed him. The men came in too and sat around in the kitchen.

"Do you think Felix will have the sense to come home?" asked Madame.

Joseph shook his head and spat skilfully into the brown earthenware spittoon.

"No fear," he answered. "He says in the States they have more sense than to believe all those old stories."

"If Felix stays on in the woods, harm will certainly come to him," said Me'mère, "I tell you the Hibou Blanc always brings disaster."

"Why don't you go and speak to the Curé?" said Madame Blais.

"He's away at Rimouski for a retreat," answered Exdras. "I saw his housekeeper, Philomène, yesterday, and she told me. They had sent for him to bring the last rites to old Audet Lemay who was dying, but he was away and they had to send for the Curé of St. Anselm instead."

"Well, it's time to get the cows," said Monsieur Blais. "Go along and get them, Joseph."

Joseph got up and went out. The children and Puppay joined him.

Me'mère went back to her spinning. Madame Blais put p'tit Charles back in his cradle, then went off to milk the cows. There were ten cows to milk. Her husband and Joseph did the milking with her and up to a year before Me'mère had always helped too.

The autumn evenings close in quickly in the north. By the time the cows were milked and supper finished, the clear cold green of evening had swept up over the sky; the stars were out, and the little silver crescent of the moon had risen over the maple wood. Joseph was sitting out on the step of the little gallery, his eyes fastened on the break in the maple wood that marked the road leading to the sugar cabin. Every now and then his father went out and joined him. They were both watching for Felix.

As the kitchen clock began to strike eight Madame put down her work. "It's time for the Rosary," she said. "Tell Joseph to come in." Her husband opened the door and called to Joseph. He came in, followed by Puppay.

The family pulled their chairs up round the stove, for the evenings were beginning to be chilly, and it was cold away from the stove.

Me'Mère began the Rosary: "*Je crois en Dieu, le Père tout-puissant. . . .*" The quiet murmur of their voices filled the kitchen.

When the Rosary was said Madame sent the children off to bed. Then she went to the salon and got a *cierge bénit*, lit it, and put it in the kitchen window. "May God have pity on him," she said. Then she picked up p'tit Charles and went off to bed with her husband, while Me'Mère went to her little room next to the salon.

It was bright and cold the next day, and the ground was covered with white hoar-frost.

Joseph was the first to speak of Felix. "He may have gone and slept with one of the neighbours," he said.

"If he did he'd be back by now," answered his father.

They were still eating their breakfast when Exdras Boulay came into the kitchen.

"Felix hasn't come back?" he asked.

Before anyone could answer, the door opened and two other neighbours came in. The news of Felix and the Hibou Blanc had already spread along the road. Soon there were eight men and boys in the kitchen and half a dozen excited children.

The men sat round in the kitchen smoking. Old Alphonse Ouellet did most of the talking. He was always the leader in the parish.

"We'll have to go and find him," he said.

"It's too bad the Curé isn't here to come with us. Well, we might as well start off now. Bring your rosary with you," he told Monsieur Blais.

Madame Blais and Me'Mère and a group of the children stood on the kitchen gallery watching the men as they tramped off along the rough track to the maple wood.

"May God have them in His care," said Madame.

"And may He have pity on Felix," added Me'Mère, and she crossed herself.

In the maple wood the ground was still covered with frost. Every little hummock of fallen leaves was white with it, and the puddles along the track were frozen solid. The men walked in silence. A secret fear gripped each one of them that they might suddenly see the Hibou Blanc perched on some old stump, or one of the snow-covered hummocks. A few hundred yards from the sugar cabin they found Felix. He was lying on his back. His red shirt looked at first like a patch of red maple leaves lying in the hoar-frost. A great birch had fallen across his chest, pinning him to the ground. One of his hands was grasping a curl of the bark — his last mad effort to try and free himself.

The men stood round staring down at him, the immense silence of the woods surrounding them. Then from far away in the distance came a thin whinnying note, the shrill triumphant cry of *Le Hibou Blanc*.

The Red River Valley

TRADITIONAL

From this valley they say you are going;
I shall miss your bright eyes and sweet smile,
For alas you take with you the sunshine
That has brightened my pathway awhile.

CHORUS:
Come and sit by my side if you love me,
Do not hasten to bid me adieu,
But remember the Red River Valley
And the girl who has loved you so true.

For this long, long time I have waited
For the words that you never would say,
But now my last hope has vanished
When they tell me that you're going away.

Oh, there never could be such a longing
In the heart of a white maiden's breast
As there is in the heart that is breaking
With love for the boy who came west.

When you go to your home by the ocean
May you never forget the sweet hours
That we spent in the Red River Valley,
Or the vows we exchanged 'mid the bowers.

Will you think of the valley you're leaving?
Oh, how lonely and dreary 'twill be!
Will you think of the fond heart you're breaking
And be true to your promise to me?

The dark maiden's prayer for her lover
To the spirit that rules o'er the world:
His pathway with sunshine may cover,
Leave his grief to the Red River girl.

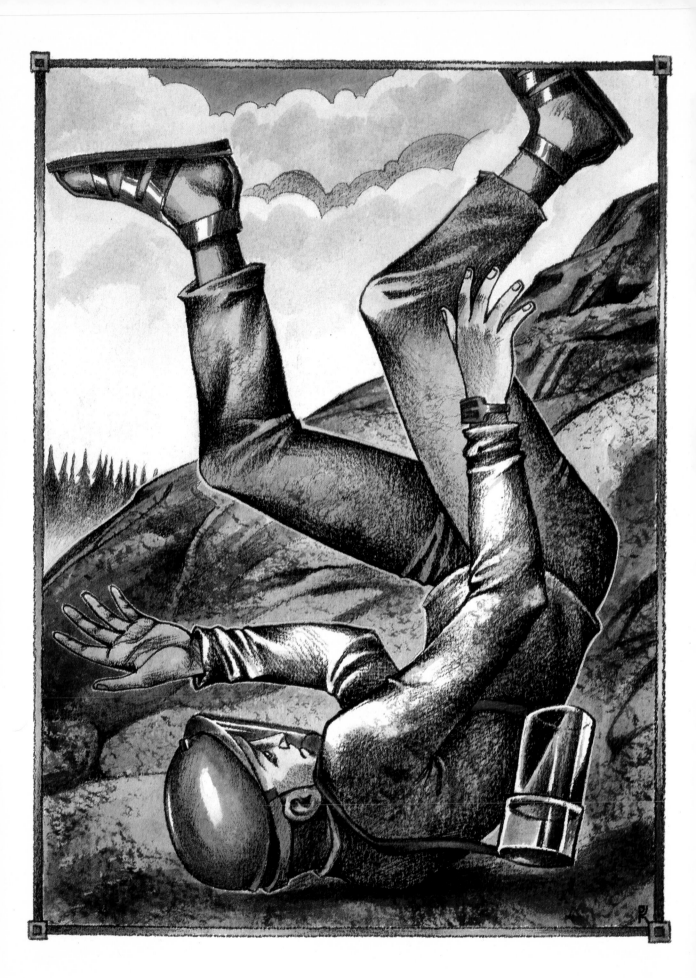

Luke in the Forest

SUZANNE MARTEL

In Surréal, the underground city beneath Mount Royal, flowers are extinct, hair no longer grows on people's heads, and children eat pills instead of food. It is the year 3000.

When Luke discovers a passage leading out of Surréal, he ventures into what remains of our world — a world that was devastated by nuclear war one thousand years before.

Meantime, Luke was off on one of his dangerous expeditions. Every afternoon after school, he had made his way to the open air — to the edge of the fascinating outer world. Now that he knew the way, it took him less than an hour to reach the mouth of the tunnel to which he had taken his friend Eric.

Today the sky was heavy, but no rain was falling. He could see the edge of the forest a hundred feet below him at the foot of the mountain. The grayness reassured him more than the vivid blues and greens of his earlier expeditions. The sun did not shoot out menacing rays, the rain did not chill him, and mist shrouded the frighteningly wide horizon.

Ideal weather for an underground boy! Luke decided to venture beyond the safe threshold of the tunnel. He took a few shaky steps on the steep slope; pebbles flew out from under his feet and, unaccustomed to rough ground, he lost his balance and rolled to the bottom of the hill.

Looking dizzily around, he saw that he had landed near those tall, sharp-needled trees that the ancient botany books called *pines*. Putting his hand to his face, he made sure that his gas mask was secure. Then he examined himself nervously. Falls were rare on the gentle slopes of Surréal and, except for speleologists exploring the grottoes, nobody had ever had a chance to roll to the bottom of a mountain. The novelty pleased Luke and helped to make up for the pain of his descent.

Above him, the entrance to the tunnel yawned in the side of the mountain. Since he had come so far, he might as well go all the way.

Picking up his ray helmet, he put it back into its plastic tube. Then he started off, taking cautious little steps and stopping every minute to consider something new. The song of a bird enchanted him, and its rapid flight was even more marvelous. The deep silence of the natural world amazed him after the mechanical sounds of a world run by motors. His sandals trod lightly on the spongy earth of the pine forest. He touched the rough bark of a tree, and blackened his finger in the shining gum. Like Adam in his earthly paradise, Luke discovered the magnificent world that God had created.

Suddenly, a savage-sounding cry reached his ears and froze him with fright. Who lives on the surface of the earth? What terrible danger lurks near? Luke was not accustomed to wide spaces, and his senses could not determine the source of the howl. He suddenly realized how far he had traveled from his protective cave. Would he perish alone without anyone ever knowing what became of him?

For the second time he felt frightened and overawed in his new world. Sitting with his back to a tree, he sent a call for help to the Prime Mover, which he had been taught to look upon as the all-powerful and kindly source of life. But even as he prayed, his prayer seemed hopeless. How could a great underground power help a boy in distress?

He heard sounds coming closer, branches crackling underfoot — and suddenly a great furry beast threw himself on the terrified boy and rolled him over. A long tail thrashed menacingly in the air, and a hot tongue licked his cheek. His eyes closed, and Luke waited stoically for death.

But suddenly, from where he did not know, a feeling of security came over him. He had been terrified at first, but now he felt calm. He opened his eyes and lifted up his head as the enemy leaned over him, panting, its long tongue hanging out, its silky ears framing a long-nosed face — and its dangerous tail thrashing about.

"Don't be frightened!"

"I'm *not* frightened." Luke answered as if it were perfectly natural for someone in this supposedly uninhabited world to start a conversation with him.

"Your *thoughts* are frightened, though. I felt them!"

Luke looked at the great beast sitting beside him. "Then you must also know that I've stopped being frightened." At twelve, a boy has his pride and is quick to defend it.

"Where are you?" asked the voice. "I don't see you anywhere."

Luke snorted. "I'm here in front of you — are you blind?" He was almost ready to sympathize with this unfortunate specimen of an unknown rarity — a furry creature with a perpetually moving tail who could not see something right under his nose. He continued questioning it. "Are there a lot of you on earth — where do you live?"

A shriek of laughter just behind him made him scramble to his feet, ready for a new attack. But there was no enemy facing him. Instead he saw a girl as tall as himself, dressed in brown homespun, and with long red hair. She was shaking with gay but mocking laughter.

"You were talking to Bark, but he can't very well answer you."

"He was very polite, though," Luke said, annoyed as the creature bounded over to the newcomer and licked her hand submissively.

"How funny you are," the girl said. "You have no hair, and you're wearing a mask. Did you come from the moon?"

Luke was too dumbfounded to answer. This was an astonishing moment. All the theories he had been taught since babyhood were turning out to be wrong. A world supposed to be deserted and scorched was inhabited. Yet animals roamed through it, and human beings walked in its green forests. Strangely enough, though, he felt as if he were coming back to his own land after a long absence.

But the girl's superior tone annoyed him, so he turned to his four-footed listener again. "Do you belong to the wolf family?" he asked politely. "Like Red Riding Hood's attacker?" He had a feeling that he was being rather tactless in reminding him of his wicked ancestor, but he wanted to show off his literary knowledge.

"He won't answer you, you know," the girl said. "He's my dog, Bark." And, as if in agreement, the dog barked shortly.

"That's what *you* think. As a matter of fact, Bark and I had a very nice chat — before you came along."

The girl shook her head. "No, you didn't! I was the one who was communicating with you. We were exchanging ideas by telepathy."

Luke, a child of the ultramodern age, was immediately interested. "Show me your apparatus, then," he said — and frowned as the girl laughed at him again.

"There isn't any apparatus. My ideas simply flash to your brain, and yours answer them. You ought to understand because you're a telepathist yourself — and quite a good one. You communicate very clearly, even from a long distance away."

Luke flushed with pride. Nothing would have made him admit that he didn't know anything about this faculty. He was a telepathist, she said. And a good one! For once, this strange girl was admiring him, and he certainly wasn't going to spoil it by admitting the truth.

"What's more," the girl said, dropping down beside him on the grass, "we don't even speak the same language." And for the first time Luke realized that this was true; when the girl spoke aloud, strange sounds came out of her mouth. They reminded him of the dead languages studied by his brother, Paul. But fortunately, thanks to this phenomenon of telepathy, they could communicate even through the language barrier.

The girl flashed a friendly smile. "My name's Agatha. What's yours?"

"Luke 15 P 9. And I live in Surréal, under the mountain." He pointed to Mount Royal and the opening to the tunnel.

Agatha accepted this calmly. "I live behind the mountain myself, on the bank of the river. Our tribe settled Laurania." She leaned forward curiously. "Why are you wearing that mask? And what are you doing in these woods? Bark and I often come here, but we've never seen you before."

"This is the first time I've come down the mountain," Luke said, without telling her how he had managed it. He didn't like to explain that he was wearing a mask because the open air was poisonous; he felt that such a remark might hurt her feelings. "I'm used to synthetic air — that's why I wear a mask. Now tell me what you're doing so far from your home."

"My father and brother went out hunting, and I decided to pick some blueberries." She ran to the edge of the forest and came back, holding a leather pouch full of tiny bluish globules. "Here, do you want some?"

Luke took one courteously. Raising his mask, he gulped it down the way he gulped his tea pill.

"Go on," Agatha urged, "have some more."

"No thanks. It's not good to take more than one pill."

Agatha shrugged and went on eating berries until her mouth was stained blue. The sight piqued Luke's curiosity; he had always enjoyed getting to the bottom of things. Now he wanted to know all about these strange capsules.

"Do you find these capsules ready-made?" he asked eagerly. What a find his discovery would be for the dietetic service! Before she could answer, he demanded, "Is that all you eat?"

Agatha stared at him, amazed. "Why no, of course not! We eat the game we catch, and fish from the river — and bread, naturally."

"*Bread*? What's that?"

Agatha took a peace of bread out of her pocket, divided it into two, and gave half to Luke. He examined the dry crust and tender white crumbs.

"That's my snack," Agatha said, biting into it with her shining teeth. And Luke, who had never seen anyone eat so much in his life, feared for her health.

Always adventurous, he risked nibbling the slice of dough. But first he asked, "What's it made of?"

"It's made of flour."

"Flour? Where do you get that from?"

"From wheat, you idiot! Don't you know anything at all?"

Luke reddened; he did not realize that what he *did* know would amaze this girl far more than what he *didn't* know. To hide his embarrassment, he started another line of inquiry. "Is that a hat, that fur stuff you're wearing?"

Agatha put a hand to her head as if to find out. "Of course not," she said. "Can't you see I'm bareheaded?"

Luke began to remember his ancient history. "Then it must be fur, like the skins our ancestors used to wear."

But Agatha shook her head. "You really don't know much, I see," she said. "This is *hair*." And she shook her magnificent red mop.

Luke stared at it, marveling. "Don't you — don't you ever take it off, even when you go to bed?"

Agatha smiled. "No, never. Not even in summertime."

"It must be very hot," Luke sympathized; actually, though it was certainly strange, he found this decoration rather pretty.

"It's no hotter than your mask." She pointed at the dog, then, and the two friends watched Bark; he was running around, looking for a scent, drunk with space and freedom.

"You live *under* the mountain?" Agatha said, as if the strangeness of such an idea had just struck her. "Under the *earth*?" What an incredible notion!

For a long time, the two youngsters sat under the pines, comparing their different ways of life, the scientific knowledge of Surréal, with all its restrictions, and the simplicity and freedom of Laurania. Luke told her about the origin of his people, about the Great Destruction, and how the refugees from the mountain had built a magnificent underground city. He had learned all this during his childhood and, like a true patriot, he was proud of his country.

Agatha's story was simpler. She could remember a legend about a fiery disaster and a terrible plague; it had been handed down by word of mouth. "The survivors made their homes in the devastated lands," she explained. "First they lived like animals. Then they formed bands and began to live in tribes so that they could help one another in storms, and against diseases and wild animals."

"Are there many tribes like yours?" Luke wanted to know.

Agatha considered. "Our bravest men, the ones who have been on long journeys, say there is a group living near the mouth of three rivers, south of here. And there may be others on a big cape, far down the river."

They didn't always understand each other clearly. Telepathy could not always cross the language barrier, and Luke's technical terms were as difficult to explain as the natural wonders that Agatha described. But the two youngsters, instinctively drawn together, trusted each other and accepted the most surprising ideas quite calmly.

Agatha, a child of nature, could not understand how the subterranean people could be so resigned. "Hasn't anyone ever tried to get out?" she asked.

"Yes. Twice they even managed to make an opening to the outside."

"And then?" It all seemed so simple to this child of the sun.

"Well, the first time the ice-ax started a waterfall. The men were drowned and part of the city was flooded."

"They must have been chopping under the river," Agatha said logically. "What happened the next time?"

"The next time, our Great Council studied the problem thoroughly in advance. They opened the leaden boundary gate, and volunteers went through it. They had to break through a wall of ice and snow; the air froze their lungs and they heard the wind howling. The Council decided that a new glacial age had begun, and that the surface of the earth was uninhabitable. So everyone calmed down, and they locked the leaden gates again."

"What bad luck," Agatha said. "They must have been digging during a winter storm! Hasn't anyone tried since?"

"Not that I know of."

"Well, what made *you* come out?"

"Oh, that was just chance!" A modest boy, Luke did not want to boast about his exploit. "I happened to find an opening. And I — I felt *drawn*."

"That was probably me calling you," Agatha said wisely. "I often come to this spot with Bark — and I've often wished for a friend." Gentler and more intelligent than the other children of her tribe, Agatha did not care for their primitive and noisy pastimes. Since her mother's death, she often accompanied her father and brother when they went hunting. They entrusted her to the huge dog, knowing that Bark would guard her against dangers.

"Are there lions and tigers in these forests?" Luke asked, remembering his prehistory lessons.

Agatha shook her head. "I've never heard of any. But there are wolves and bears — and sometimes a puma."

"Aren't you afraid?" Luke, in turn, was admiring.

"No. Bark looks after me — and so does my guardian angel."

"Where's he?"

"Bark? He's over there, near the mountain."

"No, your guardian."

"Oh, you mean my guardian angel. He's invisible, of course."

"Then how can he look after you?"

"God gave him to me, to protect me. He gives everybody a guardian angel."

"Do you think He would give me one too?" Luke decided that the presence of a guardian angel would be a good thing in this frightening world where the Prime Mover didn't seem to have much influence.

"You're God's child just as I am, even if we don't breathe the same kind of air," Agatha said.

Luke was highly impressed by this benevolent God who was so kind to foreigners, but he asked one of Eric's favorite questions. "How do you know?"

"Because I believe in Him and pray to Him," Agatha said simply. "Who do *you* pray to?"

"Why, the Prime Mover, I suppose," Luke told her. But not wanting to offend the God of the outer world he added quickly, "I don't think he can hear me here, though."

Agatha looked a little scornful. "My God can hear everything," she said proudly. "Even our secret thoughts."

"You mean He's telepathic, too?"

"More than anyone in the world. It doesn't matter where you are, He hears you."

"And what is He called?"

"We call him Our Father."

"Our Father, I like the sound of that. Do you think I could call Him that when I know Him?"

Just then a soft buzz from Luke's watch-radio signaled that his brother wanted to talk to him. He held the watch to his ear and heard a faint voice. "You'd better hurry home if you want to get here before the curfew!"

Luke pressed the tiny emission button twice as a sign that he had understood. He didn't want to start a conversation which would betray how far away he was.

Agatha looked interestedly at the watch. "What a funny talking bracelet! What did it say?"

"It was my brother, wanting me to come home. But you were near me — couldn't you hear him?"

"Yes, quite plainly — but he was speaking a foreign language."

"The same as mine," Luke said.

"Well, I couldn't understand it," Agatha said. "And of course your brother is not telepathic."

Luke was surprised. "Isn't everyone?" He had not realized that he possessed an exclusive talent.

His friend chuckled. "Of course not. Only a few people — I'm the only one in my family. It's a rare gift and we don't know much about it yet. Are there many telepathists in Surréal?"

"I've never heard of any at all," Luke said in all honesty. A few minutes ago, he thought, he hadn't known anything about telepathy himself.

In the distance, a musical sound echoed through the forest. Bark replied with a deep baying. A horn was blowing.

"It's the hunters coming home. I'll have to join them," Agatha said. "I'll see you tomorrow, Luke." To seal the pact, they shook hands; then each started off on the path to his home, happy in the secret of their new friendship.

North Lay Freedom

BARBARA SMUCKER

Julilly, Adam and Lester were sold by their original owner in Virginia to the much harsher owner of a Mississippi cotton plantation, Massa Riley. Here, Julilly makes friends with Liza, a slave of about her own age who once attempted to escape, was caught, and beaten so brutally by the overseer, Sims, that she is now crippled.

Both Julilly and Liza have heard that there is a country to the north of them, called Canada, where there are no slaves. When a Canadian, Mr. Alexander Ross, appears on the scene, the girls are naturally curious. Both long to be free.

The coming of Mr. Ross unsettled the slaves. Julilly felt it like a spark, flitting up and down the rows of cotton. There was something about the way the heavy-chested Canadian had grabbed Sims' upraised hand when he aimed to strike her again that roused a hope in Julilly's mind.

She couldn't talk with Liza. Sims was too close. She began picking quickly, and when she thought it safe, stuffed extra cotton bolls into Liza's low-slung sack. Without moving her head, she could see Mr. Ross talking with one slave and then another. It was a long time before he finally walked from the field with two of them.

The slaves he chose were Lester and Adam. Julilly stopped picking for an instant just to watch. Big, fast-moving Mr. Ross from Canada had chosen Lester and Adam to help him look for birds.

Julilly knew she must talk with Lester soon. Sometimes on Sundays, she met him in the yard of the slave quarters. He was always angry, but he listened when she talked of home. Once she had told him what Mammy Sally said about Canada. He had listened hard then. His eyes were excited and he had given Julilly that same cautious look of approval that came over his face the day she helped him from the swamp in the rain.

"Don't you talk about this to no one — just to me and to your friend, Liza," he had cautioned.

Tomorrow was Sunday. She would find Lester and ask him about Alexander Ross.

Julilly and Liza finished picking their row. Far ahead of them they could see the big Canadian with Lester and Adam enter the Piney Woods and disappear.

It was dusk when the picking and weighing of the cotton was finished. Sims was nervous and uneasy as he checked the scales. Mr. Ross was back and Lester and Adam had been sent to carry baskets of picked cotton. Mr. Ross held his shotgun loose. The grey wings of a dead mockingbird stuck out from a bag that he hung over his big shoulders. Even though he had been tramping about most of the hot afternoon hunting birds, his thick brown hair and preacher-looking suit were as neat and orderly as though he'd been sitting under the shade trees of the Big House lawn.

He stood near Sims.

"Now tell me, Mr Sims," he asked with his fast clipped Canadian accent, "how much does each slave pick during the day?"

Sims mumbled an answer.

"An amazing crop." The Canadian patted his great stomach and chest. "You know it's too cold in Canada to raise cotton."

Sims perked up with this comment.

"I heard tell," Sims grinned, his upper lip flattened against his yellow, uneven teeth, "it's such a cold place that nothin' but black-eyed peas can be raised there."

Julilly saw a smile flicker on the big man's face.

Julilly and Liza, with the other slaves, trudged back along the dusty path to the slave quarters with lighter steps that evening. As though in some kind of celebration, a large black kettle swung over a crackling flame in the yard. It bubbled with greens and sparse strips of salt pork. There hadn't been greens to eat since Julilly came to the Riley plantation on the first day. She reached inside her crocker bag for the gourd that she always carried with her, ladled out a portion for herself and poured some for Liza into a tin plate.

"Without you, Julilly" — Liza raised her tired head where she sat resting against the trunk of a thick oak tree — "I'd starve to death."

That night in the long slave cabin, all the girls whispered about Canada and Mr. Ross. Most of them knew about the place. Word of it had crept along the plantation "grapevines" in the places where they came from — in Virginia and North Carolina. They shared what they had heard.

Liza knew the most. Usually she was quiet and sullen after the day's work, but tonight she felt like talking. She hunched her crippled back against the pile of rags to ease the constant pain.

"This country is far away under the North Star," she whispered hoarsely. "It's run by a lady named Queen Victoria. She made a law there

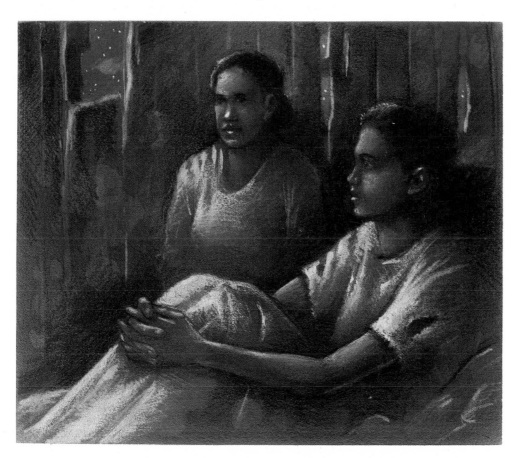

declarin' all men free and equal. The people respects that law. My daddy told me that, and he was a preacher."

A girl down the line named Bessie, who was tall and strong like Julilly, moved near Liza.

"How you know where to find that North Star, girl?" she asked.

Liza answered with certainty and precision. "You look in the sky at night when the clouds roll back. Right up there, plain as the toes on my feet, are some stars that makes a drinking gourd." Night after night Julilly and Liza had been watching it when the stars hung low, sparkling and glistening.

"The front end of that drinking gourd," Liza went on, "points straight up to the North Star. You follow that. Then you get to Canada and you are free."

"Don't you talk so much, girl." Bessie's whisper was sharp now and strained with fear. "Look what happened to you when you tried to get your freedom. You got a bent back and your legs got all beat up. I ain't lookin' for no more whippin's than I already got." She rolled onto her rags and was soon asleep.

Another girl near by crept close to Liza and Julilly. She was a timid girl, hunched up like a little mouse caught in a corner.

"I'm afraid," she shivered. "I heard a man say once that Canada is a cold country. Only the wild geese can live there. I'm afraid to go. I'm always afraid." She began to whimper. Julilly reached for her hand and held it until the girl went to sleep.

By now the other girls, sprawled along the floor, were too drained and dulled by the daily work and scant food to care or listen. Their exhausted bodies needed sleep. Like work-horses, they found their stalls each night and fell exhausted into the heap of tangled, ragged blankets.

But Liza hadn't moved from her hunched position against the wall. She wasn't asleep. Julilly could see her open eyes in the soft moonlight that spread through the cracks and open doorway of the cabin. It was late. The only night sounds were the chirping of the crickets.

Every muscle in Julilly's body ached. She spread out flat on her back close to Liza, unable to close her eyes. The thoughts in her head jumped around like grasshoppers. Was Liza trying to reach Canada and freedom when Sims tracked her down?

Free, thought Julilly. Free must be like a whippoorwill that could fly here and there and settle where it pleased . . . free could mean to get paid for your work like white folks . . . free was like the free black boy who stood beside the tall Abolitionist on the road to Mississippi and gave her water . . . if you were free, you wouldn't be whipped.

Julilly couldn't stop her thoughts.

She finally murmured to the silent, staring Liza.

"Liza." Julilly barely moved her lips. "You thinkin' of tryin' to run away to Canada again?"

She felt Liza's body twitch. Slowly the crippled girl slid to the floor and put her mouth against Julilly's ear.

"You is my friend, Julilly." She barely made a sound. "What I is goin' to say must not be told to anyone."

Julilly nodded her head.

"Before the cotton is finished bein' picked, I am gonna slip away from here some night."

"Are you afraid?" Julilly had to know.

"I am afraid, and I am not afraid." Liza's bony fingers clasped Julilly's arm. "Like my daddy said to me, 'Liza, in the eyes of the Lord, you is somebody mighty important. Don't you ever forget that.'"

Julilly nodded again.

"I'm scrawny, Julilly, but I'm tough. I think the Lord put that North Star up in the sky just for us poor niggers to follow, and I intends to follow it."

There was a long silence between them.

Finally Julilly said slowly, her heart beating so fast she thought it might snap off from whatever held it in her chest. "I am goin' with you, Liza. I'm afraid and I'm not afraid, same as you."

Chris and Sandy

MONICA HUGHES

"What are you studying in school today?" Father asked politely. He asked this same question every morning before returning to his study to work on the long mathematical calculations that would one day set the world right.

"Act Two of *Hamlet*. Plane Geometry. The causes of the First World War. Father, we're out of jam."

"Jam?" Father looked vaguely surprised, as if jam were a substance he had never heard of before. "Jam. I suppose we could have run out. We should go through the storeroom and bring our list up to date some time." He wandered off, his thumb marking the place in the book he had been reading during breakfast.

Too bad you couldn't hold a normal conversation with Father. It wasn't his fault. He was just too far inside his own head. Chris sighed. He tidied the kitchen and made a note to himself to check through the stores one day soon. Thank goodness for Sandy. Without Sandy he'd go crazy for sure.

He found his books, sat down at the table, and tapped EM Four's code into the computer. "Hello, EM Four. Chris ready for work. Is Sandy there yet?" Sandy was always late.

"Good morning, Chris. Please open your book at page fourteen. Act Two, Scene One: a room in Polonius's house. . . . Here is Sandy."

On the TV screen appeared a picture of a freckled boy, about twelve or thirteen years old, with a wide grin.

"Hi, Chris, what's cooking?"

"Hi, Sandy. Not much. Did you get all your homework done last night?"

The voice of the computer cut in. "Shall we begin, boys? Chris, explain the meaning of the scene between Ophelia and her father. How does it advance the plot?"

"Well, I guess Ophelia's scared of Hamlet because he's — "
On the TV screen Sandy crossed his eyes, wiggled his ears, and put out his tongue. Chris snorted with laughter and wondered if EM Four knew what games Sandy got up to when they were supposed to be working.

"I don't think Hamlet's mad. I think it's just a put-on," Sandy interrupted.

"Give me your reasons, Chris," EM Four said calmly.

"Oh, I don't know. It just strikes me that way, that's all."

The lesson finished, and Chris reached over to the cupboard and got a glass of synthetic milk and a protein cracker. Sandy said he'd go and get a snack too. Chris stared at the blank screen while he drank his milk and wished it would show the inside of Sandy's house. There was only a blank wall behind Sandy's cheery face, and Chris had never seen his friend's home.

When he got back, Chris asked him, "Exactly where do you live?"

"On top of the hill. Not far."

"It'd be such fun if we could get together."

"We're together now. There's school and chess games and — "

"It's not the same thing. You know, Sandy, sometimes I get absolutely squirrelly, stuck in the house all day with just Father."

"You have me for company too," EM Four put in. "No more talking now, boys. Time for Geometry. Chris, will you enumerate the properties of triangles?"

After Math there was History, and then the TV closed down. Chris picked a package marked "SKL#1" for his lunch and sat down at the table to eat it, staring at the empty screen. He wished Sandy would stay and have lunch with him, but always, as soon as lessons were over, he vanished and only reappeared when Chris coded "Games Time" into the computer. A long, empty afternoon stretched in front of him. He sighed and pushed away the rest of his lunch.

"I wish I could go over to his house. Give him one heck of a surprise if

I turned up there." He found himself walking out of the room and staring at the big front door.

For years there had been a red light over it, but about five months ago the light had turned green. When Chris had told Father, he had said vaguely, "It makes no difference. We have all we need here."

Maybe it was true for him, but it sure wasn't for Chris — thirteen years old, skinny, and growing fast, needing leg room.

Almost without meaning to, he began to turn the great wheel in the centre of the door. The first half-turn was almost more than he could manage, but then it became easier. He spun it round and round, and at last, with a faint creak, the door swung inward.

He stepped through, his heart beating hard, into a masonry shaft with metal hoops set into the wall. They led, like a staircase, up into the gloom, where he could faintly see another door, really more of a lid, sealing the top of the shaft.

Chris hesitated. Should he tell Father what he planned to do? But the study door was firmly shut. Even as a little boy, when Mother was still alive, the one rule had been: Father must never be disturbed.

"But why? I need him to play with us, Mom."

"He's working on special problems, and when he's got the answers, the world will be a safer place to live in. He's a genius, Chris, and he mustn't be disturbed."

He could almost hear Mother's voice. He set his foot to the first hoop and reached up for a handhold. Rust came off bright orange, and the hoops trembled beneath his weight, but they held. He climbed up into the shadows that came down over his shoulders like a dusty shawl.

At the top he spun the wheel in the lid and set his shoulder to it. The hoop on which he was standing bent beneath the pressure, and he grabbed at the wheel, sweating and trembling. It was a very long way down. Then he set his feet apart, one on each of two hoops, to spread the weight of his body, and tried again, heaving with all his strength against the metal lid.

It creaked, moved, lifted, and he straightened his back and pushed with both hands. It fell back with a clang, a clatter of stones, and a cloud of bitter stone dust. Slowly Chris climbed out into sunlight.

It shone in bright bars through a broken wall with dust dancing in it. The light was so strong, his eyes ran and he sneezed. He crawled cautiously between two jagged segments of wall like ruined teeth and looked around.

Below him was a desolate expanse of grey, the grey of powdered concrete and brick, grey as thick as a carpet, curved by the wind into frozen waves that seemed to beat silently against the hill on which he stood.

"Up on the hill." "Not far." "The house on the corner with the red roof and the black trim." "With the white picket fence." Chris remembered the small descriptions Sandy had let slip over the years of their friendship. Even, long ago, "A tree in the backyard with a super swing."

There were no trees up here. No swings. No houses. No streets.

The wind shivered and lifted the dust around his bare ankles. The sky was cloudless, a bowl of harsh blue from the centre of which the sun burned down.

Chris climbed down the shaft, carefully closing the lid behind him. There would be no visitors. He brushed the dust off his legs before entering the house and shutting the big front door. The house hummed quietly. The lights shone, comfortably dim.

He hesitated at the door of the study. But what was the use? He went into the other room and slumped at the table. After a time he punched EM Four's code into the computer.

"Hello, Chris. What can I do for you?"

"You lied to me."

"I? In what way?"

"I've been outside. Sandy's not real. He never could have been there, could he? My only friend, and he's not real." He put his head down on his arms.

"He is real, Chris, truly."

"Oh, sure. Where does he live then? Come on, EM Four, I'm not stupid."

"Sandy is here in this shelter."

"What?" Chris jumped to his feet. "Where? How could he be? Come on, show me where he is."

"He is difficult to reach sometimes. When you are angry — "

"I'm not angry. I am *not* angry." Chris pounded his fist on the table.

"It was not good for you to grow up alone. After your mother's death you needed a companion to keep you healthy and happy, to give meaning to your life."

"Then you *did* invent him. He *is* a lie."

"No. All I did was bring him out."

Chris slumped at the table. "Are you trying to be difficult? No, don't answer that, I can't stand it. EM Four, how many people are still living?"

"You and your father are the only life forms I have been able to detect. But my range is quite limited. There is no reason to doubt — "

"Then you lied. Sandy isn't real." Tears leaked through his closed lids, and he put his head down again.

"Sandy *is* real. Listen to me, Chris. Sandy is *you*. The part of yourself that liked to have fun, that didn't want to study — the adventurous part. The part that remembered a swing and a picket fence. Sandy is *inside you*."

Chris stared through his tears at the blank screen, remembering the freckled boy who could wiggle his ears. He felt as if someone he loved had died.

That night he lay in his narrow bunk above the table and listened to the steady whisper of the air conditioner. When the clock told him it was morning, he got up and made breakfast for Father and himself, as he had done every other day.

"What are you studying today?" Father asked, his eyes still on the papers he had brought from his study. Chris thought of telling him about Sandy, but it seemed kind of useless.

"How close are you?"

"Eh?"

"To a solution, Father."

"Oh, my goodness, that's hard to say. I see a glimmer, you know, at the end of the tunnel. A glimmer."

"What'll you do with the solution when you've found it?"

"Do? Why . . . I don't know . . . . That is for others to decide — physicists, astronomers. My work is to advance the frontier of knowledge. What other people do with it is up to them." He wandered back to his study. The door shut.

Chris cleared away the breakfast dishes and sat down at the computer terminal. He sighed and then punched in EM Four's code. "Ready for work," he said and reached for his *Hamlet*.

As he read, he found himself looking at the empty TV screen. When he stared at the printed page, dust motes danced in the golden sun at the top of the shaft. He shut the book.

"EM Four, is Sandy there?"

At once Sandy's face filled the screen — the wide grin, the twinkle in the eyes. "Hi, fella, I thought you'd given up on me."

"Fat chance. Listen, Sandy, I'm sick of *Hamlet* and Geometry and the causes of World War One. What about a study on how to find other people and learn to start living again?"

"I thought you'd never ask, Chris. EM Four, are you listening? Help! We've got a lot to learn."

Sarah from Long Ago

MARGARET LAURENCE

Sal and her parents are spending Christmas at her grandmother's house. On Christmas Eve, Sal is looking through some photograph albums in Gran's shed when she comes across an old coat in the bottom of a trunk. It seems to be just the right size for a ten-year-old, but when she puts it on an amazing thing happens. Sal is transported back in time to a Christmas Eve long ago. She meets a girl named Sarah and rides with her in an old-fashioned cutter, or horse-drawn sleigh.

The horses plunged onward, their harness bells jangling. The cutter sped through stands of spruce and pine, glittering and shimmering with the snow on their boughs. Sal thought it was the most exciting ride she'd ever had in her entire life, even counting the Giant Ferris Wheel at the Exhibition.

"I've been over to my best friend's house," Sarah was saying. "I wanted to show her my Early Present. We're always allowed to open one before Christmas Day."

"Oh, do you do that?" Sal cried. "We always have an Early Present, too."

This detail made her feel quite close to Sarah, and she sensed that Sarah felt the same.

"What was your Early Present, Sarah?" Sal asked curiously.

Sarah dug in her coat pocket, holding the horses' reins easily with one hand, and brought out a small object wrapped in red tissue paper. She handed it to Sal.

"Here — look. Papa carved it for me, and Mama did the painting. I shall cherish it always. I'll hand it on, I really will, to my children and their children. Papa and Mama laughed when I said that, but I think they were a bit pleased, too."

Sal unfolded the paper carefully. Inside was a carved wooden box. On the top, its wings delicately shaped in wood and painted a glowing orange and black, was a Monarch butterfly. Sal knew it was a Monarch, because her dad had pointed out that kind of butterfly to her on a visit to the village last spring. They were called Monarchs, Dad had said, because they were like the kings and queens of all the butterflies. On the underside of the box were these words — *To Sarah, from her loving parents.*

"It's beautiful," Sal said. "I've never seen anything like it."

"Won't you come and meet my family, Sal?" Sarah asked. "They'd be glad to meet you, I know, and your folks wouldn't worry for a little while, would they? I could take you back to the village later on."

Sal gulped. *Danger.* Meeting Sarah had been like getting a special and unexpected Christmas present. But going to New Grange Farm — that was something different. She just could not do it. But how could she get out of doing it?

If Sal went to the farm, as soon as she undid the olden days coat Sarah and her family would see that Sal's clothes were not at all the kind worn here in this place. They wouldn't understand, and how could she ever explain? You couldn't go into a welcoming house and not take off your coat, that was for sure. But she could not take the coat off *there.* She mustn't. It was her only chance of getting back home, and if she tried it at the wrong moment and in the wrong place —

Sal was all at once terrified.

She might never be able to return to her own place, her own family. Sal felt tears wanting to come into her eyes. She blinked them back furiously. This was no time for feeling sorry for herself. Action was what was needed, and that action had to be her own. Sarah was totally unaware of the danger, and she must remain so. It was up to Sal to find a solution.

What was she to say to Sarah? How could she, without being unkind and ungrateful, get out of the sleigh? She certainly could use a little help, Sal thought.

Sal had just handed the carved wooden box back to Sarah, and was frantically searching for an answer to Sarah's invitation, when a shower of huge icicles, sharp swords of frozen water, snapped and fell from a tree bough, directly in front of the horses.

CRASH!

The horses reared in fright, and bolted away down the snow path. The carved box flew out of Sarah's hands as she grabbed for the reins that had been torn from her grasp. She snatched the reins back again, and pulled hard. But the box was gone.

"My box!" Sarah shouted. She soothed the horses then, her voice coaxing them out of their fear, and finally she brought the cutter to a halt.

"I'm going to go and look for it," Sal offered quickly. "You hold the horses, eh?"

Sarah agreed, and Sal ran back along the path through the forest. To find the box seemed an impossible task in all that snow. Supposing it had fallen into one of the deep drifts? No one would ever be able to find it. Sal located the place where the horses had reared, and began looking.

Hopeless.

Then she noticed a bluejay, hovering a few inches above the snow, darting down, searching for something. The bird settled and began to explore the snow.

Sal rushed over and shooed the bird away. *Sorry, bird*, she whispered under her breath, *better luck to you next time, but thanks*. She scooped away the soft light snow with her hands. And there it was. Nestling in the snow, quite unharmed, was the precious box. Sal snatched it up and ran back to Sarah.

"The jay found it, Sarah! The jay found it! He thought it was food, and he found it. Here it is!"

Sarah took the box and grinned.

"Oh Sal, how can I ever thank you? Now you'll surely come home with me."

Sal remained standing on the path. This was her only chance, and she knew it. Now if she could just do it right.

"Sarah, I'd love to, I really would. But I can't. My family will be worried. No — I know what you're going to say — you don't have to drive me back, but thanks anyway. It's not that far, and not that cold. I have to go. But I'll always be glad I met you."

No lies there. Not a one. Now if only the rest of it would work out.

Sarah nodded in understanding. The horses wanted to be going on again, so she drew gently in a little on the reins, reassuring them that they'd soon be off and away.

"Maybe we'll see each other, over Christmas, then," Sarah said.

"Maybe," Sal said doubtfully. She wished with all her heart that such a meeting could be.

The two girls said a warm goodbye, and Sarah turned to flick the reins and tell the horses to go on.

Now was the moment for Sal's desperate plan. The timing had to be absolutely right, or she was done for. It had certainly been the putting-on of the olden days coat that had brought her here. It must be the taking-off of the coat that would take her home again. But the coat had to be tossed into the back of the cutter for the plan to work. Would she be able to do it swiftly enough, before the sleigh sped away? And would she be able to do it so that Sarah would not notice? She had to risk it.

Sal had already untied the red wool sash of the coat. As the cutter started up again, she slithered speedily out of the coat. In a flash, she had flung it into the back seat of the sleigh. It landed with a plop. The sleigh bells were ringing out. The horses were dashing along. Sarah, guiding the horses, didn't notice the thrown coat and didn't look back at Sal shivering without a coat in the snow.

Sal had a split second to realize that the coat would go to New Grange Farm, and that there would be some good reason, unknown to her, for its being there. It would travel through history until —

BLACKNESS. Sal lost track of time. Everything blurred and faded.

Sal opened her eyes.

She was sitting on the shed floor with her coat beside her. How come? And yet she didn't feel cold. She put on her coat and looked around her. The photograph albums of long ago were spread out on the floor. She picked them up and began putting them back in the trunk. As she did so, she noticed something.

There, on the bottom of the trunk, neatly folded, was an olden days coat, a girl's coat. It was a dark navy blue, with a hood, and at the waist there was attached a narrow red wool sash. It looked as though it might fit

Sal, and for a moment she thought of trying it on. But just then a voice boomed into the shed.

"Hey! So this is where you've been all this time. Did you go to sleep, or what? Lucky it's fairly warm out for this time of year. We've been a little worried about you."

Dad was standing in the shed doorway, grinning.

"I — I don't know," Sal said. "I was looking at the old albums, and I guess I sort of lost track of time. What time is it now, anyway?"

"Just time to open your Early Present," Dad said.

Gran and Mother were sitting in the living room. Sal had to admit that the tree that they'd decorated since she'd been out was really splendid, even though the ornaments were not those she was used to. Then she saw the peacock and the silver bells and the small Santa, there on the tree. Her own ornaments were there.

"You brought them!" she cried.

"We thought you'd like to see them on the tree as usual," Mother said, hugging Sal.

Gran was tall and thin, and her hands were gnarled like old tree branches. She was wearing her favourite brown and blue silk dress and the gold necklace that Grandad had given her long ago. Her hair was a feathery white. She didn't look a bit old-fashioned. She just looked like herself. Her eyes had the same brown warmth they'd always had.

"What is your Early Present to be, then, Sal?" Gran asked.

"The one from you," Sal said instantly, not knowing why that was the one she wanted most to see.

"Well, it's not anything new or glamorous," Gran said, a bit mischievously.

She handed Sal a small package, wrapped in bright paper. Sal opened it slowly, making it last a long time.

When the wrapping was off at last, Sal stared. There, in her hands, was a carved wooden box. On the top, its wings delicately shaped in wood and painted a glowing orange and black, was a Monarch butterfly.

"I've been saving it," Gran said. "Your Grandad and I didn't have a daughter, but your Dad and Mother gave us a very fine granddaughter. I've kept this to give you the year you were ten. My father carved it and my mother painted it, and they gave it to me the year I was ten."

Sal turned the box over in her hands. She read the words on the underside. *To Sarah, from her loving parents.* Only now did she recall whom she had been named after. The name Sal was short for Sarah.

Sal looked at Gran, and her heart thudded.

"Gran, it's beautiful. I'll always cherish it."

Where did those words come from? Sal knew they didn't sound exactly like her, and yet she knew she meant them. She'd heard somebody say them, and now she couldn't quite remember who or when. She knew only that this Christmas was one she would remember all her life.

"I know you will," Gran said. "It's what I guess you could call a family heirloom, now. You know, I nearly lost it, the very day I was first given it. Nearly lost it in the snow."

"How did you find it?" Sal asked curiously.

Gran smiled. It was a faraway smile, and yet it was close as well.

"It's the oddest thing," Gran said. "I never could quite remember, afterwards."

ANIMAL LIVES

In the Deep of the Grass

CHARLES G. D. ROBERTS

Misty gray green, washed with tints of the palest violet, spotted with red clover-blooms, white oxeyes, and hot orange Canada lilies, the deep-grassed levels basked under the July sun. A drowsy hum of bees and flies seemed to distil, with warm aromatic scents, from the sun-steeped blooms and grass-tops. The broad, blooming, tranquil expanse, shimmering and softly radiant in the heat, seemed the very epitome of summer. Now and again a small cloud-shadow sailed across it. Now and again a little wind, swooping down upon it gently, bent the grass-tops all one way, and spread a sudden silvery pallor. Save for the droning bees and flies there seemed to be but one live creature astir between the grass and the blue. A solitary marsh-hawk, far over by the rail fence, was winnowing slowly, slowly, hither and thither, lazily hunting.

All this was in the world above the grass-tops. But below the grass-tops was a very different world — a dense, tangled world of dim green shade, shot with piercing shafts of sun, and populous with small, furtive life. Here, among the brown and white roots, the crowded green stems, and the mottled stalks, the little earth kindreds went busily about their affairs and their desires, giving scant thought to the aerial world above them. All that made life significant to them was here in the warm green gloom; and when anything chanced to part the grass to its depths they would scurry away in unanimous indignation.

On a small stone, over which the green closed so thickly that, when he chanced to look upward, he caught but the scantiest shreds of sky, sat a half-grown fieldmouse, washing his whiskers with his dainty claws. His tiny, bead-like eyes kept ceaseless watch, peering through the shadowy tangle for whatever might come near in the shape of foe or prey. Presently two or three stems above his head were beaten down, and a big green grasshopper, alighting clumsily from one of his blind leaps, fell sprawling on the stone. Before he could struggle to his long legs and climb back to the safer region of the grass-tops, the little mouse was upon him. Sharp, white teeth pierced his green mail, his legs kicked convulsively twice or thrice, and the faint iridescence faded out of his big, blank, foolish eyes. The mouse made his meal with relish, daintily discarding the dry legs and wing-cases. Then amid the green debris scattered upon the stone, he sat up, and once more went through his fastidious toilet.

But life for the little mouse in his grass-world was not quite all watching and hunting. When his toilet was complete, and he had amiably let a large black cricket crawl by unmolested, he suddenly began to whirl round on the stone, chasing his own tail. As he was amusing himself with this foolish play, another mouse, about the same size as himself, and probably of the same litter, jumped upon the stone, and knocked him off. He

promptly retorted in kind; and for several minutes, as if the game were a well-understood one, the two kept it up, squeaking soft merriment, and apparently forgetful of all peril. The grass-tops above this play rocked and rustled in a way that would certainly have attracted attention had there been any eyes to see. But the marsh-hawk was still hunting lazily at the other side of the field, and no tragedy followed the childishness.

Both seemed to tire of the sport at the same instant; for suddenly they stopped, and hurried away through the grass on opposite sides of the stone, as if remembered business had just called to them. Whatever the business was, the first mouse seemed to forget it very speedily, for in half a minute he was back upon the stone again, combing his fine whiskers and scratching his ears. This done to his satisfaction, he dropped like a flash from his seat, and disappeared into a small hollow beneath it. As he did so, a hairy black spider darted out, and ran away among the roots.

A minute or two after the disappearance of the mouse, a creature came along which appeared gigantic in the diminutive world of the grass folk. It was nearly three feet long, and of the thickness of a man's finger. Of a steely gray-black, striped and reticulated in a mysterious pattern with a clear whitish yellow, it was an ominous shape indeed, as it glided smoothly and swiftly, in graceful curves, through the close green tangle. The cool shadows and thin lights touched it flickeringly as it went, and never a grass-top stirred to mark its sinister approach. Without a sound of warning it came straight up to the stone, and darted its narrow, cruel head into the hole.

There was a sharp squeak, and instantly the narrow head came out again, ejected by the force of the mouse's agonized spring. But the snake's teeth were fastened in the little animal's neck. The doom of the green world had come upon him while he slept.

But doomed though he was, the mouse was game. He knew there was no poison in those fangs that gripped him, and he struggled desperately to break free. His powerful hind legs kicked the ground with a force which the snake, hampered at first by the fact of its length being partly trailed out through the tangle, was unable to quite control. With unerring instinct — though this was the first snake he had ever encountered — the mouse strove to reach its enemy's back and sever the bone with the fine chisels of his teeth. But it was just this that the snake was watchful to prevent. Three times in his convulsive leaps the mouse succeeded in touching the snake's body — but with his feet only, never once with those destructive little teeth. The snake held him inexorably, with a steady, elastic pressure which yielded just so far, and never quite far enough. And in a minute or two the mouse's brave struggles grew more feeble.

All this, however, — the lashing and the wriggling and the jumping — had not gone on without much disturbance to the grass-tops. Timothy head and clover-bloom, oxeye, and feathery plume-grass, they had bowed and swayed and shivered till the commotion, very conspicuous to one looking down upon the tranquil, flowery sea of green, caught the attention of the marsh-hawk, which at that moment chanced to be perching on a high fence stake. The lean-headed fierce-eyed, trim-feathered bird shot from his perch, and sailed on long wings over the grass to see what was happening. As the swift shadow hovered over the grass-tops, the snake looked up. Well he understood the significance of that sudden shade. Jerking back his fangs with difficulty from the mouse's neck, he started to glide off under the thickest matting of the roots. But lightning-quick though he

was, he was not quite quick enough. Just as his narrow head darted under the roots, the hawk, with wings held straight up, and talons reaching down, dropped upon him, and clutched the middle of his back in a grip of steel. The next moment he was jerked into the air, writhing and coiling, and striking in vain frenzy at his captor's mail of hard feathers. The hawk flew off with him over the sea of green to the top of the fence stake, there to devour him at leisure. The mouse, sore wounded but not past recovery, dragged himself back to the hollow under the stone. And over the stone the grass-tops, once more still, hummed with flies, and breathed warm perfumes in the distilling heat.

Dreams of the Animals

MARGARET ATWOOD

Mostly the animals dream
of other animals   each
according to its kind
      (though certain mice and small rodents
        have nightmares of a huge pink
        shape with five claws descending)

: moles dream of darkness and delicate
mole smells

frogs dream of green and gold
frogs
sparkling like wet suns
among the lilies

red and black
striped fish, their eyes open
have red and black striped
dreams   defence, attack, meaningful
patterns

birds dream of territories
enclosed by singing.

Sometimes the animals dream of evil
in the form of soap and metal
but mostly the animals dream
of other animals.

There are exceptions:

      the silver fox in the roadside zoo
      dreams of digging out
      and of baby foxes, their necks bitten

      the caged armadillo
      near the train
      station, which runs
      all day in figure eights
      its piglet feet pattering,
      no longer dreams
      but is insane when waking;

      the iguana
      in the petshop window on St. Catherine Street
      crested, royal-eyed, ruling
      its kingdom of water-dish and sawdust

      dreams of sawdust.

Helvi's Visitor

SHEILA BURNFORD

The Incredible Journey tells the story of three pet animals — a bull terrier, a Siamese cat, and a Labrador retriever — who trek across northwestern Ontario in the hope of finding their human owners again. In this episode, taken from the book, Tao, the cat, has become separated from his companions.

Many miles downstream on the side to which the dogs had crossed, a small cabin stood near the bank of the river, surrounded by three or four acres of cleared land, its solid, uncompromising appearance lightened only by the scarlet geraniums at the window sills and a bright blue door. A log barn stood back from it, and a steam-bath house at the side nearer the river. The patch of vegetable garden, the young orchard and the neatly fenced fields, each with their piles of cleared boulders and stumps, were small orderly miracles of victory won from the dark encroaching forest that surrounded them.

Reino Nurmi and his wife lived here, as sturdy and uncompromising as the cabin they had built with their own hand-hewn logs, their lives as frugal and orderly as the fields they had wrested from the wilderness. They had tamed the bush, and in return it yielded them their food and their scant living from trap lines and a wood lot, but the struggle to keep it in subjection was endless. They had retained their Finnish identity complete when they left their homeland, exchanging only one country's set of solitudes and vast lonely forests for another's, and as yet their only real contact with the new world that lay beyond their property line was through their ten-year-old daughter Helvi, who knew no other homeland. Helvi walked the lonely miles to the waiting school bus each day, and through her they strengthened their roots in the security of the New World, and were content meanwhile with horizons limited by their labour.

On the Sunday afternoon that the beaver dam broke, a day of some relaxation, Helvi was down by the river, skipping flat stones across the water, and wishing that she had a companion; for she found it difficult to be entirely fair in a competition always held against herself. The riverbank was steep and high here, so she was quite safe when a rushing torrent of water, heralded by a great curling wave, swept past. She stood watching it, fascinated by the spectacle, thinking that she must go and tell her father, when her eye was caught by a piece of debris that had been whirling around in a back eddy and was now caught on some boulders at the edge of the bank. She could see what looked like a small, limp body on the surface. She ran along by the boiling water to investigate, scrambling down the bank, to stand looking with pity at the wet, bedraggled body, wondering what it was, for she had never seen anything like it before. She dragged the mass of twigs and branches further up on land, then ran to call her mother.

Mrs. Nurmi was out in the yard by an old wood stove which she still used for boiling the vegetable dyes for her weaving, or peelings and scraps for the hens. She followed Helvi, calling out to her husband to come and see this strange animal washed up by an unfamiliar, swift-surging river.

He came, with his unhurried countryman's walk and quiet thoughtful face, and joined the others to look down in silence at the small limp body, the darkly plastered fur betraying its slightness, the frail skull bones and thin crooked tail mercilessly exposed. Suddenly he bent down and laid his hand lightly on it for a moment, then pulled back the skin above and below one eye and looked more closely. He turned and saw Helvi's anxious, questioning face close to his own, and beyond that her mother's. "Is a drowned *cat* worth trying to save?" he asked them, and when her mother nodded, before Helvi's pleading eyes, he said no more, but scooped the soaking bundle up and walked back to the cabin, telling Helvi to run ahead and bring some dry sacks.

He laid the cat down in a sunny patch by the wood stove and rubbed it vigorously with sacking, turning the body from side to side until the fur stood out in every direction and it looked like some dishevelled old scarf. Then, as he wrapped the sacking firmly around and her mother pried the clenched teeth open, Helvi poured a little warm milk and precious brandy down the pale cold throat.

She watched as a spasm ran through the body, followed by a faint cough, then held her breath in sympathy as the cat retched and choked convulsively, a thin dribble of milk appearing at the side of its mouth. Reino laid the straining body over his knee and pressed gently over the ribcage. The cat choked and struggled for breath, until at last a sudden gush of water streamed out, and it lay relaxed. Reino gave a slow smile of satisfaction and handed the bundle of sacking to Helvi, telling her to keep it warm and quiet for a while — if she was sure that she still wanted a cat.

She felt the oven, still warm though the fire had long died out, then placed the cat on a tray inside, leaving the door open. When her mother went into the cabin to prepare supper and Reino left to milk the cow,

Helvi sat cross-legged on the ground by the stove, anxiously chewing the end of one fair braid, watching and waiting. Every now and then she would put her hand into the oven to touch the cat, to loosen the sacking or to stroke the soft fur, which was beginning to pulsate with life under her fingers.

After half an hour she was rewarded: the cat opened his eyes. She leaned over and looked closely into them — their blackness now contracted, slowly, to pinpoints, and a pair of astonishingly vivid blue eyes looked up instead. Presently, under her gentle stroking, she felt a throaty vibration, then heard a rusty, feeble purring. Wildly excited, she called to her parents.

Within another half-hour the little Finnish girl held in her lap a sleek, purring, Siamese cat, who had already finished two saucers of milk (which normally he detested, drinking only water), and who had groomed himself from head to foot. By the time the Nurmi family were eating their supper around the scrubbed pine table, he had finished a bowl of chopped meat, and was weaving his way around the table legs, begging in his plaintive, odd voice for more food, his eyes crossed intently, his kinked tail held straight in the air like a banner. Helvi was fascinated by him, and by his gentleness when she picked him up.

That night the Nurmis were having fresh pickerel, cooked in the old-country way with the head still on and surrounded by potatoes. Helvi ladled the head with some broth and potatoes into a saucer and put it on the floor. Soon the fishhead had disappeared to the accompaniment of pleased rumbling growls. The potatoes followed; then, holding down the plate with his paw, the cat polished it clean. Satisfied at last, he stretched superbly, his front paws extended so that he looked like a heraldic lion, then jumped on to Helvi's lap, curled himself around and purred loudly.

The parents' acceptance was completed by his action, though there had never before been a time or place in the economy of their lives for an animal which did not earn its keep, or lived anywhere except the barn or kennel. For the first time in her life Helvi had a pet.

Helvi carried the cat up to bed with her, and he draped himself with familiar ease over her shoulder as she climbed the steep ladder stairs leading up to her little room in the eaves. She tucked him tenderly into an old wooden cradle, and he lay in sleepy contentment, his dark face incongruous against a doll's pillow.

Late in the night she woke to a loud purring in her ear, and felt him treading a circle at her back. The wind blew a gust of cold rain across her face and she leaned over to shut the window, hearing far away, so faint that it died in the second of wind-borne sound, the thin, high keening of a wolf. She shivered as she lay down, then drew the new comforting warmth of the cat closely to her.

When Helvi left in the morning for the long walk and ride to the distant school the cat lay curled on the window sill among the geraniums. He had eaten a large plate of oatmeal, and his coat shone in the sun as he licked it sleepily, his eyes following Mrs. Nurmi as she moved about the cabin. But when she went outside with a basket of washing she looked back to see him standing on his hind legs peering after her, his soundless mouth opening and shutting behind the window. She hurried back, fearful of her geraniums, and opened the door — at which he was already scratch-ing — half expecting him to run. Instead he followed her to the washing line and sat by the basket, purring. He followed her back and forth between the cabin and the wood stove, the henhouse and the stable. When she shut him out once by mistake he wailed pitifully.

This was the pattern of his behaviour all day — he shadowed the Nurmis as they went about their chores, appearing silently on some point of vantage — the seat of the harrow, a sack of potatoes, the manger or the well platform — his eyes on them constantly. Mrs. Nurmi was touched by his apparent need for companionship: that his behaviour was unlike that of any other cat she attributed to his foreign appearance. But her husband was not so easily deceived — he had noticed the unusual intensity in the blue eyes. When a passing raven mocked the cat's voice and he did not look up, then later in the stable sat unheeding to a quick rustle in the straw behind, Reino knew that the cat was deaf.

Carrying her schoolbooks and lunch pail, Helvi ran most of the way home across the fields and picked up the cat as well when he came to meet her. He clung to her shoulder, balancing easily, while she performed the routine evening chores that awaited her. Undeterred by his weight she fed the hens, gathered eggs, fetched water, then sat at the table stringing dried mushrooms. When she put him down before supper she saw that her father was right — the pointed ears did not respond to any sound, though she noticed that he started and turned his head at the vibration if she clapped her hands or dropped even a small pebble on the bare floor.

She had brought home two books from the travelling library, and after the supper dishes had been cleared away her parents sat by the stove in the short interval before bed while she read aloud to them, translating as she went. They sat, in their moment of rare relaxation, with the cat stretched out on his back at their feet, and the child's soft voice, flowing through the dark austerity of the cabin, carried them beyond the circle of light from the oil lamp to the warmth and brightness of strange lands . . .

They heard of seafaring Siamese cats who worked their passages the world over, their small hammocks made and slung by their human messmates, who held them second to none as ship's cats; and of the great proud Siamese Ratting Corps who patrolled the dockyards of Le Havre with unceasing vigilance; they saw, with eyes withdrawn and dreaming, the palace watch-cats of long-ago Siam, walking delicately on thin long simian legs around the fountained courtyards, their softly padding feet polishing the mosaics to a lustred path of centuries. And at last they learned how these nobly born Siamese acquired the kink at the end of their tails and bequeathed it to all their descendants.

And as they listened, they looked down in wonder, for there on the rag rug lay one of these, stretched out flat on his royal back, his illustrious tail twitching idly, and his jewelled eyes on their daughter's hand as she turned the pages that spoke of his ancestors — the guardian cats of the Siamese princesses. Each princess, when she came down to bathe in the palace lake, would slip her rings for safe-keeping on the tail of her attendant cat. So zealous in their charge were these proud cats that they bent the last joint sideways for safer custody, and in time the faithful tails became crooked forever, and their children's and their children's children's . . .

One after another the Nurmis passed their hands admiringly down the tail before them to feel the truth in its bent bony tip; then Helvi gave him a bowl of milk, which he drank with regal condescension before she carried him up the ladder to bed.

That night, and for one more, the cat lay curled peacefully in Helvi's arms, and in the daytime during her absence he followed her parents everywhere. He trailed through the bush after her mother as she searched for late mushrooms, then sat on the cabin steps and patted the dropped corn kernels as she shucked a stack of cobs. He followed Reino and his work horse across the fields to the wood lot and perched on a newly felled pungent stump, his head following their every movement, and he curled by the door of the stable and watched the man mending harness and oiling traps. And in the late afternoons when Helvi returned he was there waiting for her, a rare and beautiful enigma in the certain routine of the day. He was one of them.

But on the fourth night he was restless, shaking his head and pawing his ears, his voice distressed at her back. At last he lay down, purring loudly, and pushed his head into her hand — the fur below his ears was soaking. She saw their sharp black triangles outlined against the little square of window and watched them flicker and quiver in response to every small night sound. Glad for him in his newfound hearing, she fell asleep.

When she woke, later in the night, aware of a lost warmth, she saw him crouched at the open window, looking out over the pale fields and the tall, dark trees below. His long sinuous tail thrashed to and fro as he measured the distance to the ground. Even as her hand moved out impulsively towards him he sprang, landing with a soft thud.

She looked down and saw his head turn for the first time to her voice, his eyes like glowing rubies as they caught the moonlight, then turn away — and with sudden desolation she knew that he had no further need of her. Through a blur of tears, she watched him go, stealing like a wraith in the night towards the river that had brought him. Soon the low, swiftly running form was lost among the shadows.

Long Skinny Minny

GABRIELLE ROY
Translated by Joyce Marshall

As everyone knows, cats are not very fond of going for walks with their masters. They prefer to wait for them to return, sitting on the stoop. Or perhaps on a window ledge, where they are in a good position to see within and without. It is said that they are more attached to places than to people though this is far from being proved. What is certain, however, is that they love their houses dearly. For proof you need only see them on the first brisk fall days, huddled shivering on the doorstep, fur standing on end, paws tucked in, waiting perhaps a whole day for their folks to get back from visiting in some distant concession. The icy wind may be blowing from that side. No matter. They want to wait as close to the doorstep as they can.

However, there are cats that do follow their masters, very few, but there are some. Like Grisou, a little blue-grey cat that spent its entire short life trying to accompany Aimé, my neighbour, when he went each day to the mountain to chop down trees.

In the still shimmering dawn Aimé would set out along the rough path on foot. Regretfully leaving his cosy nook behind the stove, Grisou would once again manage to leave at his heels without being observed. Confronted with the huge frigid outdoors, he would hesitate for a moment, meowing with fear and shock, yet still not losing sight of Aimé striding ahead. The freshly fallen snow often engulfed the little cat to his eyes. He would extricate himself with an effort and catch up with his master, then rub against Aimé's leg in contentment, wasting his energy trying to purr. So that once again he was left behind. He would try to find short cuts, plunge into the soft snow once more, call for help, mewing desperately, overtake his master again and lose him again and finally sit down, very small and frightened, wailing among the dark tree trunks. At this Aimé, who'd hoped to exhaust the patience of the little cat and force him to return home, would retrace his steps, take poor cold-stiffened Grisou and set him on his shoulder. Together the two would continue the ascent, Aimé's breath in a white cloud, the little cat clinging with all his claws to his master's woollen jacket. Even so he would appear to be dancing on Aimé's shoulder as it rose and fell with the rhythm of the walk. And as soon as the terrain became smoother and the cat's equilibrium more secure, he would begin to purr in his master's ear.

"Crazy little fool," Aimé would say. "When will you learn to stay home?"

This was quite an exceptional case among cats and, if I've described it, that was only to show the difference between Grisou and, for instance, his own mother, who was as stay-at-home a beast as you could find.

Called Long Skinny Minny, she was not in the least handsome. A scrawny attenuated cat with a crooked tail, she had irregular splotches of bluish grey scattered haphazardly over her white fur, which I must in fairness say she kept scrupulously clean.

By nature she was sullen, morose, stubborn and always fidgety.

Either she was about to have kittens and was turning over her old hiding places in her mind, those that had succeeded and those that had been discovered, with an air of complete distraction as she asked herself, "Are the oldest ones now sufficiently old to be safe to use again? Or would it be better to find one that was brand new?" But she had already had almost sixty offspring. The farm was running out of secure places for the first days of the kittens. Once their eyes were open, they were safe: too cute to be disposed of.

Or if she wasn't about to produce a litter, she'd just had one. But she'd be as distrustful as ever, taking a new complicated way to her hiding place each time. So that she sometimes became completely muddled and lost her way.

However — how strange was the nature of that cat — the moment her kittens were able to fend for themselves, she again took her place firmly among the humans. Henceforth the single thought in her head was to live in the house with the people, installed among them in the best chair, lending an ear to all conversations. And she was constantly at one door or another, begging to be let in.

Now Berthe and her brother Aimé have a strict rule: in summer cats are best outdoors. So they are not readily admitted to the house.

Scarcely had Long Skinny Minny contrived to sneak into the kitchen on someone's heels than she would find herself unceremoniously back outside. No matter. She would hear Aimé coming from the barn with the milk pails. Immediately she was at the back door and had managed to get in, Aimé having no free hand to prevent her. If he tried to bar her way with his foot, she vaulted it easily.

"The cat's in again, put her out," Berthe would say, busy frying a pan of salmon trout or slices of bread soaked in maple syrup.

Naturally it was at the most enticing hour that Long Skinny Minny always deployed all her efforts to reach the kitchen. In the bustle of supper hour with everyone occupied, she more than once succeeded in leaping onto the table and devouring an entire trout right under our noses before we could recover from our surprise enough to shout, "Shoo! Thief!" which didn't disconcert her in the least.

"That cat has no pride," Berthe decided one day.

Seated rocking while everything was being made ready, I went somewhat mildly to the defence of the cat.

"She may be hungry."

"I've just fed her the heads and guts of the fish," said Berthe. "Scat! Out!"

And she dispatched the cat outdoors.

As we were on the point of sitting down to eat, in came the baker and Long Skinny Minny entered triumphantly behind him since he hadn't thought to slam the door in her face.

He sat down. She also.

Two minutes later Berthe accompanied the baker to his van to choose some cakes and took the opportunity to put the cat back out, and the cat took the opportunity of Berthe's return with loaded arms to enter anew.

She eventually wore people down. Aimé's house is lively with many visitors. In the course of a single evening I've seen the cat put to the door twenty or even thirty times. Towards eleven o'clock it was not unusual to see her ensconced in the best chair, pretending to be asleep. From time to time she would open her eyes and bestow upon the company a strange glance in which there was less friendliness than a stubborn need, I think, to establish her importance and her place among us.

Nowhere in the world, I imagine, was there a more stay-at-home-and-sit-by-the-fire cat than this. Unlike Tontine, the little dog of the household, who went into a frenzy of joy whenever she was invited to go for a walk, Long Skinny Minny on her cushion always seemed eager to see us depart. Stretching indolently from head to toes, she would toss us a queer look, at once detached and a shade impatient, as if she were saying, "Why can't you be off then? It's never so nice as when the masters are out and you have the house to yourself."

No doubt it must also have been pleasant for her to be free for an hour or so from the perpetual humiliations and insults of that detestable Tontine.

Be that as it may, this cat, hitherto so set in her ways, finally did something one day that she had never done before and thus dumbfounded us completely.

Berthe and I were getting ready that day to go down to the river to fish for tommycod and Tontine was dancing around, beside herself with joy, giving piercing cries, "Yes! Yes! Let's go down to the river! Let's hurry!"

The small dog with the long reddish fur, half mongrel, half Pekinese, was so passionately fond of going down to the river that she'd learned to recognize the word. If we as much as uttered it in conversation, even though Tontine seemed to be sound asleep, she would immediately open her eyes, lift her head and half rise, already excited by the hope of going with us.

But why she so doted upon going down to the river remained puzzling. For once she'd reached its banks, she didn't even look at the water. Nor did she listen to what was for Berthe and me an inexhaustible joy: the infinite sound of the waves, forever dispersing, forever gathering themselves together again. And she certainly never went swimming but was careful to recoil sharply when, some time after the passage of a ship, a long wave broke unexpectedly on the shore. Moreover, she never went down there on her own as she might have done a hundred times a day. I decided finally that it was seeing us, human beings, made happy by this surprising expanse of water that in the end won over the little dog. "Since they like it so much," she perhaps said to herself, "let's give it a try too." For she had a warm heart, though dreadfully jealous.

So as we had been on our way for several minutes, we suddenly observed Long Skinny Minny trying to follow us and already entangled in the long grass. She must have managed to sneak out behind us without being noticed as she'd managed to sneak in a thousand times.

"This is a surprise," I said. "What's come over her?"

"She's getting old," said Berthe. "And when she's expecting kittens now, you'd think she no longer knows what she wants — to stay or follow, be with people or alone."

And she called over her shoulder to the cat, "You'd better go back to the house. It's too far for you."

That was a mistake, for Tontine had also turned and had seen the cat, who at once flattened herself in the grass, trying to disappear. Tontine raced up the hill like a meteor and repeated the advice in her own way, eyes furious, lip drawn back. For once Long Skinny Minny seemed about to turn on her old enemy. She spat three or four times in Tontine's face. Caught for a moment between these deplorable manners and Berthe's remonstrances, "Ah, bad girl! Come here, bad girl!" Tontine eventually obeyed and returned to our side.

But snarling still, she threatened in an undertone, "Just as long as she doesn't come any closer, for then I promise nothing."

After a moment we saw that Long Skinny Minny was still following us but at a distance, ready to flatten herself in the grass as soon as Tontine glanced in her direction.

"Between the slinking cat and the growls of the dog, we're going to have a cheerful walk," I said.

Berthe also seemed disappointed. But she said with a sort of compassion, "It's pitiful just the same."

And she tried again, gently, to send the cat back.

"You'd be much better off at home. Go on. Go home."

Halfway up the hill the head of the cat, scarcely higher than the grass, shook in negation, rather sadly.

We found it inexplicable that Long Skinny Minny should apparently be every bit as attached to us today as she had previously been to the house.

"You'd think she was afraid to be alone these days," said Berthe. "And as for getting her to change her mind, if she's taken a notion to follow us, you might as well try to move the mountain."

So we went on, more or less together, a drawn-out line with Long Skinny Minny far at the rear.

But matters became even worse. For to reach the river you have to go down a steep hill. Great rocks pierce the surface, which is rough and uneven at best. In spots the path is dry, in others always wet. You need to be appropriately shod. Long Skinny Minny kept cutting her paws on the sharp edges of the rock. She got them wet in the damp places, which seemed to displease her even more for she kept drawing one or other of them from the water and shaking it vigorously. At intervals the poor creature sat down to lick the tender cushions of her injured paws. With a helpless look she inquired of us, whimpering, "Couldn't you at least slow down? You know perfectly well I'm not wearing good heavy shoes like you."

Tontine, still nursing her rancour, raced up at once to laugh in her face.

"What came over you to decide to follow us to the river? The river isn't for you. Now put up with it."

Berthe and I finally sat down to enable Long Skinny Minny to rest for a while. Clearly the harder the way became, the less she would consent to give up. It was as if she were trying to tell us with her big eyes, so full of fatigue and stubbornness, "Do you folks think now that I've managed all this difficult bit I have any intention of returning?"

Tontine made a detour and sat down some distance from the cat, ostentatiously turning her back. And she gave a great sigh of repressed ill-temper.

The place where we were sitting is leafy and shadowy: a narrow clearing between the tangled alders and a few birch trees whose white bark relieves this slightly too sombre wood. We had seated ourselves on a smooth rock and in some connection that escapes me now began to talk

about life, how it changes as we advance, as we ourselves change, how hard it is at times to find ourselves again.

Already we could hear, rather faintly, the beating of the water against the shore and the sound became linked with what we were saying. The river and life, both in motion, seemed very close to one another, though the movement of the river soothes us and life often gives us pain as we try to follow it.

"When I was a child," Berthe told me, "my mother used to send me to the spring in this wood with butter, milk and cream. Now we have a refrigerator to keep things cool. It's a thousand times more convenient but we've lost the pleasure of the spring."

"Where is it?" I asked.

She showed me. We uncovered it under some tall dark-green ferns. It made only a tiny sound, scarcely louder than that of the hand of a clock marking the time. It was gentle and enigmatic, as mysterious as at the beginning of its life.

"It's years since I've seen it," said Berthe. "Now that we don't need it any more."

Leaning over the water, we could see very dimly our own darkened faces.

"You can only wonder," I said, "whether what we gain in living is worth what is lost."

At this Tontine, her muzzle flat on the ground but her eyes wide open and her ears impatient, barked briefly as if trying to say, "Do stop talking about life. What's the use? What can you change? Come on, let's get down to the river."

But Long Skinny Minny appeared happy to hear us speaking about the difficulties of living with ourselves and with others. She was lying on her side, still panting slightly, and from time to time she half opened her eyes to give us a golden look that was beginning to grow peaceful.

"That's it," she seemed to be saying. "Talk about life, which is hard to understand and hard to live."

And she turned to Tontine a face of stone.

When we had all four rested, we resumed our descent. The cat lamented less. Doubtless she thought the roughest part of the journey was over and she had a chance of seeing the end. But as if to taunt her by showing how easy the path was for anyone who had the hang of it, Tontine had taken to a cruel game. She raced up the hill and down just as quickly, then raced up again, each time circling the cat, yapping. With more dignity than one would have believed possible, Long Skinny Minny no longer spat or even answered this provocation but simply withdrew a single step from the brazen Tontine.

Then we came out onto the beach with its scattering of great rocks. Beyond lay the accustomed splendour of the river — to which, however, one never grows accustomed. For the thousandth time it gripped our hearts. At the same time the murmuring of the water, the most ancient song of Earth, welcomed and enfolded us. Tontine gave us a knowing look, assuring herself that it was the same as on all the other occasions, we were already solaced. Then she found herself a nice dry spot behind one of the boulders, turned in a circle and lay down with another sigh, this time of relief.

"At last you'll be quiet for a moment. I'll avail myself of the opportunity to have a rest myself," she told us with a look in which all her concern for us was gradually borne away by a need for sleep.

A little higher up the cat stretched to her full length, scrawny everywhere except for her almost constantly swollen belly. She cast a vague, somewhat bored look at all that water stretching into infinity. What a detestable element! And to think there are people who'll go right to the edge of it — or into it even! She panted gently, composing herself after the emotions of the journey, then she too closed her eyes.

For Berthe and for me, time was of little account, we scarcely see it pass when we are beside the river. It drifts into the song of the tide, which rises and falls, almost the same always. The eternal has seemingly no need to change. To our animal friends also time doesn't seem long near the water, provided we are with them. While we dream, released and marvellously free, they sleep, their minds finally reassured on our account.

Why then did I suddenly break the spell that day by suggesting, "Berthe, suppose we walk along the track?"

Tontine rose to go with us, resigned to follow because she must, but with a rather cross expression.

"What a notion, when we're so comfortable here in the cool, to seek misery elsewhere! How like that curious friend of my mistress who's never happy anywhere for long."

As for Long Skinny Minny, she looked utterly horror-stricken. "What sort of surface will I find there for my already sorely tried paws? And what's the track? Why are they now talking about such an unheard-of place?"

To tell the truth, with her crooked tail, her frantic expression, the amazement in her eyes at wakening here beside the water, she looked crazier than ever.

Yet — what else could she do once launched upon such a foolhardy escapade — she went a little way back with us. There, on a narrow bit of level ground parallel to the river, lies the railroad track.

Berthe and I moved haltingly over the ties, which are set irregularly, as if to discourage people from walking there. The body quickly becomes weary. However, the spirit rejoices, as if it imagined itself freer here than on the road of everyone else.

We had covered a fair bit of ground before we noticed that our animals were — as the saying goes — dragging their feet. Even for Tontine the rough ballast was painful. She was walking like an arthritic with short steps, head down, but without complaint. You have to give Tontine her due, she's not a whiner. But Long Skinny Minny, seated between the rails, eyes bewildered, looked as if she were on the point of giving up but, perhaps not remembering the way or simply too tired to go in either direction, she lamented at the top of her lungs.

"Where have we got to now? Where are we going? Where can it lead, a road like this? Oh why didn't anyone tell me we were going to the back of beyond?"

Tontine gave her a brief glance and a brief growl.

"We did tell you. If you don't like it here, go back. It's hard enough on this road as it is without having to listen to your doleful wails as well."

Poor Long Skinny Minny. To think that she was about to demonstrate a rare and unsuspected talent just when we, in our ignorance, thinking her too stupid, were ready to turn back. But happily I became a child again and had an impulse to try to walk on a single rail, as I used to do when I was seven or eight.

Arms extended to either side for balance, I at first managed only six or seven steps. I got back up and did a little better. Still nothing brilliant. Berthe passed me on the other rail. I began to feel jealous. We then joined hands across the roadbed, trying to support one another. In a moment we were laughing. Life suddenly seemed tender, comic, amusing. Were two slim little girls who had run nimbly along the rail looking at us across the years with a touch of pity? The dog and cat were astonished, in any case. Tontine, who had never seen her mistress give way to such whimsy, was dumbfounded. And as always when she can no longer understand the actions of those she loves, she was whimpering. However, Long Skinny Minny, seated again between the rails but not wailing any more, was watching us, her small narrow face now all attention, all shrewdness, all intelligence.

And suddenly she took off. She passed us easily, tail held high. That perfectly erect tail gave her an entirely new personality. Never would I have thought that the mere angle of a tail could make such a difference.

A short distance ahead of us she jumped onto the rail and continued along at the same speed, tail still high and straight. She didn't even waver but proceeded as if it were nothing. Then, without slowing down, she tossed us a look over her shoulder.

"So this is what you find so difficult! But it's perfectly simple!"

We were thunderstruck. She went on at her ease. A nice firm little trot that never varied. And all this time her head assured, ears erect, tail high.

"That's marvellous!" we congratulated her. "No one on earth is better at running the rail."

Modestly, as if not to claim more than her due, she granted us a brief glance that said, "Ah, that's because you have such wide feet and, poor souls, you only have two."

Despite her unassuming air, we could see that she was rather proud of herself.

The one who looked small at this moment was Tontine.

One ear drooping, tail brushing the ground, an expression of complete incredulity on her face, she watched her bitter enemy continue on her way with such sovereign ease. She gave sighs of envy and grief that reached their height when, without thought for Tontine's feelings, we once more congratulated the cat, "Bravo! Bravo!"

Then Tontine committed the folly of follies. She pulled herself onto the rail and immediately fell off. Obstinately, she tried again and with great difficulty achieved four heavy hesitant steps.

The polished steel provided no purchase for her clumsy claws. The poor stubborn creature teetered and landed on her back.

The sole comment of the cat, which had all the cards in hand for a magnificent revenge, was a sort of shrug. She was still running along ahead of us, with an occasional look behind that said mockingly, "Are you still hale and hearty? Shall we go as far as the eel fishing at l'Abatis? To Sault-au-Cochon?"

She seemed suddenly to know the whole region, its peculiarities, its geography.

"Or even to Petit Cap at the bottom of the old seigneury? How long is it now that I've heard you say you'd go there on foot one of these days?"

We had to call her back. Drunk with her success, she was capable of leading us right to Québec. At first she played deaf and wouldn't even hear of leaving the rail. But when she saw us already halfway up the hill, she decided to return.

No doubt it was not so much running on the rail that intoxicated her

as the fact that she'd astonished us. For she had further prowess to display.

In three bounds she ascended the steep hill, stomach on the ground, tail in a straight line with her nose.

At the top, however, she had the good grace to wait for us. There she sat with her tail wrapped around her paws, gazing at the river, the clouds and, far away, between blinks of her eyes, our little procession laboriously climbing.

And on her features was that vaguely amiable expression that comes to people as to animals when for once in their lives they have been admired.

Then There Were Three

R. D. LAWRENCE

Cry Wild *is the story of a Canadian timber wolf. Although the story is imaginary, it is based on the author's close observation of wolves and his long experience in the north country. In this excerpt the pup, Silverfeet, and his brother and sisters, have their first, brutal encounter with another inhabitant of the wilderness — a black bear.*

Silverfeet was nine days old when his eyes began to open. The cubs were alone in the den that afternoon, for the bitch wolf had gone on a hunt with her mate. She had been forced by hunger to abandon the young ones. Had she been with a pack, she would not have gone and there would have been no hunger in the den; but although her mate was a good hunter he had been unable, alone, to bring down enough game for their needs. The dog had brought hares and groundhogs, and now and then a grouse, but such fare is meagre for two full-grown timber wolves, inadequate for a she-wolf nursing young. In the middle of plenty, these two efficient, powerful hunters were suffering want. Yet there was nothing really unusual about this. Wolves were created to hunt in packs; they are sociable animals that band together for survival. The dog and his mate, before the coming of the pups, had made an efficient, if small, hunting pack, but the dog alone could not hope to provide enough of the big game needed for the survival of the cubs. So the two had paired again and they had gone to hunt, perforce leaving the cubs unguarded.

Silverfeet and his brother and sisters were unaware of these things. They had nursed from their mother before she left the den, and now they made small dog-noises as they huddled together. Silverfeet had one of his black sister's ears clamped firmly in his mouth, and he was sucking it, comforting himself as a human baby might do with his thumb. At first, when the gummy lids of his right eye separated just a crack, exposing the eye to the sunlight that slanted into the cave, panic seized him and he let go of his sister's ear and tried to bury his head beneath the squirming bodies of the others. For some moments he continued to try to escape the light and then his second eyelid parted a little, chasing away more darkness. Fear was overcome by curiosity. Silverfeet withdrew his head from the bundle of living fur into which he had thrust it, and blinked owlishly towards the cave mouth. The strong light hurt his eyes and he turned away, but there was a fascination in that light. He had to stare at it. Slowly the pain of the light became less and less, until at last it left him altogether and for the first time he could see, though dimly.

That afternoon all the wolf pups gained their vision. Until then they had been guided by their ears and by their nostrils. They had crawled around and over one another, and had wandered aimlessly around the den chamber. Now they had eyes to guide them. They discerned each other for the first time and they recognized the smells and sounds of the den with their eyes. It was a wonderful experience. And if it frightened them at first, it held new promise.

The four rose to unsteady legs and peered at one another, smelling each other and sniffing about the chamber. They were small and feeble and their muscles would not co-ordinate properly, but the light drew them. Silverfeet was the first to make for it — slowly, wobbling, as often crawling as walking, but determined to reach the daylight that beckoned so persuasively. And the others followed. The four inched their way towards the outside on their short, rubbery legs, ignorant of the dangers that lurked there. Now and then one would sit down and rest a moment before setting off again.

Their progress was uneven but it took them closer and closer to their objective. Finally they were at the den entrance. Silverfeet stopped abruptly, dazzled by the sun. The others huddled around him, small, scared, and excited; four precocious animal children reaching too soon the great, green world. Silverfeet's chubby little body was toppled forward by the combined weight of the others. He rolled a little way outside, stopped, recovered, and scrambled slowly to his feet. He moved two steps forward, paused undecided, and peered back to see what the others were doing. The small gray bitch was just then moving, intent on following Silverfeet; the black bitch was sprawled flat on her belly at the cave mouth; the brindled little dog was still framed by the opaqueness of the cave, but he, too, was beginning to follow.

At last the four cubs were outside. They again huddled together, fear beginning to crowd their senses. They were so small and so unsure, and this new world was so big, even to their myopic sight. Silverfeet, not really knowing why, felt the urge to return to the safe darkness of the den and he began to walk again, but his senses were too weak and he did not know which way to go. Instead of retracing his steps, he moved farther away from the cave. His brother and sisters followed, a ragged little group that travelled but inches at a time. Some instinct warned Silverfeet that he was going in the wrong direction; perhaps the smell of the den became weaker in his nostrils, perhaps fear sharpened his senses. He stopped and the others stopped with him. They sat undecided.

The squirrel that lived near the den had been watching the young wolves. Squatting lazily on his nesting branch he had followed their ungainly progress from the cave mouth with the intent curiosity that all wild things display towards newness in their territory. Suddenly he sat upright and riveted his gaze upon an area of tangled scrubland a bare quarter of a mile from the den. The cubs continued with their antics, still trying to return to the security of their nursery.

The squirrel had lost all interest in them; his entire attention was devoted to the place he was watching. From his high vantage point he could see the brush moving. His keen ears caught a heavy sound coming from the area. Suddenly the squirrel chittered his alarm cry. He kept up the churring for perhaps half a minute, then he bolted up the tree and disappeared into his nesting hole. The cubs were oblivious of this. They heard the noise that the squirrel made, but they did not know that this was an alarm, alerting the forest to the presence of a dangerous prowler.

Silverfeet had succeeded in pointing himself in the right direction at last. Wobbling, he was slowly making his way towards the cave mouth. His sisters were following, but his brother had lost his bearings and was wandering farther away.

From the direction of the scrub patch a pig-like grunt disturbed the stillness of the afternoon. On its heels came the crackling of brush. Presently, the shaggy bulk of a black bear emerged into view. The bear's shambling course was erratic. He paused now and then to snuffle at something on the ground. Once he stopped at a dead log; with two slow smashes of his powerful forepaws, he tore it to pieces and stooped to lick up the ants from within the rotting wood, enjoying the pungent taste of the acidy bodies. When he had lapped up the last scurrying ant, he ambled up the hill towards the wolf den. Suddenly he stopped. Wolf scent had penetrated his nostrils. He was interested and cautious. He knew the smell of the wolf den, and he knew that in that den he could expect to find some young; these would be delicate mouthfuls for the still winter-hungry bear. But he knew also the savagery of timber wolves protecting their young, and so he paused, advanced a couple of steps, and paused once more, working his nostrils and flicking his ears, trying to locate the adult wolves. A few yards farther on he detected the smell of the cubs. He squinted, trying with his poor vision to locate their whereabouts, at the same time deciding that the parent wolves were not present. He quickened his steps, and the scent of the pups guided him unerringly towards the feebly-moving shape of the brindled male.

Returning home from a successful deer hunt, the parent wolves had picked up the scent of the bear. Now they were rushing towards the den, pausing occasionally to track the bear's progress, aware that he was heading directly for their den. The wolves were half a mile from home, but their progress was swift. They raced in their fastest gallop, jumping deadfalls, smashing their way through brush in an effort to get to their pups ahead of the marauding bear.

They burst out of the forest in view of their den just as the black bear seized the body of the brindled cub. The big bear stood on all fours, facing the cave entrance and eyeing the remaining pups. The little male was entirely hidden within his great jaws. He bit down, and the life was crushed from the little brindled body. At this moment two furious, savage things unleashed themselves upon the bear.

With flashing fangs and upcurled lips the wolves bore into the attack, smashing into the bear from either side. The bitch seized the bear's left

hind leg, the dog sank his teeth into the hairy right flank. The bear whirled, shaking off both wolves with ease. He dropped the body of the pup. The wolves attacked again, their throaty growls of rage mingled with the bear's roar of surprise. The bear rushed the dog, trying to clasp him in his strong arms and crush him to death. While he was doing this the bitch struck him hard in the shoulder, knocking him off his feet. In a trice the dog wolf hit again and slashed a furrow in one of the bear's ears.

The bear was nimble. Quickly he regained his feet and charged the she-wolf; the tactic was repeated. While the she retreated out of reach, the dog bore in from the other side. Slowly the two wolves were easing the bear away from the cubs. The fight was fierce, and the noise of it filled the forest with fear. The three remaining pups, meanwhile, lay as though frozen, their instincts telling them to stay that way while the life and death struggle raged on; not even a whimper escaped them.

The bear was trying to run from the wolves now. Repeatedly he sought to gallop away, but each time he was met by one of the charging wolves. Again and again they bit at him. Time after time the bear tried to crush them. If he was slow with his biting jabs, he was fast with his forepaws. The fight seemed to have come to an impasse. But if the bear wanted to escape, the wolves wanted even more to get him away from the den.

Step by step, yard by yard, they drew him away, until at last they were down the slope and close to the brush out of which the bear had come. The dog had a wound on his right shoulder, where one of the bear's claws had raked him. Blood came, but the wound was not serious. The bear was bleeding from several bites, but these, too, were only superficial. His shaggy coat of matted hair made him almost impervious to the fangs of the wolves.

The wolves paused for a fraction of time, and the bear took advantage of the moment to wheel and charge into the heavy brush. The dog pursued him. The bitch hesitated, the mother instinct conquering her desire for vengeance. She climbed the slope to her pups.

She went first to the three, and smelled them and licked them, noting that they were unharmed. She turned to the dead cub then, licked it all over, and nuzzled it as though urging it to move. The bitch whined and licked her baby again. Carefully she opened her mouth and picked it up. It looked at first as though she were going to eat it, for the small body hardly protruded from either side of her jaws, but this is the way in which wolves carry their young. She turned and entered the den and deposited the dead pup in the nesting chamber. In a moment she was back outside, and one by one she carried her other pups to safety. She lay down with them, and Silverfeet and his sisters suckled from her. The dead pup lay on his back near her front paws; she nuzzled him and pushed him towards her dugs. She looked to the cave mouth and listened to the progress of the chase.

The dog wolf had no desire now to attack the bear, but he kept chasing him, pushing him out of his country, always near but never actually closing with him. They ran in this fashion for about two miles. At last the dog stopped. The bear kept travelling, grotesquely agile, looking like a moving black ball as he raced at top speed to disappear over a hilltop. The dog waited a few moments and listened, and when he could hear the bear no more he turned and raced for home.

The Springfield Fox

ERNEST THOMPSON SETON

The hens were disappearing. My uncle was wrathy. He determined to conduct the war himself, and sowed the woods with poison baits, trusting to luck that our own dogs would not get them. He indulged in contemptuous remarks on my by-gone woodcraft, and went out evenings with a gun and the two dogs, to see what he could destroy.

Vix knew right well what a poisoned bait was; she passed them by or else treated them with active contempt, but one she dropped down the hole of an old enemy, a skunk, who was never afterward seen. Formerly old Scarface was always ready to take charge of the dogs, and keep them out of mischief. But now that Vix had the whole burden of the brood, she could no longer spend time in breaking every track to the den, and was not always at hand to meet and mislead the foes that might be coming too near.

The end is easily foreseen. Ranger followed a hot trail to the den, and Spot, the fox-terrier, announced that the family was at home, and then did his best to go in after them.

The whole secret was now out, and the whole family doomed. The hired man came around with pick and shovel to dig them out, while we and the dogs stood by. Old Vix soon showed herself in the near woods, and led the dogs away off down the river, where she shook them off when she thought proper, by the simple device of springing on a sheep's back. The frightened animal ran for several hundred yards, then Vix got off, knowing that there was now a hopeless gap in the scent, and returned to the den. But the dogs, baffled by the break in the trail, soon did the same, to find Vix hanging about in despair, vainly trying to decoy us away from her treasures.

Meanwhile Paddy plied both pick and shovel with vigor and effort. The yellow, gravelly sand was heaping on both sides, and the shoulders of the sturdy digger were sinking below the level. After an hour's digging, enlivened by frantic rushes of the dogs after the old fox, who hovered near in the woods, Pat called:

"Here they are, sor!"

It was the den at the end of the burrow, and cowering as far back as they could, were the four little woolly cubs.

Before I could interfere, a murderous blow from the shovel, and a sudden rush from the fierce little terrier, ended the lives of three. The fourth and smallest was barely saved by holding him by his tail high out of reach of the excited dogs.

He gave one short squeal, and his poor mother came at the cry, and circled so near that she would have been shot but for the accidental protection of the dogs, who somehow always seemed to get between, and whom she once more led away on a fruitless chase.

The little one saved alive was dropped into a bag, where he lay quite still. His unfortunate brothers were thrown back into their nursery bed, and buried under a few shovelfuls of earth.

We guilty ones then went back into the house, and the little fox was soon chained in the yard. No one knew just why he was kept alive, but in all a change of feeling had set in, and the idea of killing him was without a supporter.

He was a pretty little fellow, like a cross between a fox and a lamb. His woolly visage and form were strangely lamb-like and innocent, but one could find in his yellow eyes a gleam of cunning and savageness as unlamb-like as it possibly could be.

As long as anyone was near he crouched sullen and cowed in his shelter-box, and it was a full hour after being left alone before he ventured to look out.

My window now took the place of the hollow basswood. A number of hens of the breed he knew so well were about the cub in the yard. Late that afternoon as they strayed near the captive there was a sudden rattle of the chain, and the youngster dashed at the nearest one and would have caught him but for the chain which brought him up with a jerk. He got on his feet and slunk back to his box, and though he afterward made several rushes he so gauged his leap as to win or fail within the length of the chain and never again was brought up by its cruel jerk.

As night came down the little fellow became very uneasy, sneaking out of his box, but going back at each slight alarm, tugging at his chain, or at times biting it in fury while he held it down with his forepaws. Suddenly he paused as though listening, then raising his little black nose he poured out a short quavering cry.

Once or twice this was repeated, the time between being occupied in worrying the chain and running about. Then an answer came. The far-away *yap-yurrr* of the old fox. A few minutes later a shadowy form appeared on the wood-pile. The little one slunk into his box, but at once returned and ran to meet his mother with all the gladness that a fox could show. Quick as a flash she seized him and turned to bear him away by the road she came. But the moment the end of the chain was reached the cub was rudely jerked from the old one's mouth, and she, scared by the opening of a window, fled over the wood-pile.

An hour afterward the cub had ceased to run about or cry. I peeped out, and by the light of the moon saw the form of the mother at full length on the ground by the little one, gnawing at something — the clank of iron told what, it was the cruel chain. And Tip, the little one, meanwhile was helping himself to a warm drink.

On my going out she fled into the dark woods, but there by the shelter-box were two little mice, bloody and still warm, food for the cub brought by the devoted mother. And in the morning I found the chain was very bright for a foot or two next the little one's collar.

On walking across the woods to the ruined den, I again found signs of Vixen. The poor heart-broken mother had come and dug out the be-draggled bodies of her little ones.

There lay the three little baby foxes all licked smooth now, and by them were two of our hens fresh killed. The newly heaved earth was print-ed all over with tell-tale signs — signs that told me that here by the side of her dead she had watched like Rizpah. Here she had brought their usual meal, the spoil of her nightly hunt. Here she had stretched herself beside them and vainly offered them their natural drink and yearned to feed and warm them as of old; but only stiff little bodies under their soft wool she found, and little cold noses still and unresponsive.

A deep impress of elbows, breast, and hocks showed where she had laid in silent grief and watched them for long and mourned as a wild mother can mourn for its young. But from that time she came no more to the ruined den, for now she surely knew that her little ones were dead.

Tip the captive, the weakling of the brood, was now the heir to all her love. The dogs were loosed to guard the hens. The hired man had orders to shoot the old fox on sight — so had I, but was resolved never to see her. Chicken-heads, that a fox loves and a dog will not touch, had been poisoned and scattered through the woods; and the only way to the yard where Tip was tied, was by climbing the wood-pile after braving all other dangers. And yet each night old Vix was there to nurse her baby and bring it fresh-killed hens and game. Again and again I saw her, although she came now without awaiting the querulous cry of the captive.

The second night of the captivity I heard the rattle of the chain, and then made out that the old fox was there, hard at work digging a hole by the little one's kennel. When it was deep enough to half bury her, she gathered into it all the slack of the chain, and filled it again with earth.

Then in triumph thinking she had gotten rid of the chain, she seized little Tip by the neck and turned to dash off up the wood-pile, but alas! only to have him jerked roughly from her grasp.

Poor little fellow, he whimpered sadly as he crawled into his box. After half an hour there was a great outcry among the dogs, and by their straight-away tonguing through the far woods I knew they were chasing Vix. Away up north they went in the direction of the railway and their noise faded from hearing. Next morning the hounds had not come back. We soon knew why. Foxes long ago learned what a railroad is; they soon devised several ways of turning it to account. One way is when hunted to walk the rails for a long distance just before a train comes. The scent, al-ways poor on iron, is destroyed by the train and there is always a chance of hounds being killed by the engine. But another way more sure, but harder to play, is to lead the hounds straight to a high trestle just ahead of the train, so that the engine overtakes them on it and they are surely dashed to destruction.

This trick was skilfully played, and down below we found the mangled remains of old Ranger and learned that Vix was already wreaking her revenge.

That same night she returned to the yard before Spot's weary limbs could bring him back and killed another hen and brought it to Tip, and stretched her panting length beside him that he might quench his thirst. For she seemed to think he had no food but what she brought.

It was that hen that betrayed to my uncle the nightly visits.

My own sympathies were all turning to Vix, and I would have no hand in planning further murders. Next night my uncle himself watched, gun in hand, for an hour. Then when it became cold and the moon cloud-ed over he remembered other important business elsewhere, and left Paddy in his place.

But Paddy was "onaisy" as the stillness and anxiety of watching worked on his nerves. And the loud bang! bang! an hour later left us sure only that powder had been burned.

In the morning we found Vix had not failed her young one. Again next night found my uncle on guard, for another hen had been taken. Soon after dark a single shot was heard, but Vix dropped the game she was bringing and escaped. Another attempt made that night called forth another gun-shot. Yet next day it was seen by the brightness of the chain that she had come again and vainly tried for hours to cut that hateful bond.

Such courage and staunch fidelity were bound to win respect, if not toleration. At any rate, there was no gunner in wait next night, when all was still. Could it be of any use? Driven off thrice with gun-shots, would she make another try to feed or free her captive young one?

Would she? Hers was a mother's love. There was but one to watch them this time, the fourth night, when the quavering whine of the little one was followed by that shadowy form above the wood-pile.

But carrying no fowl or food that could be seen. Had the keen huntress failed at last? Had she no head of game for this her only charge, or had she learned to trust his captors for his food?

No, far from all this. The wild-wood mother's heart and hate were true. Her only thought had been to set him free. All means she knew she tried, and every danger braved to tend him well and help him to be free. But all had failed.

Like a shadow she came and in a moment was gone, and Tip seized on something dropped, and crunched and chewed with relish what she brought. But even as he ate, a knife-like pang shot through and a scream of pain escaped him. Then there was a momentary struggle and the little fox was dead.

The mother's love was strong in Vix, but a higher thought was stronger. She knew right well the poison's power; she knew the poison bait, and would have taught him had he lived to know and shun it too. But now at last when she must choose for him a wretched prisoner's life or sudden death, she quenched the mother in her breast and freed him by the one remaining door.

It is when the snow is on the ground that we take the census of the woods, and when the winter came it told me that Vix no longer roamed the woods of Erindale. Where she went it never told, but only this, that she was gone.

Gone, perhaps, to some other far-off haunt to leave behind the sad remembrance of her murdered little ones and mate. Or gone, maybe, deliberately, from the scene of a sorrowful life, as many a wild-wood mother has gone, by the means that she herself had used to free her young one, the last of all her brood.

Mutt Makes His Mark

FARLEY MOWAT

Mutt was a real dog. He lived in Saskatoon with the author when the author was just a boy. But Mutt was not convinced that he was a dog — he thought that he was a human. Some people sometimes seemed to think so, too. This story is from The Dog Who Wouldn't Be.

It all began on one of those blistering July days when the prairie pants like a dying coyote, the dust lies heavy, and the air burns the flesh it touches. On such days those with good sense retire to the cellar caverns that are euphemistically known in Canada as beer parlors. These are all much the same across the country — ill-lit and crowded dens, redolent with the stench of sweat, spilled beer, and smoke — but they are, for the most part, moderately cool. And the insipid stuff that passes for beer is usually ice cold.

On this particular day five residents of the city, dog fanciers all, had forgathered in a beer parlor. They had just returned from witnessing some hunting-dog trials held in Manitoba, and they had brought a guest with them. He was a rather portly gentleman from the state of New York, and he had both wealth and ambition. He used his wealth lavishly to further his ambition, which was to raise and own the finest retrievers on the continent, if not in the world. Having watched his own dogs win the Manitoba trials, this man had come on to Saskatoon at the earnest invitation of the local men, in order to see what kind of dogs they bred, and to buy some if he fancied them.

He had not fancied them. Perhaps rightfully annoyed at having made the trip in the broiling summer weather to no good purpose, he had become a little overbearing in his manner. His comments when he viewed the local kennel dogs had been acidulous, and scornful. He had ruffled the local breeders' feelings, and as a result they were in a mood to do and say foolish things.

The visitor's train was due to leave at 4 P.M., and from 12:30 until 3 the six men sat cooling themselves internally, and talking dogs. The talk was as heated as the weather. Inevitably Mutt's name was mentioned, and he was referred to as an outstanding example of that rare breed, the Prince Albert retriever.

The stranger hooted. "Rare breed!" he cried. "I'll say it must be rare! I've never even heard of it."

The local men were incensed by this big-city skepticism. They immediately began telling tales of Mutt, and if they laid it on a little, who can blame them? But the more stories they told, the louder grew the visitor's mirth and the more pointed his disbelief. Finally someone was goaded a little too far.

"I'll bet you," Mutt's admirer said truculently, "I'll bet you a hundred dollars this dog can outretrieve any damn dog in the whole United States."

Perhaps he felt that he was safe, since the hunting season was not yet open. Perhaps he was too angry to think.

The stranger accepted the challenge, but it did not seem as if there was much chance of settling the bet. Someone said as much, and the visitor crowed.

"You've made your brag," he said. "Now show me."

There was nothing for it then but to seek out Mutt and hope for inspiration. The six men left the dark room and braved the blasting light of the summer afternoon as they made their way to the public library.

The library stood, four-square and ugly, just off the main thoroughfare of the city. The inevitable alley behind it was shared by two Chinese restaurants and by sundry other merchants. My father had his office in the rear of the library building overlooking the alley. A screened door gave access to whatever air was to be found trapped and roasted in the narrow space behind the building. It was through this rear door that the delegation came.

From his place under the desk Mutt barely raised his head to peer at the newcomers, then sank back into a comatose state of near oblivion engendered by the heat. He probably heard the mutter of talk, the introductions, and the slightly strident tone of voice of the stranger, but he paid no heed.

Father, however, listened intently. And he could hardly control his resentment when the stranger stooped, peered beneath the desk, and was heard to say, "*Now* I recognize the breed — Prince Albert rat hound did you say it was?"

My father got stiffly to his feet. "You gentlemen wish a demonstration of Mutt's retrieving skill — is that it?" he asked.

A murmur of agreement from the local men was punctuated by a derisive comment from the visitor. "Test him," he said offensively. "How about that alley there — it must be full of rats."

Father said nothing. Instead he pushed back his chair and, going to the large cupboard where he kept some of his shooting things so that they would be available for after-work excursions, he swung wide the door and got out his gun case. He drew out the barrels, fore and end, and stock and assembled the gun. He closed the breech and tried the triggers, and at that familiar sound Mutt was galvanized into life and came scuffling out from under the desk to stand with twitching nose and a perplexed air about him.

He had obviously been missing something. This wasn't the hunting season. But — the gun was out.

He whined interrogatively and my father patted his head. "Good boy," he said, and then walked to the screen door with Mutt crowding against his heels.

By this time the group of human watchers was as perplexed as Mutt. The six men stood in the office doorway and watched curiously as my father stepped out on the porch, raised the unloaded gun, leveled it down the alley toward the main street, pressed the triggers, and said in a quiet voice, "Bang — bang — go get 'em boy!"

To this day Father maintains a steadfast silence as to what his intentions really were. He will not say that he expected the result that followed, and he will not say that he did not expect it.

Mutt leaped from the stoop and fled down that alleyway at his best speed. They saw him turn the corner into the main street, almost causing two elderly women to collide with one another. The watchers saw the people on the far side of the street stop, turn to stare, and then stand as if petrified. But Mutt himself they could no longer see.

He was gone only about two minutes, but to the group upon the library steps it must have seemed much longer. The man from New York had just cleared his throat preparatory to a new and even more amusing sally, when he saw something that made the words catch in his gullet.

They all saw it — and they did not believe.

Mutt was coming back up the alley. He was trotting. His head and tail were high — and in his mouth was a magnificent ruffed grouse. He came up the porch stairs nonchalantly, laid the bird down at my father's feet, and with a satisfied sigh crawled back under the desk.

There was silence except for Mutt's panting. Then one of the local men stepped forward as if in a dream, and picked up the bird.

"Already stuffed, by God!" he said, and his voice was hardly more than a whisper.

It was then that the clerk from Ashbridge's Hardware arrived. The clerk was disheveled and mad. He came bounding up the library steps, accosted Father angrily, and cried:

"That damn dog of yours — you ought to keep him locked up. Come bustin' into the shop a moment ago and snatched the stuffed grouse right out of the window. Mr Ashbridge's fit to be tied. Was the best bird in his whole collection. . . ."

I do not know if the man from New York ever paid his debt. I do know that the story of that day's happening passed into the nation's history, for the Canadian press picked it up from the *Star-Phoenix*, and Mutt's fame was carried from coast to coast across the land.

That surely was no more than his due.

HERE, NOW

Matthew Cuthbert Is Surprised

L. M. MONTGOMERY

Matthew Cuthbert is getting on in years. His heart troubles him a good deal, and he is not as spry as he used to be. He and Marilla have decided to adopt a boy to help with the chores. This is the beginning, not just of one book — Anne of Green Gables, *but of a series of books that has brought joy to countless readers over the years.*

Matthew Cuthbert and the sorrel mare jogged comfortably over the eight miles to Bright River. It was pretty road, running along between snug farmsteads, with now and again a bit of balsamy fir wood to drive through or a hollow where wild plums hung out their filmy bloom. The air was sweet with the breath of many apple orchards and the meadows sloped away in the distance to horizon mists of pearl and purple; while

"The little birds sang as if it were
The one day of summer in all the year."

Matthew enjoyed the drive after his own fashion, except during the moments when he met women and had to nod to them — for in Prince Edward Island you are supposed to nod to all and sundry you meet on the road whether you know them or not.

Matthew dreaded all women except Marilla and Mrs. Rachel; he had an uncomfortable feeling that the mysterious creatures were secretly laughing at him. He may have been quite right in thinking so, for he was an odd-looking personage, with an ungainly figure and long iron-gray hair that touched his stooping shoulders, and a full, soft brown beard which he had worn ever since he was twenty. In fact, he had looked at twenty very much as he looked at sixty, lacking a little of the grayness.

When he reached· Bright River there was no sign of any train; he thought he was too early, so he tied his horse in the yard of the small

Bright River hotel and went over to the station-house. The long platform was almost deserted; the only living creature in sight being a girl who was sitting on a pile of shingles at the extreme end. Matthew, barely noting that it *was* a girl, sidled past her as quickly as possible without looking at her. Had he looked he could hardly have failed to notice the tense rigidity and expectation of her attitude and expression. She was sitting there waiting for something or somebody and, since sitting and waiting was the only thing to do just then, she sat and waited with all her might and main.

Matthew encountered the station-master locking up the ticket-office preparatory to going home for supper, and asked him if the five-thirty train would soon be along.

"The five-thirty train has been in and gone half an hour ago," answered that brisk official. "But there was a passenger dropped off for you — a little girl. She's sitting out there on the shingles. I asked her to go into the ladies' waiting-room, but she informed me gravely that she preferred to stay outside. 'There was more scope for imagination,' she said. She's a case, I should say."

"I'm not expecting a girl," said Matthew blankly. "It's a boy I've come for. He should be here. Mrs. Alexander Spencer was to bring him over from Nova Scotia for me."

The station-master whistled.

"Guess there's some mistake," he said. "Mrs. Spencer came off the train with that girl and gave her into my charge. Said you and your sister were adopting her from an orphan asylum and that you would be along for her presently. That's all *I* know about it — and I haven't got any more orphans concealed hereabouts."

"I don't understand," said Matthew helplessly, wishing that Marilla was at hand to cope with the situation.

"Well, you'd better question the girl," said the station-master carelessly. "I dare say she'll be able to explain — she's got a tongue of her own, that's certain. Maybe they were out of boys of the brand you wanted."

He walked jauntily away, being hungry, and the unfortunate Matthew was left to do that which was harder for him than bearding a lion in its den — walk up to a girl — a strange girl — an orphan girl — and demand of her why she wasn't a boy. Matthew groaned in spirit as he turned about and shuffled gently down the platform towards her.

She had been watching him ever since he had passed her and she had her eyes on him now. Matthew was not looking at her and would not have seen what she was really like if he had been, but an ordinary observer would have seen this:

A child of about eleven, garbed in a very short, very tight, very ugly dress of yellowish gray wincey. She wore a faded brown sailor hat and beneath the hat, extending down her back, were two braids of very thick, decidedly red hair. Her face was small, white and thin, also much freckled; her mouth was large and so were her eyes, that looked green in some lights and moods and gray in others.

So far, the ordinary observer; an extraordinary observer might have seen that the chin was very pointed and pronounced; that the big eyes were full of spirit and vivacity; that the mouth was sweet-lipped and expressive; that the forehead was broad and full; in short, our discerning extraordinary observer might have concluded that no commonplace soul inhabited the body of this stray woman-child of whom shy Matthew Cuthbert was so ludicrously afraid.

Matthew, however, was spared the ordeal of speaking first, for as soon as she concluded that he was coming to her she stood up, grasping with one thin brown hand the handle of a shabby, old-fashioned carpet-bag; the other she held out to him.

"I suppose you are Mr. Matthew Cuthbert of Green Gables?" she said in a peculiarly clear, sweet voice. "I'm very glad to see you. I was beginning to be afraid you weren't coming for me and I was imagining all the things that might have happened to prevent you. I had made up my mind that if you didn't come for me tonight I'd go down the track to that big wild cherry-tree at the bend, and climb up into it to stay all night. I wouldn't be a bit afraid, and it would be lovely to sleep in a wild cherry-tree all white with bloom in the moonshine, don't you think? You could imagine you were dwelling in marble halls, couldn't you? And I was quite sure you would come for me in the morning, if you didn't tonight."

Matthew had taken the scrawny little hand awkwardly in his; then and there he decided what to do. He could not tell this child with the glowing eyes that there had been a mistake; he would take her home and let Marilla do that. She couldn't be left at Bright River anyhow, no matter what mistake had been made, so all questions and explanations might as well be deferred until he was safely back at Green Gables.

"I'm sorry I was late," he said shyly. "Come along. The horse is over in the yard. Give me your bag."

"Oh, I can carry it," the child responded cheerfully. "It isn't heavy. I've got all my worldly goods in it, but it isn't heavy. And if it isn't carried in just a certain way the handle pulls out — so I'd better keep it because I know the exact knack of it. It's an extremely old carpet-bag. Oh, I'm very glad you've come, even if it would have been nice to sleep in a wild cherry-tree. We've got to drive a long piece, haven't we? Mrs. Spencer said it was eight miles. I'm glad because I love driving. Oh, it seems so wonderful that I'm going to live with you and belong to you. I've never belonged to anybody — not really. But the asylum was the worst. I've only been in it four months, but that was enough. I don't suppose you ever were an orphan in an asylum, so you can't possibly understand what it is like. It's worse than anything you could imagine. Mrs. Spencer said it was wicked of me to talk like that, but I didn't mean to be wicked. It's so easy to be wicked without knowing it, isn't it? They were good, you know — the asylum people. But there is so little scope for the imagination in an asylum — only just in the other orphans. It *was* pretty interesting to imagine things about them — to imagine that perhaps the girl who sat next to you was really the daughter of a belted earl, who had been stolen away from her parents in her infancy by a cruel nurse who died before she could confess. I used to lie awake at nights and imagine things like that, because I didn't have time in the day. I guess that's why I'm so thin — I *am* dreadful thin, ain't I? There isn't a pick on my bones. I do love to imagine I'm nice and plump, with dimples in my elbows."

With this Matthew's companion stopped talking, partly because she was out of breath and partly because they had reached the buggy. Not another word did she say until they had left the village and were driving down a steep little hill, the road part of which had been cut so deeply into the soft soil that the banks, fringed with blooming wild cherry-trees and slim white birches, were several feet above their heads.

The child put out her hand and broke off a branch of wild plum that brushed against the side of the buggy.

"Isn't that beautiful? What did that tree, leaning out from the bank, all white and lacy, make you think of?" she asked.

"Well now, I dunno," said Matthew.

"Why, a bride, of course — a bride all in white with a lovely misty veil. I've never seen one, but I can imagine what she would look like. I don't ever expect to be a bride myself. I'm so homely nobody will ever want to marry me — unless it might be a foreign missionary. I suppose a foreign missionary mightn't be very particular. But I do hope that some day I shall have a white dress. That is my highest ideal of earthly bliss. I just love pretty clothes. And I've never had a pretty dress in my life that I can remember — but of course it's all the more to look forward to, isn't it? And then I can imagine that I'm dressed gorgeously. This morning when I left the asylum I felt so ashamed because I had to wear this horrid old wincey dress. All the orphans had to wear them, you know. A merchant in Hopeton last winter donated three hundred yards of wincey to the asylum. Some people said it was because he couldn't sell it, but I'd rather believe that it was out of the kindness of his heart, wouldn't you? When we got on the train I felt as if everybody must be looking at me and pitying me. But I just went to work and imagined that I had on the most beautiful pale blue silk dress — because when you *are* imagining you might as well imagine something worth while — and a big hat all flowers and nodding plumes, and a gold watch, and kid gloves and boots. I felt cheered up right away and I enjoyed my trip to the Island with all my might. I wasn't a bit sick coming over in the boat. Neither was Mrs. Spencer, although she generally is. She said she hadn't time to get sick, watching to see that I didn't fall overboard. She said she never saw the beat of me for prowling about. But if it kept her from being seasick it's a mercy I did prowl, isn't it? And I wanted to see everything that was to be seen on that boat, because I didn't know whether I'd ever have another opportunity. Oh, there are a lot more cherry-trees all in bloom! This Island is the bloomiest place. I just love it already, and I'm so glad I'm going to live here. I've always heard that Prince Edward Island was the prettiest place in the world, and I used to imagine I was living here, but I never really expected I would. It's delightful when your imaginations come true, isn't it? But those red roads are so funny. When we got into the train at Charlottetown and the red roads began to flash past I asked Mrs. Spencer what made them red and she said she didn't know and for pity's sake not to ask her any more questions. She said I must have asked her a thousand already. I suppose I had, too, but how are you going to find out about things if you don't ask questions? And what *does* make the roads red?"

"Well now, I dunno," said Matthew.

"Well, that is one of the things to find out sometime. Isn't it splendid to think of all the things there are to find out about? It just makes me feel glad to be alive — it's such an interesting world. It wouldn't be half so interesting if we knew all about everything, would it? There'd be no scope for imagination then, would there? But am I talking too much? People are always telling me I do. Would you rather I didn't talk? If you say so I'll stop. I *can* stop when I make up my mind to it, although it's difficult."

Matthew, much to his own surprise, was enjoying himself. Like most quiet folks he liked talkative people when they were willing to do the talking themselves and did not expect him to keep up his end of it. But he had never expected to enjoy the society of a little girl. Women were bad enough in all conscience, but little girls were worse. He detested the way they had of sidling past him timidly, with sidewise glances, as if they expected him to gobble them up at a mouthful if they ventured to say a word. This was the Avonlea type of well-bred little girl. But this freckled witch was very different, and although he found it rather difficult for his slower intelligence to keep up with her brisk mental processes he thought that he "kind of liked her chatter." So he said as shyly as usual:

"Oh, you can talk as much as you like. I don't mind."

"Oh, I'm so glad. I know you and I are going to get along together fine. It's such a relief to talk when one wants to and not be told that children should be seen and not heard. I've had that said to me a million times if I have once. And people laugh at me because I use big words. But if you have big ideas you have to use big words to express them, haven't you?"

"Well now, that seems reasonable," said Matthew.

"Mrs. Spencer said that my tongue must be hung in the middle. But it isn't — it's firmly fastened at one end. Mrs. Spencer said your place was named Green Gables. I asked her all about it. And she said there were trees all around it. I was gladder than ever. I just love trees. And there weren't any at all about the asylum, only a few poor weeny-teeny things out in front with little whitewashed cagey things about them. They just looked like orphans themselves, those trees did. It used to make me want to cry to look at them. I used to say to them, 'Oh, you *poor* little things! If you were out in a great big woods with other trees all around you and little mosses and Junebells growing over your roots and a brook not far away and birds singing in your branches, you could grow, couldn't you? But you can't where you are. I know just exactly how you feel, little trees.' I felt sorry to leave them behind this morning. You do get so attached to things like that, don't you? Is there a brook anywhere near Green Gables? I forgot to ask Mrs. Spencer that."

"Well now, yes, there's one right below the house."

"Fancy. It's always been one of my dreams to live near a brook. I never expected I would, though. Dreams don't often come true, do they? Wouldn't it be nice if they did? But just now I feel pretty nearly perfectly happy. I can't feel exactly perfectly happy because — well, what colour would you call this?"

She twitched one of her long glossy braids over her thin shoulder and held it up before Matthew's eyes. Matthew was not used to deciding on the tints of ladies' tresses, but in this case there couldn't be much doubt.

"It's red, ain't it?" he said.

The girl let the braid drop back with a sigh that seemed to come from her very toes and to exhale forth all the sorrows of the ages.

"Yes, it's red," she said resignedly. "Now you see why I can't be perfectly happy. Nobody could who had red hair. I don't mind the other things so much — the freckles and the green eyes and my skinniness. I can imagine them away. I can imagine that I have a beautiful rose-leaf complexion and lovely starry violet eyes. But I *cannot* imagine that red hair away. I do my best. I think to myself, 'Now my hair is a glorious black, black as the raven's wing.' But all the time I *know* it is just plain red, and it breaks my heart. It will be my lifelong sorrow. I read of a girl once in a novel who had a lifelong sorrow, but it wasn't red hair. Her hair was pure gold rippling back from her alabaster brow. What is an alabaster brow? I never could find out. Can you tell me?"

"Well now, I'm afraid I can't," said Matthew, who was getting a little dizzy. He felt as he had once felt in his rash youth when another boy had enticed him on the merry-go-round at a picnic.

"Well, whatever it was it must have been something nice because she was divinely beautiful. Have you ever imagined what it must feel like to be divinely beautiful?"

"Well now, no, I haven't," confessed Matthew ingenuously.

"I have, often. Which would you rather be if you had the choice — divinely beautiful or dazzlingly clever or angelically good?"

"Well now, I — I don't know exactly."

"Neither do I. I can never decide. But it doesn't make much real difference for it isn't likely I'll ever be either. It's certain I'll never be angelically good. Mrs. Spencer says — oh, Mr. Cuthbert! Oh, Mr. Cuthbert!! Oh, Mr. Cuthbert!!!"

That was not what Mrs. Spencer had said; neither had the child tumbled out of the buggy nor had Matthew done anything astonishing. They had simply rounded a curve in the road and found themselves in the "Avenue."

The "Avenue," so called by the Newbridge people, was a stretch of road four or five hundred yards long, completely arched over with huge, wide-spreading apple-trees, planted years ago by an eccentric old farmer.

Overhead was one long canopy of snowy fragrant bloom. Below the boughs the air was full of a purple twilight and far ahead a glimpse of painted sunset sky shone like a great rose window at the end of a cathedral aisle.

Its beauty seemed to strike the child dumb. She leaned back in the buggy, her thin hands clasped before her, her face lifted rapturously to the white splendour above. Even when they had passed out and were driving down the long slope to Newbridge she never moved or spoke. Still with rapt face she gazed afar into the sunset west, with eyes that saw visions trooping splendidly across that glowing background. Through Newbridge, a bustling little village where dogs barked at them and small boys hooted and curious faces peered from the windows, they drove, still in silence. When three more miles had dropped away behind them the child had not spoken. She could keep silence, it was evident, as energetically as she could talk.

"I guess you're feeling pretty tired and hungry," Matthew ventured at last, accounting for her long visitation of dumbness with the only reason he could think of. "But we haven't very far to go now — only another mile."

She came out of her reverie with a deep sigh and looked at him with the dreamy gaze of a soul that had been wandering afar, star-led.

"Oh, Mr. Cuthbert," she whispered, "that place we came through — that white place — what was it?"

"Well now, you must mean the Avenue," said Matthew after a few moments' profound reflection. "It is a kind of pretty place."

"Pretty? Oh, *pretty* doesn't seem the right word to use. Nor beautiful, either. They don't go far enough. Oh, it was wonderful — wonderful. It's the first thing I ever saw that couldn't be improved upon by imagination. It just satisfies me here" — she put one hand on her breast — "it made a queer funny ache and yet it was a pleasant ache. Did you ever have an ache like that, Mr. Cuthbert?"

"Well now, I just can't recollect that I ever had."

"I have it lots of times — whenever I see anything royally beautiful. But they shouldn't call that lovely place the Avenue. There is no meaning in a name like that. They should call it — let me see — the White Way of Delight. Isn't that a nice imaginative name? When I don't like the name of a place or a person I always imagine a new one and always think of them so. There was a girl at the asylum whose name was Hepzibah Jenkins, but I always imagined her as Rosalia DeVere. Other people may call that place the Avenue, but I shall always call it the White Way of Delight. Have we really only another mile to go before we get home? I'm glad and I'm sorry. I'm sorry because this drive has been so pleasant and I'm always sorry when pleasant things end. Something still pleasanter may come after, but you can never be sure. And it's so often the case that it isn't pleasanter. That has been my experience anyhow. But I'm glad to think of getting home. You see, I've never had a real home since I can remember. It gives me that pleasant ache again just to think of coming to a really truly home. Oh, isn't that pretty."

They had driven over the crest of a hill. Below them was a pond, looking almost like a river so long and winding was it. A bridge spanned it midway and from there to its lower end, where an amber-hued belt of sand-hills shut it in from the dark blue gulf beyond, the water was a glory of many shifting hues — the most spiritual shadings of crocus and rose and ethereal green, with other elusive tintings for which no name has ever been found. Above the bridge the pond ran up into fringing groves of fir and maple and lay all darkly translucent in their wavering shadows. Here and there a wild plum leaned out from the bank like a white-clad girl tiptoeing to her own reflection. From the marsh at the head of the pond came the clear, mournfully-sweet chorus of the frogs. There was a little gray house peering around a white apple orchard on a slope beyond and, although it was not yet quite dark, a light was shining from one of its windows.

"That's Barry's pond," said Matthew.

"Oh, I don't like that name, either. I shall call it — let me see — the Lake of Shining Waters. Yes, that is the right name for it. I know because of the thrill. When I hit on a name that suits exactly it gives me a thrill. Do things ever give you a thrill?"

Matthew ruminated.

"Well now, yes. It always kind of gives me a thrill to see them ugly white grubs that spade up in the cucumber beds. I hate the look of them."

"Oh, I don't think that can be exactly the same kind of a thrill. Do you think it can? There doesn't seem to be much connection between grubs and lakes of shining waters, does there? But why do other people call it Barry's pond?"

"I reckon because Mr. Barry lives up there in that house. Orchard Slope's the name of his place. If it wasn't for that big bush behind it you could see Green Gables from here. But we have to go over the bridge and round by the road, so it's near half a mile further."

"Has Mr. Barry any little girls? Well, not so very little either — about my size."

"He's got one about eleven. Her name is Diana."

"Oh!" with a long indrawing of breath. "What a perfectly lovely name!"

"Well now, I dunno. There's something dreadful heathenish about it, seems to me. I'd ruther Jane or Mary or some sensible name like that. But when Diana was born there was a schoolmaster boarding there and they gave him the naming of her and he called her Diana."

"I wish there had been a schoolmaster like that around when *I* was born, then. Oh, here we are at the bridge. I'm going to shut my eyes tight. I'm always afraid going over bridges. I can't help imagining that perhaps, just as we get to the middle, they'll crumple up like a jack-knife and nip us. So I shut my eyes. But I always have to open them for all when I think we're getting near the middle. Because, you see, if the bridge *did* crumple up I'd want to *see* it crumple. What a jolly rumble it makes! I always like the rumble part of it. Isn't it splendid there are so many things to like in this world? There, we're over. Now I'll look back. Good night, dear Lake of Shining Waters. I always say good night to the things I love, just as I would to people. I think they like it. That water looks as if it was smiling at me."

When they had driven up the further hill and around a corner Matthew said:

"We're pretty near home now. That's Green Gables over —"

"Oh, don't tell me," she interrupted breathlessly, catching at his partially raised arm and shutting her eyes that she might not see his gesture. "Let me guess. I'm sure I'll guess right."

She opened her eyes and looked about her. They were on the crest of a hill. The sun had set some time since, but the landscape was still clear in the mellow afterlight. To the west a dark church spire rose up against a marigold sky. Below was a little valley and beyond a long, gently-rising slope with snug farmsteads scattered along it. From one to another the child's eyes darted, eager and wistful. At last they lingered on one away to the left, far back from the road, dimly white with blossoming trees in the twilight of the surrounding woods. Over it, in the stainless southwest sky, a great crystal-white star was shining like a lamp of guidance and promise.

"That's it, isn't it?" she said, pointing.

Matthew slapped the reins on the sorrel's back delightedly.

"Well now, you've guessed it! But I reckon Mrs. Spencer described it so's you could tell."

"No, she didn't — really she didn't. All she said might just as well have been about most of those other places. I hadn't any real idea what it looked like. But just as soon as I saw it I felt it was home. Oh, it seems as if I must be in a dream. Do you know, my arm must be black and blue from the elbow up, for I've pinched myself so many times today. Every little while a horrible sickening feeling would come over me and I'd be so afraid it was all a dream. Then I'd pinch myself to see if it was real — until suddenly I remembered that even supposing it was only a dream I'd better go on dreaming as long as I could; so I stopped pinching. But it *is* real and we're nearly home."

With a sigh of rapture she relapsed into silence. Matthew stirred uneasily. He felt glad that it would be Marilla and not he who would have to tell this waif of the world that the home she longed for was not to be hers after all. They drove over Lynde's Hollow, where it was already quite dark, but not so dark that Mrs. Rachel could not see them from her window vantage, and up the hill and into the long lane of Green Gables. By the time they arrived at the house Matthew was shrinking from the approaching revelation with an energy he did not understand. It was not of Marilla or himself he was thinking or of the trouble this mistake was probably going to make for them, but of the child's disappointment. When he thought of that rapt light being quenched in her eyes he had an uncomfortable feeling that he was going to assist at murdering something — much the same feeling that came over him when he had to kill a lamb or calf or any other innocent little creature.

The yard was quite dark as they turned into it and the poplar leaves were rustling silkily all round it.

"Listen to the trees talking in their sleep," she whispered, as he lifted her to the ground. "What nice dreams they must have!"

Then, holding tightly to the carpet-bag which contained "all her worldly goods," she followed him into the house.

Auction Fever

W. O. MITCHELL

Jake, the hired man on a prairie farm, and the kid, his friend and companion, are the main characters in a series of stories that were originally written as radio plays. In this story, Jake demonstrates his remarkable ability to escape from awkward predicaments that he creates himself.

I had the measles and the prairie itch once and the mumps on both sides. I had the black crowing, Ma says, but I never had the worst of all. Jake says it often hits our district, sometimes in the spring and sometimes in the fall; it knocks folks over like the disease that runs through jack rabbits every seven years: Auction fever.

A lot of folks must have figured it got Jake this spring, but that wasn't auction fever at all; that was the Duke of Broomhead. A person couldn't say Jake caught auction fever off of a snuffy York boar, could they? If the Duke of Broomhead hadn't bit Jake between the household goods and the red weeder, we would have had lots of money left over for the little buckskin colt. You'll see what I mean, later.

Colonel Hepworth held the sale in the back of Hig Wheeler's lumberyard, where it says, "We built the West." "Hup-an'-a-whiddle-eeee-diddle-ho-riddle-hum — who'll bid me five an' a five an' a five?" There is the way Colonel Hepworth sells stuff for folks. He is a long thin fellow with the build of a Kentucky whip; he has a long, thin horse face too, and he wears a coat with a velvet collar, and a bowler hat. He waves a cane around all the time. He makes the folks laugh a lot.

Ma gave Jake fifty dollars to buy her a stove; she didn't come into Crocus with us; she knows Jake is a good trader. Jake says once he started out with only a cotter pin and he ended up with a burning harrow, a bull calf, and ten dollars to boot; he did it in thirty-one trades. That will show you.

At the sale we ran across all kinds of folks from our district, all of them with stuff hanging out of their hands: slop pails, picture frames, lanterns, disk plates, bridles. Old Man Gatenby he had a lamp under one arm; the shade was shaped like a long haystack, only you don't see many pink haystacks with tassels hanging around them. I better not say what he had under his other arm.

Jake asked him where was the stove at, because Ma's grate had burned out. He said over behind the implements.

It is bad enough in spring with the air sort of soft and sweet and you feel lazy in your knees; but with an auction sale besides, it is no wonder folks feel like kicking over the britching.

Kids were playing tag all around their folks' legs; the cows and calves were bawling, and the chickens in their crates were cut-cutting to beat anything. We could hear Colonel Hepworth's voice coming floaty to us: "Huppy-oh-whiddle-eeee-diddle-hoo-a ten an' a ten, but what I want is fif- teen!" Like a circus. Just like a circus.

"Holy diddle!" Jake had a look on his face like he didn't believe what he saw. "Thinka anybuddy havin' a shaganappy thing like that in their house!"

One of her legs was off, so she leaned to one side like a horse resting on a hot day; she was all scuffed up and carved up and battered up. Springs hung out of her bottom; they were poking out her top. I guess she was a couch.

Jake bent down for a closer look. Her back was curved out in two places, just about right to catch a person between the shoulder blades. Along the front were baby angels with their cheeks blown out, and in the middle of the top were two black hawks. They must have been mad at each other, because they were pointed in the opposite direction.

Jake straightened up and he had a look on his face like his gums were hurting him. "Ain't that enuff tuh give a badger thuh heartburn!" he said.

"Pore thing ain't ever had a chance tuh heal up!"

"What is it, Jake?"

"Search me," Jake said. "Could call her a gosh-hawk couch, I guess."

That was when Jake saw the stove over by the cream separator. While he looked inside her, I headed for the stock pens.

Then I saw the colt.

I don't even remember climbing up to sit on the rail of his pen. All I know is that I was up there with my toes hooked around the rail, and I was looking down on that colt, soaking him in, his shaggy coat the colour of pull taffy, his silver mane and tail, and his hoofs just like Ma's teacups.

I never said to myself, I want him. It was quicker than thinking, quick as a gopher down a hole. I wanted him so bad I hurt, the funny kind when you can't tell where you hurt but you sure know you do.

I could feel the spring chinook soft at my nose and hear it in my ears. It was whispering in the long grass at the side of the pen! It had come clear across the prairie to me and my buckskin colt.

I got down off of that fence and I headed for Jake. He knows what to get for a kid.

I found him on the edge of all the folks ringed around Colonel Hepworth and looking up at him.

"Jake!" I said. "I just been over to the stock pens and I saw a buckskin colt!"

"Did yuh now?"

"He's a buckskin, Jake, I'd like for you to look at him — he's a buckskin with a real light mane and a tail!"

"Look kinda funny without one," Jake said. "There ain't no —"

" — sold to thuh fella in thuh trainman's cap!" yelled Colonel Hepworth. "An' now, gen'lemen, let us turn to thuh pigs!"

" — jist talkin' about it thuh other day. Yer maw figgers it's about time fer yuh to have a horse-a yer own." Jake had a real pleased look on his face. "Got yer maw's stove — Pride-a the Prairies — hot-water ressy-voar on her — on'y thirty dollars — leaves twen'y left over."

"Jake, do you think — could — I want that there colt, Jake — I want — "

"Ain't no harm in takin' a look at him," Jake said.

Whilst Jake looked at the colt I stood there and hoped like anything he would be all right so Jake would buy him.

"Risin' a year," Jake said. "Nice put-up colt."

"Can I — will you buy him for me, Jake?"

Jake spit. "I will," he said, "if he don't go over twenty."

"Do you think he — "

"Nope — I don't think he will. C'mon — we'll stick close to thuh colonel till he gits tuh that there colt."

Colonel Hepworth was standing up on the seat of an old MacDougall tractor next to the hogpens. He was pointing to the Duke of Broomhead with his cane, and he had an envelope in his hand.

"This here pig, gen'lemen, is thuh Duke-a Broomhead — pure-blood registered York boar with a stringa folks from here tuh thuh correction line. Take a look at that there royal pig!"

I could see the Duke of Broomhead's angry little eyes looking out between the rails of his pen. He was chomping and breathing real mad. I took a couple of steps back from the pen. Jake didn't. Jake isn't scared of anything.

"Now whut am I bid for this here pig, gen'lemen — hup — let her go — huppa-diddle-eee-hi-widdle-ho — thanks for thuh five-dollar bid — thuh ree-dickalus sum-a five dollars fer — who'll gimme ten — an' a ten an' a ten — ten I am give!"

I didn't see anybody make a five- or a ten-dollar bid; a person doesn't dare spit when Colonel Hepworth is selling.

"An' fifteen — five an' a ten an' a ten an' a five — an' a huppy-eye-oh-ring-a-dang-doh! Fifteen ain't enuff — my heart bleeds fer the pig a-holdin' his noble head low in shame — blue blood, gen'lemen, blue as the ink in yer fountain pen, gen'lemen!"

"Lard!" Jake snorted.

"Lard, Jake?"

"All he's good for — that's a five-year-old boar — too old — he ain't no good for — "

"Who'll gimme two more — more — two more — fifteen an' a two — "

"Then what are they bidding for, Jake?"

"Auction fever, Kid — that pig ain't worth thuh haulin' away."

"One dollar is all I ask — one dollar more tuh save that there pig's pride — huppy-oh-whiddle-eeee-rum — don't nobody feel sorry fer that there pig?"

Jake was leaning against the Duke of Broomhead's pen with his elbow on the top rail.

"Thuh papers ain't extra!" yelled Colonel Hepworth waving the envelope around. "All fer thuh price-a fifteen dollars — fifteen once an' a fifteen twice — who'll bid me fifty cents more — four bits more — "

"Hey — ow — uh!" Just like the four-ten on a clear fall night, Jake let a whoop out of him and jumped like a startled jack rabbit.

Colonel Hepworth's cane came down with a bang. "Sold!" he shouted. "Sold tuh Jake Trumper fer fifteen an' a half — an' a very fine buy you've — "

Jake quit dancing around with his hand on the back of his leg.

"Hey — wait a minnit — I ain't bought nothin'! I didn't bid on no worn-out — "

"Thuh bid wuz made an' Pete's a-markin' her down — cash bag's to yer right. Now, gen'lemen, let us turn tuh — "

"You ain't gonna stick me with — " Jake had quit rubbing the seat of his overalls. "That there damn boar jist tooka chunk outa my — "

"Terms is strickly cash," said Colonel Hepworth. "You wouldn't be tryin' tuh back out, would yuh?"

"No, I ain't," said Jake; "I'm jist tryin' tuh tell yuh I —"

"If yuh ain't satisfied, yuh kin put him up fer rebiddin'."

"But I didn't bid in thuh first pl — "

"Yuh want him up ag'in?"

"Hell, no! He ain't even mine!"

"He sure is! Make up yer mind — we ain't got all day — there's a lotta stuff tuh go yet. Thuh steers is next. Yes er no?"

Jake he looked sort of helpless and mad at the same time. He jerked his head up and down. He was too mad to talk.

The Duke of Broomhead sold to Magnus Petersen for five dollars.

Whilst Jake collected five dollars off of Magnus and forked out fifteen fifty to Pete Stover, I thought about my little buckskin colt. I thought about the sunlight on the real fine hairs bearding under his chin and the wind lifting his woolly tail. I didn't feel so good. Ten fifty from twenty is nine fifty. That won't buy any colt.

"Nine fifty isn't enough for any colt, Jake!"

Jake looked down at me and he said, "I'm sorry, Kid." That was all he said. Me, I could feel my arm around that colt's neck, and my throat started to get all plugged up.

"But — can't — couldn't — "

"Ain't nothin' we kin do, Kid. Yuh heard him say — she's strickly cash."

"Couldn't we go downtown an' — "

"Ain't no time fer that," Jake said. He looked down at the nine fifty he had in his hand.

"Could we trade around a little, Jake, and — like that there cotter — "

"He's startin' on them cows an' steers — "

"Couldn't we trade around — "

"Huh?"

"I said — couldn't we trade around, the way you did when you ended up with the — "

Jake stared at me. "We might," he said. "Nine fifty — that there colt might go at twen'y. Kid, we're gonna haftuh work fast. We — Hey, Johnny!"

That was Johnny Totcoal, and he was carrying a big moose's head.

"You got papers fer him, Johnny?"

Johnny was looking kind of disgusted. "Missus is gonna snatch me bald-headed when she sees this here critter."

"Why did yuh buy him for?"

"I dunno — just seemed like a real good buy at eight fifty."

"Was yuh wantin' tuh sell him — "

"I sure was."

"Whatta yuh want?"

"I'd kinda like tuh git what I paid fer him, Jake."

"He's missin' one eye, ain't he, Johnny?"

"I'd let him go fer seven fifty."

"Moths bin tuh work on that left ear."

"Seven dollars'd be a real good price on him," Johnny said.

"I might give yuh five."

"Make her six, Jake."

"Ain't that there stuffin' comin' outa his neck?"

"I'd be takin' a two-fifty loss."

"Give yuh five."

"Make her six, Jake."

"Five fifty."

"He's yores."

When Johnny had left, Jake turned to me. "Up fifty — down three — that's thuh way tuh do her, Kid."

It was Old Man Gatenby we ran into next, and Jake said to him, "When did yuh git thuh power line intuh yore place?"

"We ain't got her," Old Man Gatenby said.

"Looks like that there 'lectric lamp's gonna come in real handy," Jake said. "Gonna put in wind ee-lectric, are you?"

"Can't till after thuh war," Gate said.

"Well," Jake said, "she'll look nice anyways — even if yuh can't light her up."

"You wouldn't be int'rested, would yuh?"

"Hell, no — we ain't got ee-lectricity neither. Fella's gotta be real careful round a auction, Gate. Take me — I come here fer one thing — jist one thing — this here gen-you-wine moose's head — I got him."

Gate set his lamp down on the ground and he stared at the moose's head, and he scratched his jaw slow like your nail on sandpaper. "Wut thuh hell fer?"

"Why, deckeration," Jake said. "He's gonna look real nice up on thuh wall — over thuh fireplace. Go real nice over a fella's fireplace, wouldn't he?"

"He might," Old Man Gatenby said.

"Kinda keep a fella comp'ny, I figger."

"Ummm," said Old Man Gatenby.

"Too bad about that there lamp, Gate."

"Yeah — uh — don't wanta make a trade, do yuh?"

"Nope," Jake said. "We ain't got ee — "

"Give yuh two dollars tuh boot," said Gate.

Jake didn't even say yes. He dropped the moose's head and he grabbed that lamp. Gate gave him two dollars, and we started off.

"Hey!" yelled Gate. "I jist remembered — I ain't got no fireplace neither!"

We kept right on going.

Mrs. Biggs was standing beside a washtub, two slop pails, a bed spring, and a brass bedstead.

"Nice day," Jake said with his eye on the bed.

"Cer'n'y is," Mrs. Biggs said. She lives in town.

"Nice crowd," Jake said.

"Cer'n'y is," Mrs. Biggs said.

"Nice lamp here," Jake said.

"Cer'n'y is," Mrs. Biggs said.

"Go real nice with alla that lovely furniture-a yores," Jake said.

"'T might," said Mrs. Biggs.

"Nice bedstead yuh got there, Mrs. Biggs."

"'T ain't what I told Charlie tuh git," she said. "I told him a Winnipeg couch fer when Florence come tuh stay with us, an' he went an' — "

"P'r'aps yuh could use this here lamp better," said Jake. "She's double-lined silk, yuh know — quit makin' 'em sence thuh war."

I looked at the lamp, and I was wondering did Jake mean the last war or the Boer War. And then I wasn't caring about any lamp, because I could hear Colonel Hepworth yelling, "Hup — an' this's thuh lasta thuh cows —. " I started in thinking how that colt's nose would be real velvet against a person's neck, and I was thinking how I always was fussy about a horse with a white blaze in the middle of his forehead.

"C'm'on, Kid." Jake had one end of the bedstead, and he wanted for me to help him haul her off a ways. Over by our wagon box, Jake counted up our money. He'd given two dollars to boot for the bed; that left four dollars.

"She's worth about fifteen bucks," Jake said. "We're gittin' within strikin' distance-a that colt."

"But, Jake, he's finishin' up the cows already!"

"I know it. All we gotta do is find somebuddy wants a bed an' — "

"Just whut I'm lookin' fer."

Jake and me turned. It was Mr. Ricky. Nobody gets the best of Mr. Ricky.

"Yuh wanta buy a bed?" Jake said.

"Shore do," said Mr. Ricky. "Not buy exac'ly — figgered tuh trade."

"Yuh kin have her fer sixteen dollars," Jake said.

Mr. Ricky shook his head. "Give yuh six dollars an' a dye-van."

"A whut!"

"A dye-van — high-class piece-a furniture. Mind yuh, she ain't A-one."

"Whut is it?"

"A sorta chesterfield — ain't new — kinda scuffed up some — "

"Jake! He's startin' in on the colt — he's sellin' — "

"Springs is all there. I paid twelve dollars fer her."

"Where is she?"

"I ain't got thuh time ner thuh energy tuh take yuh over — I tell yuh she's a good trade — six dollars tuh boot."

"I'd like tuh see her first," Jake said.

"We haven't got time, Jake!"

" — five I am bid an' that don't nearly pay thuh stud fee alone on this here colt — hup — look at him, gen'lemen — right next door tuh a Palomino — five an' a five. Who'll gimme ten?"

"Hurry, Jake."

"O.K.," Jake said.

Mr. Ricky handed him six dollars.

We ran for the other corner of the lot where Mr. Ricky said the thing was. And then we saw it.

Jake had traded us right into the gosh-hawk couch.

I felt kind of sick. Jake didn't look so good either. He said:

"Jist goes tuh show, Kid. When yuh trade, take yer time. Take — yer — damn — time!"

"But — what can we — "

"Here." Jake handed me our ten dollars. "You git over there an' start biddin' on that there colt. I'll see what I kin do about this here couch. Day, Mrs. Fotheringham."

That was Mrs. Fotheringham. She is married to Dr. Fotheringham. Her chest sticks out like on some pigeons.

"You haven't seen the doctor, have you?" she said to Jake.

"No, I ain't, Mrs. Fotheringham," said Jake.

"Hup — an' I got six fifty — six fifty bid for the colt — hup — gimme eight — an' eight an' eight — "

"Seven!" I yelled and I hadn't reached the edge of the crowd.

"Huppy-oh-seven I got — seven an' I asked fer eight — eight ain't enuff fer that blocky little colt. Who'll gimme eight? Who'll gimme eight? Eight I got — eight fer thuh colt."

"Eight an' twen'y-five cents!" I yelled.

"Two bits from thuh kid that wants that colt — two bits from the boy with the freckles on his nose — eight twen'y-five!"

"Nine!"

It was Mr. Ricky bidding against me. He knows a good thing when he sees it. Mr. Ricky sold us the gosh-hawk couch.

"Nine an' a quarter!" I shouted.

"An' a quarter from thuh two-bit kid — hup another bid — hup — gimme ten — "

Mr. Ricky nodded.

"Ten I got. Ten is all I got, an' thuh colt's worth thirty. If she goes fer a cent under thirty, I'll never sell another horse!"

"Twelve!" That was me did that, and I didn't care if I didn't have the money to pay. Mr. Ricky wasn't going to get my buckskin colt. That is the way auction fever gets a person.

"Fifteen!"

"Now we're comin' fine, gen'lemen — fifteen — five an' a ten an' a ten an' a five — five more fer thuh colt — five more fer — "

"Twenty!" That was me again with ten dollars in my pocket.

"Twen'y-one." Mr. Ricky didn't sound so anxious. Like Jake said, that colt would go near twenty.

I didn't know what to do. All I knew was I didn't want to live any more if I didn't get my colt. But I couldn't say it; I couldn't say twenty-two.

"Twenty-two!"

"Another bidder — twen'y-two he's give me — twen'y-two dollars — huppy-eye-oh-diddle-riddle-eee-hum — who'll gimme twen'y-five — five an' a twen'y — twen'y an' a five!"

It sure was a new bidder. It was Jake; I could tell his voice anywhere. Jake has sold the gosh-hawk couch. Jake is smart. Jake is the smartest there is!

"Twen'y-two once — twen'y-two twice — twen'y-two fer thuh third an' last time! Sold! Sold tuh Jake Trumper, owner-a thuh Duke-a Broomhead an' — "

"Not no more I ain't!"

He was standing over beside Pete Stover and the cash bag. I headed for Jake.

He was counting out the money for my colt, and when he was through counting he still had a handful of bills.

"Jake, where did you — what — "

"Thuh gosh-hawk couch, Kid. Gen-you-wine Eyetalyun carvin' — Renny-saunce — Eyetalyun walnut. Mrs. Fotheringham's bin waitin' forty years tuh git her han's on that there couch. Doc wuz supposed tuh git it fer her whilst she was at Auxill'ary. Reel valuable that there stuff, she said — seventy-five dollars' valuable."

"You mean we got — "

"Yore maw's stove an' thuh colt an' thuh fifty dollars we come with an' thirteen dollars tuh boot."

I didn't say anything. I just looked at my colt with his proud neck and the wind in his mane.

"Pretty fussy about that there colt, Kid?"

"Oh, Jake! — he — I got a name for him."

"Have you now?"

"Fever, Jake — Auction Fever."

The Conjurer's Revenge

STEPHEN LEACOCK

"Now, ladies and gentlemen," said the conjurer, "having shown you that the cloth is absolutely empty, I will proceed to take from it a bowl of goldfish. Presto!"

All around the hall people were saying, "Oh, how wonderful! How does he do it?"

But the Quick Man on the front seat said in a big whisper to the people near him, "He — had — it — up — his — sleeve."

Then the people nodded brightly at the Quick Man and said, "Oh, of course"; and everybody whispered round the hall, "He — had — it — up — his — sleeve."

"My next trick," said the conjurer, "is the famous Hindostanee rings. You will notice that the rings are apparently separate; at a blow they all join (clang, clang, clang) — Presto!"

There was a general buzz of stupefaction till the Quick Man was heard to whisper, "He — must — have — had — another — lot — up — his — sleeve."

Again everybody nodded and whispered, "The — rings — were — up — his — sleeve."

The brow of the conjurer was clouded with a gathering frown.

"I will now," he continued, "show you a most amusing trick by which I am enabled to take any number of eggs from a hat. Will some gentleman kindly lend me his hat? Ah, thank you — Presto!"

He extracted seventeen eggs, and for thirty-five seconds the audience began to think that he was wonderful. Then the Quick Man whispered along the front bench, "He — has — a — hen — up — his — sleeve," and all the people whispered it on. "He — has — a — lot — of — hens — up — his — sleeve."

The egg trick was ruined.

It went on like that all through. It transpired from the whispers of the Quick Man that the conjurer must have concealed up his sleeve, in addition to the rings, hens, and fish, several packs of cards, a loaf of bread, a doll's cradle, a live guinea-pig, a fifty-cent piece, and a rocking-chair.

The reputation of the conjurer was rapidly sinking below zero. At the close of the evening he rallied for a final effort.

"Ladies and gentlemen," he said, "I will present to you, in conclusion, the famous Japanese trick recently invented by the natives of Tipperary. Will you, sir," he continued, turning toward the Quick Man, "will you kindly hand me your gold watch?"

It was passed to him.

"Have I your permission to put it into this mortar and pound it to pieces?" he asked savagely.

The Quick Man nodded and smiled.

The conjurer threw the watch into the mortar and grasped a sledge hammer from the table. There was a sound of violent smashing. "He's — slipped — it — up — his — sleeve," whispered the Quick Man.

"Now, sir," continued the conjurer, "will you allow me to take your handkerchief and punch holes in it? Thank you. You see, ladies and gentlemen, there is no deception, the holes are visible to the eye."

The face of the Quick Man beamed. This time the real mystery of the thing fascinated him.

"And now, sir, will you kindly pass me your silk hat and allow me to dance on it? Thank you."

The conjurer made a few rapid passes with his feet and exhibited the hat crushed beyond recognition.

"And will you now, sir, take off your celluloid collar and permit me to burn it in the candle? Thank you, sir. And will you allow me to smash your spectacles for you with my hammer? Thank you."

By this time the features of the Quick Man were assuming a puzzled expression. "This thing beats me," he whispered, "I don't see through it a bit."

There was a great hush upon the audience. Then the conjurer drew himself up to his full height and, with a withering look at the Quick Man, he concluded:

"Ladies and gentlemen, you will observe that I have, with this gentleman's permission, broken his watch, burnt his collar, smashed his spectacles, and danced on his hat. If he will give me the further permission to paint green stripes on his overcoat, or to tie his suspenders in a knot, I shall be delighted to entertain you. If not, the performance is at an end."

And amid a glorious burst of music from the orchestra the curtain fell, and the audience dispersed, convinced that there are some tricks, at any rate, that are not done up the conjurer's sleeve.

Going Up North

DENNIS LEE

I'm going up north and live in the bush
Cause I can't stand parents that nag and push!

I'm going up north and live in a shack,
So tell my parents that I'm never coming back!
And I won't write letters,
    But I think I'll take a snack.

I'm going up north and I'll see strange sights.
I'll be all on my own with the Northern Lights.
I shall whistle to myself
    When the grizzly bears prowl,
And they'll say to one another
    As they snuffle and growl,
"I think I hear a tea kettle
    Coming to the boil,
Or maybe it's a radio
    That's going for a stroll,
Or an operatic porcupine
    Practising a role;
Imagine that — a porcupine
    Practising a role!"
Then the bears will start to fidget
    As they're lolloping along,
Cause a porcupine's ferocious

If you interrupt his song;
And they'll mutter back and forth,
    "This is not the place for me —
I don't *want* to eat a porcupine —
    I think it's time to flee!"
And I'll squeak a sort of YES!
    And I'll maybe whistle less
And they'll never even guess
    That it's me.

Then I'll sneak back home in the dark of night
And I'll see my parents taking fits with fright
And I won't say Sorry.
    Or, Glad to be back,
But I'll give them a squeeze
    And quickly remark,
"What *marvellous* weather
    We're having today!

Did anything happen
    While I was away?
The grizzlies were great;
    And oh, by the way,
I hope you'll be nicer
    than yesterday."

Stephen's Whistle

JOY KOGAWA

The Second World War was fought by Canada and her allies against Germany and Japan. Many Canadians whose parents or grandparents had originally come from Japan were suspected, wrongly, of being enemy spies. Their homes were taken away from them by the Canadian government, and they were forced to move to remote regions of the Canadian west.

This story, from the book Naomi's Road, *is about a girl who, with her brother Stephen, has been separated from her parents because they came from Japan. Naomi is now cared for by her aunt, whom she calls "Obasan". They have just been moved from British Columbia to a farm on the prairies.*

Finally we come to our new home. What a dusty, lonely place. The air here is angry and hits out suddenly like a wild man. It blows dust into your eyes and your hair. You turn around and turn around and squeeze your eyes shut. But you can't escape. The flat brown earth stretches on and on till it meets the sky. Dried bunches of scratchy weeds tumble along the fields and roads. They get stuck on the miles and miles of barbed-wire fences. No trees can stand this awful place.

Our hut is even smaller than the one in Slocan. There's just one room. Out of one window we can see the huge farm machines. They look like skeletons of dinosaurs. From the other window we can see the straight road with the ditch beside it.

Obasan puts rags and newspapers around the bottom of the door and the windows. She's trying to keep out the dust and the flies. But they keep coming in anyway. In summer the windows are covered with them. The horrible flies walk on your arms with their sticky hairy feet. They stick in your hair and land in your food. Ugh! Why don't they just go away?

We don't have a bathhouse here. Our bath is a round tub. Getting water is such hard work, especially in winter. We put on our boots and coats, and out we go with our buckets. The hole always gets frozen over and Uncle has to chop it open with a long-handled axe. I can hardly lift the heavy pails. The water sometimes spills down my boots and my feet get itchy and bumpy and red.

After we all take our baths, Obasan washes the clothes in the same water. They hang outside in the icy wind, stiff as cardboard. It's so cold your face stings and your eyelids freeze.

I hate it here. I hate it so much that I want to run away. So does Stephen.

"Why can't we go away?" I ask Uncle. "Even if we can't go back to our first house, can't we go back to Slocan?"

"Someday. Maybe someday," Uncle says. But "someday" never comes.

In the spring we have to work, work, work. The field stretches on forever and is full of rows of plants. All day long we hoe the weeds. It gets so hot it feels like an oven. We're gingerbread cookies baking to bits.

Sometimes I get sick from the heat and lie down in the dirt. Then Uncle comes running across the field. He carries me to the root cellar or to the ditch water. The root cellar is cool, but the rotten potatoes smell horrible. I'd rather sit under the bridge in the muddy water.

"Careful," Uncle says as he helps me into the brown water. The thistles growing on the ditch bank sting your feet.

The school in Granton is different from the one in Slocan. Most of the children don't have black hair like Stephen and me. And they don't have to stay home to work like us either. Only the children like Stephen and me have to work. The teachers send us our homework to do at night.

In harvest time, Obasan wraps rags around all our wrists. She says it helps to lift the heavy beets. But I don't like the rags. I don't like us looking dirty and ragged and ugly in the dusty field. I have to wear Stephen's old clothes. None of my dresses and skirts fit anymore and I don't have

pretty clothes. For school, Obasan fixes her old dresses to fit me. But they don't fit. She says they are beautiful silk. But I hate them. I want store-bought dresses like the other girls.

I write long letters to Daddy in the hospital. He can't come to be with us, Stephen says, until the doctor says he can work. Daddy always sends music to Stephen.

Stephen saves Daddy's sheets of music and ties them all together with shoelaces. One evening he's finally finished helping Uncle with the irrigating job. He takes out all Daddy's music and kneels to get the flute from under the bunk bed.

"Uncle!" Stephen cries out. He holds the flute up for Uncle to see. There is a long crack all the way down the side.

"Ah, the air is too dry," Uncle says sadly.

Stephen and Uncle try tying it together and taping it. But when he plays it, it just sounds windy. He tries and tries until Uncle says finally, "We can't fix it."

Stephen takes Daddy's music and a flashlight and runs out of the house. We can hear him pushing the bike away from the house.

"Where are you going?" Obasan calls from the door. But Stephen doesn't answer. From the window we can see the light from his flashlight bouncing up and down as he goes down the road. It's the first time Stephen has gone to town on his bike at night.

Bedtime passes and still Stephen doesn't come home. He doesn't come home all night long. Early the next morning, as Uncle is getting ready to go to look for him, we can see Stephen riding his bike. He looks like a dot on the road.

"Where were you?" Obasan asks. She's been sitting up all night. She left the coal-oil lamp on in the window.

Stephen just shrugs his shoulders. He doesn't want to talk.

Uncle doesn't say anything.

The next day, when we're hoeing, Stephen tells me he went to the United Church in Granton. A window was open. He climbed in and felt around till he found the piano. He also found a blanket and covered the piano so it would be quieter. He was afraid he might get caught. Then he played Daddy's music until the flashlight batteries died.

"Want to hear Daddy's songs?" he asks. The tunes he whistles are so happy they make me want to dance.

Stephen says when the flashlight went dead, he took the blanket off the piano and fell asleep.

"When I grow up," Stephen says, "I'm going to have a piano and a violin and another flute. I really am, Naomi. And a trumpet too."

"I believe you, Stephen," I say as I whack out the weeds.

The Shining Red Apple

MORLEY CALLAGHAN

It was the look of longing on the boy's face that made Joe Cosentino, dealer in fruits and vegetables, notice him. Joe was sitting on his high stool at the end of the counter where he sat every afternoon looking out the window at the bunches of bananas and the cauliflowers and the tomatoes and apples piled outside on the street stand, and he was watching to see that the kids on the way home from school didn't touch any of the fruit.

This skinny little boy, who was wearing a red sweater and blue overalls, stood near the end of the fruit stand where there was a pyramid of big red apples. With his hands linked loosely together in front of him, and his head, with the straight, untidy brown hair that hung almost down to his blue eyes, cocked over to one side, he stood looking with longing at the apples. If he moved a little to the right, he would be out of sight of the window, but even so if he reached his hand out to take an apple, Joe, sitting at the end of the counter and watching, would surely see the hand. The sleeves of Joe's khaki shirt were rolled up, and as he sat on his stool he folded his hairy forearms across his deep chest. There wasn't much business, there seemed to be a little less every day, and sitting there week after week, he grew a little fatter and a little slower and ever so much more meditative. The store was untidy, and the fruit and the vegetables no longer had the cool, fresh appearance they had in the stores of merchants who were prosperous.

If the kid, standing outside, had been a big, resolute-looking boy, Joe would have been alert and suspicious, but as it was, it was amusing to sit there and pretend he could feel the kid's longing for the apple growing stronger. As though making the first move in a game, Joe leaned forward suddenly, and the boy, lowering his head, shuffled a few feet away. Then Joe, whistling thinly, as if he hadn't noticed anything, got up and went out, took out his handkerchief, and started to polish a few of the apples on the pile. They were big, juicy-looking apples, a little over-ripe and going soft. He polished them till they gleamed and glistened in the sun. Then he said to the kid, "Fine day, eh, son?"

"Yeah," the kid said timidly.

"You live around here?"

"No."

"New around here, eh?" Joe said.

The kid, nodding his head shyly, didn't offer to tell where he lived, so Joe, chuckling to himself, and feeling powerful because he knew so surely just what would happen, went back to the store and sat down on the stool.

At first the little kid, holding his hands behind his back now, shuffled away out of sight, but Joe knew he would go no further than the end of the stand; he knew the kid would be there looking up and down the street furtively, stretching his hand out a little, then withdrawing it in fear before he touched an apple, and always staring, wanting the apple more and more.

Joe got up and yawned lazily, wetting his lips and rubbing his hand across them, and then he deliberately turned his back to the window. But at the moment when he was sure the kid would make up his mind and shoot out his hand, he swung around, and he was delighted to see how the child's hand, empty and faltering, was pulled back. "Ah, it goes just like a clock. I know just what he'll do," Joe thought. "He wants it, but he doesn't know how to take it because he's scared. Soon he wants it so much he'll have to take it. Then I catch him. That's the way it goes," and he grinned.

But in a little while Joe began to feel that maybe he was making it far too hard for the kid, as though the apples were something precious and untouchable. So, doing a thing he hardly ever did, he went out onto the street and, paying no attention to the kid, who had jumped away nervously, he mopped his shining forehead and wiped his red mouth and lazily picked up one of the apples from the top of the pile, as though all such luxuries of the world were within his reach. He munched it slowly with great relish, spitting out bits of red skin, and gnawing it down to the core. The kid must have been very hungry, for his mouth dropped open helplessly, and his blue eyes were innocent and hopeless.

After tossing the core in a wide arc far out on the street, where it lay in the sunlight and was attacked by two big flies, Joe started back into the store thinking, "Now for sure he'll grab one. He won't wait now. He can't." Yet to tantalize him, he didn't go right into the store; he turned at the door, looked up at the sky, as though expecting it to rain suddenly.

The frightened kid had really been ready to take an apple then. He had been so ready that he couldn't turn his head away, even though he knew Joe was watching him, for the apple seemed to belong to him now that he had made up his mind to take it and it was so close to him.

While Joe was grinning and feeling pleased with his cunning, his wife came in from the room at the back of the store. She was a black-haired woman, wide-hipped and slow-moving now, with tired brown eyes. When she stood beside her husband, with her hands on her hips, she looked determined and sensible. "The baby's sleeping now, I think, Joe. It's been pretty bad the way she's been going on."

"That's good," Joe said.

"She feels a lot better today."

"She's all right."

"I feel pretty tired. I think I'll lie down," she said, but she walked over to the window and looked out at the street.

Then she said sharply, "There's a kid out there near the apples. One's gone from the top."

"I sold it," Joe lied.

"Watch the kid," she said.

"O.K.," Joe said, and she went back to the bedroom.

Eagerly Joe looked again for the kid, who stood rooted there in spite of the hostile glance of the woman. "I guess he doesn't know how to do it," Joe thought. Yet the look of helpless longing was becoming so strong in the kid's face, so bold and unashamed, that it bothered Joe and made him irritable. He wanted to quarrel openly with the boy. "Look at the face on you. Look out, kid, you'll start and cry in a minute," he said to himself. "So you think you can have everything you want, do you?" The agony of wanting was so plain in the boy's face that Joe was indignant. "Who does the kid think he is?" he muttered.

In the room back of the store there was a faint whimpering and the sound of a baby stirring. "Look at that, son," Joe said to himself, as though still lecturing the kid. "It's a nice baby, but it's not a boy. See what I mean? If you go round with that look on your face when you want things and can't get them, people'll only laugh at you." As he spoke Joe grew restless and unhappy, and he looked helplessly around the untidy store, as if looking upon his own fate.

The kid on the sidewalk, who had shuffled away till he was out of sight, came edging back slowly. And Joe, getting excited, whispered, "Why doesn't he take it when he wants it so much? I couldn't catch him if he took it and ran," and he got up to be near the corner of the window, where he could see the boy's hand if it came reaching out. "Now. Right now," he muttered, really hoping it would happen.

Then he thought, "What's the matter with him?" for the kid was walking away, brushing by the fruit stand. One of his hands was swinging loose at his side. Then Joe realized that the swinging hand was to knock an apple off the pile and send it rolling along the sidewalk, and he got up eagerly and leaned forward with his head close to the window.

The kid, looking up warily, saw Joe's face and he grew frightened. His own face was full of terror. Ducking, he ran.

"Hey!" Joe yelled, running out to the sidewalk.

In a wild way the kid looked around, but he kept on running, his legs in the blue overalls pumping up and down.

Grabbing an apple and yelling, "Hey, hey, kid, you can have it!" Joe followed a few steps, but the kid wouldn't look back.

Joe stood on the sidewalk, an awful eagerness growing in him as he stared at the shiny red apple and wondered what would happen to the kid he was sure he would never see again.

What Language Do Bears Speak?

ROCH CARRIER
Translated by Sheila Fischman

Following our own morning ritual, to which we submitted with more conviction than to the one of saying our prayers when we jumped out of bed, we ran to the windows and lingered there, silent and contemplative, for long moments. Meanwhile, in the kitchen, our mother was becoming impatient, for we were late. She was always afraid we'd be late . . . Life was there all around us and above us, vibrant and luminous, filled with trees; it offered us fields of daisies and it led to hills that concealed great mysteries.

The story of that morning begins with some posters. During the night, posters had been put up on the wooden poles that supported the hydro wires.

"Posters! They've put up posters!"

Did they announce that hairy wrestlers were coming? Far West singers? Strong men who could carry horses on their shoulders? Comic artists who had "made all America collapse with laughter"? An international tap-dance champion? A sword swallower? Posters! Perhaps we'd be allowed to go and see a play on the stage of the parish hall — if the curé declared from the pulpit that the play wasn't immoral and if we were resourceful enough to earn the money for a ticket. Posters! The artists in the photographs would gradually come down from the posters until they inhabited our dreams, haunted our games and accompanied us, invisible, on our expeditions.

"There's posters up!"

We weren't allowed to run to the posters and, trembling, read their marvellous messages; it was contrary to maternal law to set foot outside before we had washed and combed our hair. After submitting to this painful obligation we were able to learn that we would see, in flesh and blood, the unsurpassable Dr. Schultz, former hunter in Africa, former director of zoos in the countries of Europe, former lion-tamer, former elephant-hunter and former free-style wrestling champion in Germany, Austria and the United Kingdom, in an unbelievable, unsurpassable show — "almost unimaginable." Dr. Schultz would present dogs that could balance on balls, rabbit-clowns, educated monkeys, hens that could add and subtract; in addition, Dr. Schultz would brave a savage bear in an un-even wrestling match "between the fierce forces of nature and the cunning of human intelligence, of which the outcome might be fatal for one of the protagonists."

We had seen bears before, but dead ones, with mouths bleeding, teeth gleaming. Hunters liked to tell how their victims had appeared to them: ". . . standing up, practically walking like a man, but a big man, hairy like a bear; and then it came to me roaring like thunder when it's far away behind the sky, with claws like knives at the end of its paws, and then when I fired it didn't move any more than if a mosquito'd got into its fur. Wasn't till the tenth bullet that I saw it fall down . . ." Loggers, too, had spotted bears and some, so they said, had been so frightened their hair had turned white.

Dr. Schultz was going to risk his life before our eyes by pitting himself against this merciless beast. We would see with our own eyes, alive before us, not only a bear but a man fighting a bear. We'd see all of that!

A voice that reached the entire village, a voice that was magnified by loudspeakers, announced that the great day had arrived: "At last you can see, in person, the unsurpassable Dr. Schultz, the man with the most scars in the world, and his bear — a bear that gets fiercer and fiercer as the sea-son for love comes closer!"

We saw an old yellow bus drive up, covered with stars painted in red, pulling a trailer on whose sides we could read: DR. SCHULTZ AND ASSO-CIATES UNIVERSAL WONDER CIRCUS LTD. The whole thing was covered

with iron bars that were tangled and crossed and knotted and padlocked. A net of clinking chains added to the security. Between messages, crackling music made curtains open at the windows and drew the children outdoors. Then the magical procession entered the lot where we played ball in the summer. The motor growled, the bus moved forward, back, hesitated. At last it found its place and the motor was silent. A man got out of the bus. He stood on the running-board; twenty or thirty children had followed the circus. He considered us with a smile.

"Hi, kids," he said.

He added something else, words in the same language, which we'd never heard before.

"Either he's talking bear," said my friend Lapin, "or he's talking English."

"If we can't understand him," I concluded, "it must be English."

The man on the running-board was still talking; in his strange language he seemed to be asking questions. Not understanding, we listened, stupefied to see Dr. Schultz in person, alive, come down from the posters.

"We talk French here," one of us shouted.

Smiling again, Dr. Schultz said something else we didn't understand.

"We should go get Monsieur Rancourt," I suggested.

Monsieur Rancourt had gone to Europe to fight in the First World War and he'd had to learn English so he could follow the soldiers in his army. I ran to get Monsieur Rancourt. Panting behind his big belly, he hurried as fast as he could. He was looking forward to speaking this language. He hadn't spoken it for so many years he wasn't sure, he told me, that he could remember it. As soon as he saw the man from the circus he told me: "I'm gonna try to tell him hello in English."

"Good day sir! How you like it here today?" ("I remember!" Monsieur Rancourt rejoiced, shouting with delight. "I didn't forget!")

Dr. Schultz moved towards Monsieur Rancourt, holding out his hand. A hand wearing a leather glove, in the middle of summer.

"It's because of the bear bites," my friend Lapin explained to me.

"Apparently the *Anglais* can't take the cold," said one of our friends whose mother's sister had a cousin who worked in an *Anglais* house in Ontario.

The man from the circus and Monsieur Rancourt were talking like two old friends meeting after a number of years. They even laughed. In English, Monsieur Rancourt laughed in a special way, "a real English laugh," we judged, whispering. In French, Monsieur Rancourt never laughed; he was surly. We listened to them, mouths agape. This English language which we'd heard on the radio, in the spaces between the French stations when we turned the tuning knob, we were hearing now for real, in life, in our village, spoken by two men standing in the sun. I made an observation: instead of speaking normally, as in French, instead of spitting the words outside their lips, the two men were swallowing them. My friend Lapin had noticed the same thing, for he said:

"Sounds like they're choking."

Suddenly something was overturned in the trailer; we could hear chains clinking, a bump swelled out the canvas covering and we saw a black ball burst out — the head of a bear.

Dr. Schultz and Monsieur Rancourt had rolled up their shirtsleeves and they were comparing tattoos.

"The bear's loose!"

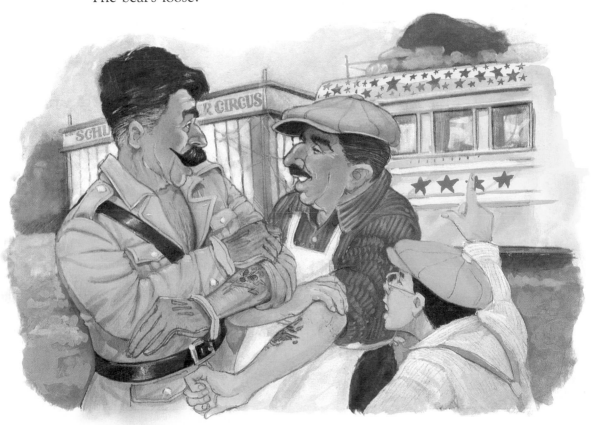

The animal ran out of the canvas, came down from the roof of the bus and jumped to the ground. How could we tell that to Dr. Schultz who didn't understand our language, whose back was turned to the trailer and who was completely absorbed in his conversation?

"Monsieur Rancourt!" I shouted. "The bear's running away!"

There was no need to translate. The man from the circus had understood. Waving a revolver, he sped towards the bear, which was fleeing into a neighbouring field. He shouted, pleaded, threatened.

"What's he saying?" we asked Monsieur Rancourt.

"Words that English children don't learn till they're men."

"He must be saying the same words my father says when a cow jumps over the fence. They aren't nice."

Dr. Schultz, whom we had seen disappear into the oats, came back after a long moment and spoke to Monsieur Rancourt, who ran to the village. The men who were gathered at the general store rushed off to find other men; they took out traps, rifles, ropes. While the mothers gathered up their children who were scattered over the village, the men set out, directed by fat Monsieur Rancourt. Because of his experience in the war, he took charge of the round-up. Dr. Schultz had confided to him, we learned later:

"That bear's more important than my own wife."

They mustn't kill it, then, but bring it back alive.

The show was to begin in the early afternoon. Dr. Schultz, who had gone with the men into the forest, came back muttering; we guessed that he was unhappy. At his trailer he opened the padlock, unfastened the crossed iron bars, pulled out the pegs and undid the chains. We saw him transform his trailer into a stage, with the help of a system of pulleys, ropes and tripods. Suddenly we were working with the circus man: we carried boxes, held out ropes, unrolled canvas, stuck pickets in the ground, lined up chairs. Dr. Schultz directed our labours. Small, over-excited men that we were, we had forgotten he was speaking a language we didn't understand.

A piece of unrolled canvas suspended from a rope, which was held in place by stakes, formed a circular enclosure. It resembled a tent without a roof; we had built it. We were proud; would we, as long as we lived, ever have another day as beautiful as this one? From now on we were part of the circus.

At last it was time for the show. The music cried out as far as the horizon. In the stands there were mostly women; the men were still pursuing the lost bear.

In gleaming leather boots, in a costume sparkling with gilt braid, Dr. Schultz walked out on the stage. He said a few words and the crowd applauded fervently; the spectators no doubt considered it a mark of prowess to speak with such ease a language of which they couldn't utter a single word.

He opened a cage and a dozen rabbits came out. On the back of each he hung a number. At the other end of the platform was a board with holes cut out of it. Above each hole, a number. The man from the circus gave an order and the rabbits ran to the holes that bore their numbers. Unbelievable, wasn't it? We all raised rabbits, but our animals had never learned anything more intelligent than how to chew clover. Our hands were burning, so much had we applauded our friend Dr. Schultz. Next came the trained dogs' act: one danced a waltz; another rode around a track on a bicycle while his twin played a drum. We applauded our great friend hard enough to break our metacarpals.

The acrobatic chimpanzee's act had scarcely begun when a great uproar drowned the music from the loudspeakers. The canvas wall shook, it opened, and we saw the captured bear come in. The men from the village were returning it to its master, roaring, furious, screaming, clawing, kicking, gasping, famished. The men from the village, accustomed to recalcitrant bulls and horses, were leading it with strong authority; they had passed ropes around its neck and paws so the furious animal had to obey. Monsieur Rancourt was speaking French and English all at once.

When he saw his bear, Dr. Schultz let out a cry that Monsieur Rancourt didn't translate. The men's hands dropped the ropes; the bear was free. He didn't notice immediately. We heard his harsh breathing, and his master's too. The hour had come: we were going to see the greatest circus attraction in the Americas, we were going to see with our own eyes the famous Dr. Schultz, our friend, wrestle a giant black bear.

No longer feeling the ropes burning its neck, no longer submitting to the strength of the men who were tearing it apart, the bear stood up, spread its arms and shot forward with a roar. The bear struck Dr. Schultz like a mountain that might have rolled onto him. The bear and our friend tumbled off the stage. There was a ripple of applause; all the men together would never have succeeded in mustering half the daring of Dr. Schultz.

The bear got up again, trampled on the great tamer of wild beasts and dived into the canvas enclosure, tearing it with one swipe of its claws before disappearing.

Dr. Schultz had lost his jacket and trousers. His body was streaked with red scratches. He was weeping.

"If I understand right," said Monsieur Rancourt, "he's telling us that the bear wasn't *his* bear . . ."

"It isn't *his* bear . . ."

The men shook and spluttered with laughter as they did at the general store when one of them told a funny story.

The men laughed so hard that Monsieur Rancourt could no longer hear Dr. Schultz's moans as he lay bleeding on the platform. The undertaker apologized for the misunderstanding.

"That bear was a bear that talked English, though, because I didn't understand a single word he said."

My Own Day

JEAN LITTLE

When I opened my eyes this morning,
The day belonged to me.
The sky was mine and the sun,
And my feet got up dancing.
The marmalade was mine and the squares of sidewalk
And all the birds in the trees.
So I stood and I considered
Stopping the world right there,
Making today go on and on forever.
But I decided not to.
I let the world spin on and I went to school.
I almost did it, but then, I said to myself,
"Who knows what you might be missing tomorrow?"

About the Authors

Margaret Atwood

Margaret Eleanor Atwood was born in Ottawa, Ontario, in 1939. Her father was an entomologist in whose company she came to know the wilderness of Quebec and northern Ontario. The family moved to Sault Ste. Marie in 1945, and to Toronto in 1946. Atwood graduated from Victoria College, University of Toronto, in 1961, and went on to do graduate work at Harvard. Atwood has been a poet, novelist, teacher, editor and critic.

Atwood's published work includes: *Double Persephone* (1961), *The Circle Game* (1966), *The Journals of Susanna Moodie* (1970), *Survival: A Thematic Guide to Canadian Literature* (1972), *Surfacing* (1972), *Life Before Man* (1979) and *The Handmaid's Tale* (1986). She wrote and illustrated one story for children, *Up in a Tree* (1978).

Hazel Boswell

Born in Quebec City in 1882, Hazel May Boswell spent her childhood summers on her grandfather's seigneury, and there came to know something of the folklore of Quebec. At 18 she began travelling. She spent two years on Canada's west coast, then studied painting in France, Germany and Italy.

Boswell was the author of two books: *French Canada: Pictures and Stories* (1938) and *Legends of Quebec: From the Land of the Golden Dog* (1966).

Sheila Burnford

Sheila Burnford was born in Scotland in 1918. She was educated in Edinburgh, in Harrowgate, Yorkshire, and in Germany. During the Second World War she served as an ambulance driver in London, and married David Burnford, a surgeon. They moved to Canada in 1951. After the success of her first novel, *The Incredible Journey*, Burnford was able to sustain herself as a writer. She divided her time between northern Ontario, and a cottage in Hampshire, where she died in 1984.

In addition to her children's books, *The Incredible Journey* (1961) and *Mr. Noah and the Second Flood* (1973), Burnford wrote a volume of autobiographical essays, *The Fields of Noon* (1964), and two books about the north, *Without Reserve* (1969) and *One Woman's Arctic* (1972).

Morley Callaghan

Morley Callaghan was born in Toronto in 1903. He graduated from St. Michael's College, University of Toronto, then studied at Osgoode Hall. He was called to the bar in 1928, but has never practiced law. As a student, he worked for the Toronto *Daily Star*, where he was encouraged to write by fellow reporter, Ernest Hemingway. Callaghan spent a year in Paris in the company of American expatriate writers, Hemingway, Stein, Fitzgerald and the rest. Callaghan is a novelist, short-story writer, journalist and sometime contributor to CBC radio.

Callaghan's published work includes: *Strange Fugitive* (1928), *A Native Argosy* (1929), *Such is My Beloved* (1934), *They Shall Inherit the Earth* (1935), *More Joy in Heaven* (1937), *The Loved and the Lost* (1951). He wrote one novel for juveniles, *Luke Baldwin's Vow* (1948).

Natalie Savage Carlson

Natalie Savage Carlson was born in Winchester, Virginia, in 1906. Her mother was of French Canadian extraction, a fact that has had a noticeable effect on Carlson's choice of subject. Carlson's first published work appeared in the *Baltimore Sunday Sun* when she was eight. The family subsequently moved to Long Beach, California, where Carlson studied journalism and worked as a reporter.

Carlson's children's stories include: *The Talking Cat and Other Stories of French Canada* (1952), *Sashes Red and Blue* (1956), *The Letter on the Tree* (1964), *The Family Under the Bridge* (1958), *Befana's Gift* (1969), *Runaway Marie Louise* (1977) and *Jaky or Dodo?* (1978).

Bliss Carman

Bliss Carman was born in Fredericton, New Brunswick, in 1861. He was educated at the University of New Brunswick, with further studies at Oxford, Edinburgh and Harvard. He became, with his first cousin, Charles G.D. Roberts, a literary journalist in New York City and, later, Boston. He undertook the first of his many successful poetry-reading tours across Canada in 1921.

Carman published over 50 volumes of poetry in his lifetime. Among the titles were: *Low Tide on Grand Pré* (1893), *The Piper of Pan* (five volumes, 1902–1905) and *Sappho* (1905).

Roch Carrier

Roch Carrier was born in 1937 in a small village in the Beauce region of Quebec. He was educated at the Université de Montréal and the Sorbonne. A teacher, poet, novelist, playwright and essayist, he now combines teaching at the Collège Militaire St. Jean with his writing career.

Carrier's publications include two volumes of poetry, *Les Jeux incompris* (1956) and *Cherche tes mots, cherche tes pas* (1958), and the following works of fiction: *Jolis deuils* (1964), *La Guerre, yes sir!* (1968), *Floralie, Where Are You?* (1971) and *Is It the Sun, Philibert* (1972).

Elizabeth Clark

Ella Elizabeth Clark was born in Summertown, Tennessee, in 1896. She studied at Northwestern and Columbia universities. She was a member of the English department of Washington State University, in Pullman, Washington, from 1927 until her retirement in 1961. Utterly devoted to the preservation of native culture, Miss Clark travelled all over North America interviewing, and recording her conversations with native elders. She died in 1984.

Clark's books include: *Indian Legends of the Pacific Northwest* (1953), *Indian Legends of Canada* (1960), *Indian Legends from the Northern Rockies* (1966) and *Sacagawee of the Lewis and Clark Expedition* (1979).

George Clutesi

A west-coast, Tse-shaht Indian, George Clutesi was born in 1905. He left school, after failing grade eight, to become a pile-driver, in which occupation he remained for 21 years. After suffering a back injury, he became the janitor of an elementary school on Vancouver Island. Clutesi is an artist — given his first set of paint brushes by the artist Emily Carr — and a writer who "got sick of what the white writers were saying about Indians."

Clutesi's two books are *Son of Raven, Son of Deer* (1967) and *Potlach* (1969).

Christie Harris

Christie Harris was born in New Jersey in 1907. While she was still young her family moved to British Columbia. She was educated in Surrey, British Columbia, and at the University of British Columbia. She has been an elementary school teacher, freelance writer, and a regular contributor to CBC radio for almost 40 years. She lives in Vancouver with her husband, Thomas.

Harris is the author of about a score of children's books. Among them are: *Cariboo Trail* (1957), *Once Upon a Totem* (1963), *You Have to Draw the Line Somewhere* (1964), *Raven's Cry* (1966), *Forbidden Frontier* (1968), *Mouse Woman and the Vanished Princesses* (1976).

Juliet Heslewood

Juliet Heslewood was born in Yorkshire in 1951. She studied English and the history of art at the University of London. She now makes her home in France.

Heslewood is the author of *Tales of Sea and Shore* (1983) and *Earth, Air, Fire and Water* (1986).

James Houston

James Houston was born in 1921 in Toronto. He studied art in the city of his birth, and in Paris and Tokyo. He served for 12 years as a Canadian government administrator on Baffin Island in the Canadian Arctic. While there, he was largely responsible for bringing to international attention the distinctive qualities of Inuit art. At the same time, he introduced Inuit artists to the techniques of printmaking. Houston writes and illustrates novels for both adults and children. He is also a filmmaker, scriptwriter and art consultant.

Houston's books include: *Tikta'liktak: an Eskimo Legend* (1965), *The White Archer* (1967), *The White Dawn* (1971), *Frozen Fire* (1977), *Spirit Wrestler* (1980), *Eagle Song* (1983) and *Whiteout* (1988).

Monica Hughes

Born in Liverpool in 1925, Monica Hughes lived in Cairo, Egypt, for part of her childhood. Her father, a mathematician and amateur astronomer, imparted to her an enthusiasm for science and a love of books. Hughes travelled widely and worked at a variety of jobs before meeting and marrying her husband in Ottawa, Ontario. The family moved to Edmonton, Alberta, in 1964, and has remained there since.

Hughes is a prolific writer of children's stories. Among her books are: *Gold-Fever Trail* (1974), *Crisis on Conshelf Ten* (1975), *Earthdark* (1977), *The Beckoning Lights* (1980), *The Keeper of the Isis Light* (1980).

sean o huigin

Born in Brampton, Ontario, in 1942, sean o huigin has been active for many years in the Toronto poetry scene. He was a minor partner in The Bohemian Embassy, a coffee house established in 1960, where he gave the first poetry readings. He has also been an enthusiastic proponent of poetry in public schools, giving readings and conducting seminars across the country. He now lives in Ireland.

o huigin's books include: *Pickles, Street Dog of Windsor* (1982), *Scary Poems for Rotten Kids* (1982), *Well, You Can Imagine* (1983), *The Ghost Horse of the Mounties* (1983), *Blink, a Strange Book for Children* (1984) and *Atmosfear* (1985)

E. Pauline Johnson

Pauline Johnson was born on the Six Nations Reserve near Brantford, Ontario, in 1861. She was the daughter of a Mohawk father and an English mother. She was, for the most part, educated informally, but she was exposed at an early age to the great Victorian poets. Her reputation as a poet owed a great deal to her popularity as a performer. She made much of her Indian heritage — often wearing Indian dress during her recitals — but her work was clearly derived from a European tradition. She died in 1913.

Pauline Johnson's books include: *The White Wampum* (1895), *Legends of Vancouver* (1911) and *Flint and Feather* (1912).

Joy Kogawa

Joy Kogawa was born in Vancouver in 1935. She moved with her family to the interior of British Columbia as a result of the government-ordered evacuation of Japanese-Canadians during the Second World War. Since then she has lived in Saskatoon, Ottawa and Toronto. She is a poet, and the author of the widely-acclaimed novel, *Obasan*.

Kogawa's books include: *The Splintered Moon* (1967), *A Choice of Dreams* (1974), *Jericho Road* (1977), *Obasan* (1981), *Woman in the Woods* (1985) and *Naomi's Road* (1986).

Margaret Laurence

Jean Margaret Wemys was born in Neepawa, Manitoba, in 1926. The town of her birth became the model for "Manawaka," the imaginary setting of her four finest novels. She was educated in Winnipeg and worked as a reporter for the *Winnipeg Citizen* before she met and married Jack Laurence, an engineer. They lived in England and Africa before they returned to Canada in 1957. Margaret Laurence moved to England in 1962 and stayed there for ten years before returning to Canada. She lived in Lakefield, Ontario, until her death in 1987.

Margaret Laurence's books include three volumes derived from her African experiences, *A Tree for Poverty* (1954), *This Side Jordan* (1960) and *The Tomorrow Tamer* (1963); the four Manawaka novels, *The Stone Angel* (1964), *A Jest of God* (1966), *The Fire-Dweller* (1969) and *A Bird in the House* (1970); and two stories for children, *Six Darn Cows* (1979) and *The Olden Days Coat* (1979).

R.D. Lawrence

Born at sea in 1921 on board a British passenger ship, R.D. Lawrence was educated in Spain. He enlisted, at the outbreak of the Spanish Civil War, in the Republican army and was wounded in 1937. He was later interned and finally released and sent to England in 1938. He served with British forces in the Second World War. After the war, he studied biology and worked as a journalist. He emigrated to Canada in 1954. Lawrence has alternately homesteaded in northern Ontario and worked as a journalist. He now lives on 100 acres in Ontario's Haliburton Highlands with two timber wolves and a variety of other fauna.

Lawrence's books include: *Wildlife in Canada* (1966), *Cry Wild* (1970), *The North Runner* (1979), *The Ghost Walker* (1983), *The Shark* (1985) and *The Natural History of Canada* (1988).

Stephen Leacock

Stephen Leacock was born in Swanmore, England, in 1869, third of 11 children. Leacock's father abandoned them after the family had settled in the Lake Simcoe district of Ontario. Leacock attended local schools and Upper Canada College in Toronto. He later taught at U.C.C. while he worked on a degree in modern languages at the University of Toronto. After further studies in political economy in Chicago, he was appointed lecturer in the department of political science at McGill, where he remained until his retirement in 1936. He died in 1944.

Leacock was the author of about 60 books. Among them were not only the humorous sketches for which he was famous, but also histories and political essays. His books include: *Elements of Political Science* (1906), *Literary Lapses* (1910), *Sunshine Sketches of a Little Town* (1912), *Arcadian Adventures of the Idle Rich* (1914), *My Discovery of the West* (1937) and *The Boy I Left Behind Me* (1946).

Dennis Lee

Born in Toronto in 1939, Dennis Lee attended University of Toronto Schools (where he attained the highest marks of any grade 13 student in Ontario) and Victoria College, University of Toronto. He taught at the University of Toronto for several years, was a co-founder of the experimental Rochdale College, and co-founder of House of Anansi Press. A poet and children's writer, Lee has also been an editor for other publishers, and lyricist for a children's television programme, *Fraggle Rock*.

Lee's adult poetry includes *Kingdom of Absence* (1967) and *Civil Elegies* (1968). For children he has written: *Wiggle to the Laundromat* (1970), *Alligator Pie* (1974), *Nicholas Knock and Other People* (1974), *Garbage Delight* (1977) and *The Ordinary Bath* (1979).

Jean Little

Jean Little was born in Formosa (now Taiwan) where her parents were medical missionaries. She has been almost blind since birth, but was encouraged by her parents to persevere despite the disability. She was educated in Guelph, Ontario, where she still lives, and at Victoria College, University of Toronto, where she obtained the highest marks in her graduating class. She is now a full-time writer and occasional lecturer in children's literature.

Little's books include: *Mine For Keeps* (1962), *Home From Far* (1965), *Spring Begins in March* (1966), *Take Wing* (1968) and *Look Through My Window* (1970).

Janet Lunn

Janet Lunn was born in Dallas, Texas, in 1928, but most of her childhood was spent in New England. She attended Queen's University in Kingston, Ontario, where she met her husband. Her writing career began with book reviews for the *Kingston Whig-Standard*. Later, when she and her husband moved to Toronto, she wrote for a variety of publications. From 1962 to 1972, she was children's book reviewer for the *Globe and Mail*. Then, for three years, she was children's editor for a Toronto publisher. Lunn now lives in a 150-year-old farmhouse in Prince

Edward County, Ontario. She continues to review books, and works as a free-lance editor and children's writer.

Her books for children include: *Double Spell* (1968), *Larger Than Life* (1979), *The Twelve Dancing Princesses* (1979), *The Root Cellar* (1981) and *Shadow in Hawthorn Bay* (1986).

Cyrus Macmillan

Cyrus Macmillan was born in 1882 in Wood Islands, Prince Edward Island. He taught for some years in Charlottetown before joining the English department at McGill University, where he remained for the rest of his career. He was Dean of Arts and Sciences from 1940 to 1947, and also served as a Member of Parliament, representing a Prince Edward Island constituency during the Second World War. He died in 1953.

Macmillan wrote *Canadian Wonder Tales* (1918) and *Canadian Fairy Tales* (1922) as well as a history of McGill. A number of the stories from the two anthologies were reprinted after his death in *Glooskap's Country* (1955).

Suzanne Martel

Born in Quebec City in 1924, Suzanne Martel was educated at the Monastery of the Ursulines in Quebec City; University of Toronto; and CEGEP Marie Victorin, Montreal. She has worked as a reporter for *Le Soleil* and as a freelance contributor to *Radio Canada*, television and print media. She was French co-ordinator for women's activities at Expo 67, and founder and editor of *Safari*, a weekly magazine for children.

Martel is the author of a score of books, including science fiction for children and historical fiction for adults. Her books include: *Jeanne, Fille du Roi* (1974), *Surréal 3000* (1980) which was translated into English as *The City Underground* (1982), *Nos Amis Robots* (1981) and *Peewee* (1982).

Eva Martin

Born in Woodstock, Ontario, in 1939, Eva Martin has lived most of her life in Toronto. From the University of Toronto she obtained a B.A. and an M.A. in library science. As a librarian with a particular interest in inner-city children, she has written playscripts, scripts for puppet shows, and articles for professional journals. She has been co-ordinator of services for children and young adults at the Scarborough Public Library for 11 years.

Her book, *Canadian Fairy Tales*, was published in 1984.

W.O. Mitchell

William Ormond Mitchell was born in Weyburn, Saskatchewan, in 1914. He spent some of his youth in Florida because of ill-health. Throughout the 1930s, he mixed travel, education and odd jobs. He studied medicine at the University of Manitoba, then education at the University of Alberta, before becoming a teacher himself in rural Alberta. After the acclaim accorded to him with the publication of *Who Has Seen the Wind?*, Mitchell gained increasing prominence as a journalist, the author of radio plays, and raconteur. He has also become well-known as a teacher of creative writing, especially at the Banff Centre School of Fine Arts.

Mitchell's books include: *Who Has Seen the Wind?* (1947), *Jake and the Kid* (1962), *The Vanishing Point* (1973), *How I Spent My Summer Holidays* (1981) and *Since Daisy Creek* (1984).

L.M. Montgomery

Lucy Maud Montgomery was born in Clifton, Prince Edward Island, in 1874, where she was raised by her maternal grandparents. After attending school in Charlottetown, and Dalhousie University in Halifax, she taught for a number of years on the island. She looked after her grandmother in Cavendish, P.E.I. for three years, then married Rev. Ewan Macdonald. His calling took them to small communities in Ontario where Montgomery kept house and pursued a writing career. She died in Toronto in 1942.

Anne of Green Gables (1908) and its seven sequels enjoyed immediate success in Canada and abroad. Montgomery wrote 22 books of fiction in all, including two novels for adults. She also wrote poetry, and ten volumes of unpublished diaries.

Farley Mowat

Farley Mowat was born in Belleville, Ontario, in 1921, and raised in Saskatoon, Saskatchewan. He attended the University of Toronto, then served with the Canadian forces (Hastings and Prince Edward Regiment) during the Second World War. After the war, he resumed his academic studies, spending two years in Canada's far north before completing his degree.

Mowat has written many books about the North, native people and wildlife. *People of the Deer* (1952), *The Desperate People* (1959), *Ordeal By Ice* (1960), *Never Cry Wolf* (1963), *Siber: My Discovery of Siberia* (1970) and *Sea of Slaughter* (1984) are a few of the many titles. Specifically for children he has written: *The Dog Who Wouldn't Be* (1957) and *Owls in the Family* (1961).

Charles G.D. Roberts

Charles George Douglas Roberts was born in Douglas, near Fredericton, New Brunswick, in 1860. He was educated at the University of New Brunswick where he obtained his B.A. in 1879, and his M.A. in 1881. He taught in Chatham and Fredericton before accepting a position as professor of English at King's College, Windsor, Nova Scotia. By 1897 he was earning his living as a freelance journalist, novelist and poet. He lived for a while with Bliss Carman in New York, then went to England, where he spent 17 years. He fought with the Canadian Forces Overseas during the First World War. He was knighted in 1935 and died in 1943.

Roberts's books include: *Orion, and Other Poems* (1880), *The Canadian Guide-Book* (1891), *The Raid from Beauséjour* (1894), *The Land of Evangeline* (1895), *A History of Canada* (1897) and *Canada in Flanders* (1918).

Gabrielle Roy

Born in St. Boniface, Manitoba, in 1909, Gabrielle Roy was raised in that province, and taught school there for nine years. When she was 28, she travelled to Europe, returning to Canada after two years because of the outbreak of the

Second World War. She settled in Montreal and made her way there as a journalist and writer. In 1947, she married a doctor. They settled in Quebec City where she died in 1983.

Bonheur d'Occasion (1945), translated into English as *The Tin Flute* (1947), sold well over a million copies. Among Roy's other books are: *La Petite Poule d'eau* (1950), *Alexandre Chenevert* (1954), *Rue Deschambault* (1955), *Cet été qui chantait* (1972) and *La montagne secrète* (1961). Virtually all of Roy's work is available in English translation.

Duncan Campbell Scott

Duncan Campbell Scott was born in Ottawa in 1862. His father was a Methodist minister. During Scott's childhood, the family moved regularly from one community to another in Ontario and Quebec. Scott attended Wesleyan College in Stanstead, but a lack of money prevented him from pursuing his ambition to study medicine. He joined the department of Indian Affairs in 1879 and remained there, a civil servant, until his retirement in 1932. He died in 1947.

Scott's books include: *The Magic House and Other Poems* (1893), *In the Village of Viger* (1896), *The Magic House: Labor and the Angel* (1898) and *The Poems of Duncan Campbell Scott* (1926).

Robert Service

Born in Preston, England, in 1874, Robert Service was educated in Glasgow. On graduation, he entered the Commercial Bank of Scotland. In 1894, he came to Canada, where he entered the service of the Canadian Bank of Commerce. He was stationed in Vancouver, Victoria, Kamloops, and finally, Whitehorse and Dawson in the Yukon. He was an ambulance driver during the First World War. Afterward, he travelled extensively in Europe, but particularly in France. He died in Monte Carlo in 1958.

Service's books include: *Songs of the Sourdough* (1907), *Ballads of a Cheechako* (1909), *Ballads of a Bohemian* (1921), *Bar-room Ballads* (1940) and *Lyrics of a Low Brow* (1951).

Ernest Thompson Seton

Ernest Thompson (he adopted the name "Seton" as an adult) was born in South Shields, Durham, England. The family moved to Canada in 1866. Seton was educated in Toronto public schools, then studied art at the Ontario College of Art in Toronto, and in schools overseas. He was appointed naturalist to the Manitoba government in 1890. In 1896 he moved to the United States. He founded a youth movement devoted to outdoors activities and was subsequently involved in the Boy Scouts of America organization. In 1930 he founded the New Mexico Institute of Wildlife and Woodcraft which remained, with his writing, the focus of his attention until his death in 1946.

Seton wrote and illustrated about 40 books. They include: *Wild Animals I Have Known* (1898), *Lives of the Hunted* (1901), *Two Little Savages* (1903), *Life Histories of Northern Animals* (1909) and *Lives of Game Animals* (four volumes, 1925–1928).

Barbara Smucker

Born in Kansas, Missouri, in 1915, Barbara Smucker studied English and journalism at the state university. A brief career as a reporter ended when she married a scholar and Mennonite pastor whose postings took them to Mississippi (where Barbara Smucker was, for a time, the only white teacher in a black high school) and to Kitchener, Ontario. She was children's librarian in the Kitchener Public Library, then head librarian at Renison College, until her retirement in 1982.

Smucker's books for children include: *Henry's Red Sea* (1955), *Wigwam in the City* (1966), *Underground to Canada* (1977), *Amish Adventure* (1983) and *White Mist* (1985).

William Toye

William Eldred Toye was born in Toronto in 1926. He was educated at Victoria College, University of Toronto, where he obtained his B.A. in 1948. On graduation, he went to Oxford University Press, where he has remained since. Toye started out as production manager. A self-taught designer, he was active in the Society of Typographical Designers, and served as its president for two years. He gradually took on other editorial tasks, from copy-editing to editing children's books. He has been editorial director since 1950.

Toye has retold a number of Indian legends for children: *The Mountain Goats of Temlahan* (1969), *How Summer Came to Canada* (1969), *The Loon's Necklace* (1977) and *The Fire Stealer* (1979). He is the general editor of *The Oxford Companion to Canadian Literature* (1983) and was a founding editor of *Tamarack Review* until its demise in 1982.

The Illustrators

Donna Gordon
"The Princess and the Geese"; "The Ships of Yule"; "The Baker's Magic Wand"; "Going Up North".

Robert Johannsen
"Akla Gives Chase"; "The Talking Cat"; "North Lay Freedom"; "Helvi's Visitor"; "Then There Were Three"; "Auction Fever"; "The Shining Red Apple".

Peter Kovalik
"The Origin of Stories"; "Goldenhair"; "The Pedler"; "Le Hibou Blanc"; "Luke in the Forest"; "Dreams of the Animals"; "Chris and Sandy".

June Lawrason
"The Boy of the Red Twilight Sky";
"Sarah from Long Ago"; "Matthew Cuthbert Is Surprised".

Paul McCusker
"How the Human People Got the First Fire"; "The Cremation of Sam McGee"; "Long Skinny Minny"; "Mutt Makes His Mark"; "The Conjurer's Revenge"; "What Language Do Bears Speak?"

Renée Mansfield
"The Song My Paddle Sings"; "The House at Hawthorn Bay"; "The Springfield Fox"; "Stephen's Whistle".

Michelle Nidenoff
"The Loon's Necklace"; "Bye Bye"; "The Red River Valley"; "In the Deep of the Grass"; "My Own Day".

Acknowledgments

Care has been taken to trace ownership of copyright material contained in this book. The publishers will gladly receive any information that will enable them to rectify any reference or credit line in subsequent editions.

"Akla Gives Chase" by James Houston (page 27). From *Long Claws: An Arctic Adventure* by James Houston. Used by permission of the Canadian Publishers, McClelland & Stewart, Toronto.

"Auction Fever" by W.O. Mitchell (page 237). From *Jake and the Kid* by W.O. Mitchell, © 1961. Reprinted by permission of Macmillan of Canada, a division of Canada Publishing Corporation.

"The Baker's Magic Wand" by Cyrus Macmillan (page 95). Reprinted from *Canadian Wonder Tales* by Cyrus Macmillan (London: The Bodley Head, 1974).

"The Boy of the Red Twilight Sky" by Juliet Heslewood (page 51). Copyright © Juliet Heslewood 1983. Reprinted from *Tales of Sea and Shore* by Juliet Heslewood (1983) by permission of Oxford University Press.

"Bye Bye" by sean o huigin (page 67). From *Scary Poems for Rotten Kids* by sean o huigin. Reprinted by permission of Black Moss Press.

"Chris and Sandy" by Monica Hughes, (page 143). Copyright © 1986 by Monica Hughes. Reprinted by permission of the author.

"The Conjurer's Revenge" by Stephen Leacock (page 253). From *Literary Lapses* by Stephen Leacock. Used by permission of the Canadian Publishers, McClelland & Stewart, Toronto.

"The Cremation of Sam McGee" by Robert Service (page 79). Reprinted from *Collected Poems* by Robert Service (New York: Dodd Mead, 1940).

"Dreams of the Animals" by Margaret Atwood (page 166). From *Procedures for Underground* by Margaret Atwood. Reprinted by permission of Oxford University Press, Canada.

"Going Up North" by Dennis Lee (page 256). From *Nicholas Knock and Other People* © 1974 by Dennis Lee. Reprinted by permission of Macmillan of Canada, a division of Canada Publishing Corporation.

"Goldenhair" by Eva Martin (page 59). Reprinted from *Canadian Fairy Tales* by Eva Martin, illustrated by Lazlo Gal, published by Groundwood Books, 1984.

"Helvi's Visitor" by Sheila Burnford (page 169). From *The Incredible Journey* by Sheila Burnford. Copyright © 1960 by Sheila Burnford. Reproduced by permission of Hodder & Stoughton Limited.

"Le Hibou Blanc" by Hazel Boswell (page 117). Reprinted from *Legends of Quebec* (Toronto: McClelland & Stewart, 1966).

"The House at Hawthorn Bay" by Janet Lunn (page 103). From *The Root Cellar* by Janet Lunn, © 1981. Reprinted by permission of Lester & Orpen Dennys Publishers Ltd., Canada.

"How the Human People Got the First Fire" by George Clutesi (page 17). Reprinted from *Son of Raven, Son of Deer*, by George Clutesi (Sidney, British Columbia: Gray's Publishing, 1967)

"In the Deep of the Grass" by Charles G.D. Roberts (page 161). Reprinted from *Watchers of the Trails* by Charles G.D. Roberts.

"Long Skinny Minny" by Gabrielle Roy (page 179). From *Enchanted Summer* by Gabrielle Roy. Used by permission of the Canadian Publishers, McClelland & Stewart, Toronto. First published in French, *Cet été qui chantait* (Montreal et

Paris, 1972). English translation: Joyce Marshall. Copyright on both French and English versions: Fonds Gabrielle Roy, 5793 Deom Ave., Montreal (Quebec).

"The Loon's Necklace" by William Toye (page 9). Copyright © Oxford University Press, 1977. Used by permission of Oxford University Press Canada.

"Luke in the Forest" by Suzanne Martel (page 125). Reprinted from *The City Under Ground* by Suzanne Martel, 1982, by permission of the publisher, Douglas & McIntyre, Vancouver.

"Matthew Cuthbert Is Surprised" by L.M. Montgomery (page 219). Reprinted from *Anne of Green Gables* with permission of Ruth Macdonald, David Macdonald and Farrar, Straus and Giroux.

"Mutt Makes His Mark" by Farley Mowat (page 211). Reprinted from *The Dog Who Wouldn't Be* by permission of Farley Mowat.

"My Own Day" by Jean Little (page 280). From *Look Through My Window* by Jean Little. Reprinted by permission of Harper & Row, Publishers, Inc.

"North Lay Freedom" by Barbara Smucker (page 137). From *Underground to Canada* by Barbara Smucker © 1977. Clarke Irwin & Co. Ltd. Used by permission of Irwin Publishing Inc.

"The Origin of Stories" by Elizabeth Clark (page 3). Reprinted by permission of the Association of American Indian Affairs, Inc.

"The Pedler" by Duncan Campbell Scott (page 85). Reprinted from *In the Village of Viger* (Boston, 1896).

"The Princess and the Geese" by Christie Harris (page 39). Copyright © 1976 by Christie Harris. Reprinted by permission of the author.

"The Red River Valley" (Traditional) (page 123). Collected by Edith Fowke and published in *The Penguin Book of Canadian Folk Songs*.

"Sarah from Long Ago" by Margaret Laurence (page 151). From *The Olden Days Coat* By Margaret Laurence. Used by permission of the Canadian Publishers, McClelland & Stewart, Toronto.

"The Shining Red Apple" By Morley Callaghan (page 265). From *Now That April's Here and Other Stories* (New York: Random House, 1936). Reprinted by permission of the author.

"The Ships of Yule" by Bliss Carman (page 90). Reprinted from *Bliss Carman's Poems* (Toronto: McClelland & Stewart, 1931).

"The Song My Paddle Sings" by E. Pauline Johnson (page 13). Reprinted from *Flint and Feather: The Complete Poems of E. Pauline Johnson (Tekahionwake)* (Toronto: Hodder & Stoughton, 1931).

"The Springfield Fox" by Ernest Thompson Seton (page 203). Reprinted from *Wild Animals I Have Known* (New York: Scribners, 1926).

"Stephen's Whistle" by Joy Kogawa (page 259). From *Naomi's Road*, published by Oxford University Press, 1986. Reprinted by permission of the author.

"The Talking Cat" by Natalie Savage Carlson (page 69). From *The Talking Cat and Other Stories of French Canada* by Natalie Savage Carlson. Copyright 1952, 1980 by Natalie Savage Carlson. Reprinted by permission of Harper & Row, Publishers Inc.

"Then There Were Three" by R.D. Lawrence (page 195). From *Cry Wild* published by Totem Books. Copyright © 1970 by R.D. Lawrence. Reprinted by permission of the author.

"What Language Do Bears Speak?" by Roch Carrier (page 271). From *The Hockey Sweater and Other Stories*, translated by Sheila Fischman. (Toronto: House of Anansi Press, 1979). Reprinted by permission of the publisher.

Index